"Stubborn? Me?"

Jason stepped inside and pushed the door shut. "You're the most hardheaded woman I've ever met. And pushy, too."

"Pushy!"

"Yeah, pushy. You keep sticking your nose in where it doesn't belong and isn't wanted."

Amanda drew herself up to her greatest height, though it was woefully short of his. "Somebody on this mountain wrote that letter to me, Mr. Kruger. Somebody wants brides up here. You'd better face that fact."

He pointed his finger at her. "I can tell you this, Miss Pierce, when I find out who wrote that letter, I'm going to fire that man so fast, he won't know what hit him."

"Oh! You pigheaded man!" Amanda jerked her chin. "Don't worry. I'm leaving for good. I won't be back, and you'll never hear from me again. You'll have your precious mountain all to yourself. I hope it keeps you warm at night...!

Dear Reader,

The perfect complement to a hot summer day is a cool drink, some time off your feet and a good romance novel. And we have four terrific stories this month for you to choose from!

We are delighted with the return of Judith Stacy, who is known for her satisfying, often humorous, Americana romances. She has outdone herself with *The Blushing Bride,* a darling tale set in the mountains of California. When Amanda Pierce, who runs a matrimonial service, receives a letter from the owner of a logging company looking for a mail-order bride, she travels to his mountain determined to match not one but several of her brides with the lonely loggers. What she doesn't count on is being "felled" herself—by the handsome boss!

In *Jake's Angel*, by newcomer Nicole Foster, an embittered—and wounded—Texas Ranger on the trail of a notorious outlaw winds up in a small New Mexican town and is healed, emotionally and physically, by a beautiful widow. Jillian Hart brings us a wonderful Medieval, *Malcolm's Honor*, in which a ruthless knight discovers a lasting passion for the feisty noblewoman he is forced to marry.

And don't miss *Lady of Lyonsbridge*, the emotional sequel to *Lord of Lyonsbridge* by Ana Seymour. In the latest novel, a marriage-shy heiress falls for an honorable knight who comes to her estate on his way to pay a kidnapped king's ransom.

Enjoy! And come back again next month for four more choices of the best in historical romance.

Sincerely,

Tracy Farrell
Senior Editor

JUDITH STACY

The Blushing Bride

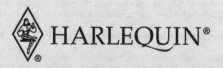

HARLEQUIN®

TORONTO • NEW YORK • LONDON
AMSTERDAM • PARIS • SYDNEY • HAMBURG
STOCKHOLM • ATHENS • TOKYO • MILAN • MADRID
PRAGUE • WARSAW • BUDAPEST • AUCKLAND

ISBN 0-373-29121-3

THE BLUSHING BRIDE

Visit us at www.eHarlequin.com

Printed in U.S.A.

Please address questions and book requests to:
Harlequin Reader Service
U.S.: 3010 Walden Ave., P.O. Box 1325, Buffalo, NY 14269
Canadian: P.O. Box 609, Fort Erie, Ont. L2A 5X3

Chapter One

California, 1886

Was it too late to run?

Amanda Pierce eyed the freight wagon and its driver across the street from her hotel, and considered turning tail and heading back to San Francisco. Back to clean sheets. Back to gentlemen of good breeding. Back home.

She drew in a deep breath and glimpsed her reflection in the cracked mirror in the corner of the hotel lobby. Blue gown, matching hat set in dark curls, kid shoes. She looked completely out of place in this wide-open, raucous little town of Beaumont at the base of the Sierra Nevada Mountains.

Back in San Francisco this had seemed like a good idea, but now…

Amanda watched her reflection in the mirror and forced herself to square her shoulders and stand a little straighter. True, she wasn't well-traveled. She wasn't wise to the ways of the world. But she was twenty-four years old, with enough good sense to accomplish this difficult trip and keep herself safe in the process. Didn't that count for something? Of course it did.

Fortified now, Amanda ventured onto the board-walk, careful to avoid the miners and loggers who passed, men in soiled work clothes with unkempt beards. She eyed the freight wagon from the Kruger Brothers' Lumber and Milling Company across the street. It was the reason she'd come to Beaumont and spent two days in the hotel, watching for its arrival.

Now it was here. Amanda pushed her chin a little higher, drawing up her courage. She could do this. She *had* to.

That thought carried Amanda across the dirt street, darting between teams of horses and mules, and big rumbling wagons.

"Excuse me, sir?" she called to the driver as she reached the safety of the boardwalk.

His back was to her as he oversaw the loading of supplies into the Kruger wagon. A bear of a man, he wore stained buckskins and a slouch hat yanked down over his unruly gray hair.

Amanda ventured closer. "Sir? Excuse me?"

He half turned, squinting hard at her. "You talk-ing to me, lady?"

Up close his face was like cracked leather, dried and hardened by the elements—at least, the portion of his face Amanda could see above his tangled beard.

"Are you Mr. Harper?" she asked. "Mr. Samuel Harper?"

His eyes narrowed. "Who wants to know?"

She gripped her handbag tighter. "I'm Miss Amanda Pierce, from San Francisco."

"Yeah, that's me, all right," he said, and hitched up his trousers. "'Cept ain't nobody called me Samuel since last time I was at Sunday services, and I don't rightly recall just how long ago that was. I go by Shady."

Amanda hoped he'd been given that nickname because of an affection for leafy trees and not as a testament to his character.

"Mr. Harper, I'm seeking—"

"Call me Shady."

Amanda managed a small smile. "Yes, certainly...Shady. As I was saying, I need transportation to the Kruger Brothers' Lumber and Milling Company, and was told you could provide that."

Shady reared back and eyed her up and down. "You want to go up to the camp?"

"Yes," Amanda said.

"Up on the mountain?"

"Well, yes," she said.

"And you want me to take you up there?"

"I was informed there was no other reliable transportation." Amanda pulled a dog-eared envelope from her handbag. "Mr. Kruger assured me of your honesty, and instructed me to wait at the hotel until you arrived in town, then ride up to the lumber camp with you."

"Yeah, I make a run up and down the mountain

every couple of days." Shady stroked his long, ragged beard. "It was Jason Kruger that sent for you?"

"Yes," Amanda said. "He's expecting me."

"You?"

She drew in a little breath. "Yes, Mr. Harper, I—"

"Shady."

"Shady." Amanda cleared her throat and pressed the envelope closer toward him. "It's all right here in his instructions."

"And you're sure it was Jason Kruger that sent for you?" he asked. "'Cause, now, there's two of them, you know. There's Jason and there's Ethan. They're brothers."

Amanda pressed her lips together and waved toward the Kruger Brothers' Lumber and Milling Company sign painted on the freight wagon in big red letters.

"Yes, I'm aware they're brothers."

"Now, Jason, he's the oldest one, but not by much, as I hear tell," Shady said. "He's the one what runs things up on the mountain, you know."

"I do know that Mr.—Shady," Amanda said. "I have business with Mr. Kruger. He wrote and asked me to come here."

"Business, huh?" Shady shrugged and turned back to the wagon. "Well, okay by me, I reckon. I'll be pulling out of here pretty quick so as to get back to the camp before dark."

"I'll get my bag from the hotel," Amanda said.

Shady turned to her once more. "If'n you're real

sure you want to meet up with Jason Kruger, that is.''

Amanda's stomach twisted into a knot as the old man squinted at her, and again she was tempted— very tempted—to head for home.

"I'm sure," Amanda said.

She'd come too far to turn back now.

"What's wrong now?''

Jason Kruger pulled his boots from the corner of his desk and rocked forward in his chair. He'd just finished his supper and didn't like the intrusion of one of his men into his office at the end of the day.

The Spartan room wasn't much to look at with its rough-hewn walls, a couple of desks and cupboards, and a potbellied stove in the corner, but Jason liked the solitude after a hard day's work. He wanted to look over his new journals, not deal with this man again.

"What is it, Duncan?" Jason asked. "Spit it out.''

The thin, wiry man lingering at the door pulled off his hat and twisted it in his hands.

"Well, boss, I'm sorry to be a bother to you, but...." Duncan shifted from one foot to the other. "Well, my Gladys is having problems with that Polly Minton, and well, this time I—''

Jason cursed and came to his feet. "I told you not to bring your wife here in the first place.''

"Well, yeah, I know, but—''

"No women in camp. That's my rule. I told you.''

"Yes, sir, and I appreciate you making an exception 'cause she's my wife, and all, but—"

"Trouble." Jason cursed again. "Women are nothing but trouble. They don't belong here. I've got no use for women in a logging camp."

Duncan twisted his hat tighter in his hands. "Yes, boss, I know that, and I'm beholden to you, but—"

"I told you when you brought her here that you were responsible for her," Jason said. "I want no part of it. You got problems, you handle them."

"Yes, sir, I know you said that, but, well…" Duncan ventured closer to the desk. "My Gladys and Polly Minton are fighting something fierce. I tried to settle it, I swear I did, but Polly's took it into her head that Gladys stole from her and they've been going at it all day now. You got to help me, Mr. Kruger, you got to."

Jason fumed silently, staring at the little man. Duncan was a good worker, nimble and surefooted in his job herding the great logs down the river to the millpond. He'd been loyal too. Turnover in the logging camps was high, but Duncan had stuck around. The only trouble he'd ever caused was bringing his wife here with him.

And now she'd been accused of stealing. Jason wouldn't tolerate theft in the camp. He needed order and discipline among his crew to bring down the giant redwoods and Douglas firs, get them out of the rugged mountains, run them through the sawmill and send them off to market.

He couldn't let a theft go unpunished. Female or not, he needed to put a stop to this.

Jason blew out his breath, tapping off some of his anger.

"All right, Duncan, I'll take care of it," he said.

"I'm beholden to you, boss, I am." Duncan eased out the door. "I'll go get my Gladys. That Miz Minton is here, too. I'll fetch them both. They're right outside."

"Women." Jason pulled on the back of his neck and dropped into his chair again. Bad enough dealing with the problems his crew created. Fights, mostly. A shooting every once in a while. Disagreements between his men could be settled quickly. But women...

Jason mumbled another curse.

The office door opened and Polly Minton and Gladys Duncan walked inside. Jason knew them both. He knew everybody in his logging camp and in the tiny town that had sprung up on its outskirts.

They were both big women. Jason was over six feet tall and Gladys could just about look him square in the eye. Polly ran the laundry and had scrubbed up some mighty impressive arm muscles.

Duncan eased between the women, still twisting his hat.

"Now, Mr. Kruger here, he's agreed to hear you both out," Duncan said, "and he's going to settle this thing once and for all."

Gladys and Polly glared at each other, then turned to Jason.

"All right," Jason said. "Tell me what happened. You go first, Mrs. Minton."

Polly Minton squared her shoulders, enjoying her moment.

"I was just doing the neighborly thing, the Christian thing," Polly said. "I invited Gladys over to my house a few days ago and we sat a spell before I had to get supper going. Then today I dropped by her place—just to be neighborly—and sitting right there on her windowsill, pretty as you please, there it was."

Jason frowned. "What?"

"She stole it!" Polly said.

"I did no such thing!" Gladys shouted.

"Stole what?" Jason asked.

"Look here. See for yourself. I brought it along for evidence." Polly pulled back the cloth cover on the small hamper she'd carried into the office with her. She lifted out a half-eaten apple pie.

"I sneaked me a bite of this pie when Gladys wasn't looking," Polly said. "It's my recipe. No two ways about it, Gladys Duncan stole me apple pie recipe!"

"I did no such thing!" Gladys declared.

"A pie recipe?" Jason got to his feet and turned to Duncan. "You've got me involved in this over some damn pie recipe?"

Polly gasped. "That recipe has been in my family for generations. It's a treasure."

"Some treasure!" Gladys tossed her head.

Jason pointed at Duncan. "I ought to fire you right now."

He twisted his hat. "But Mr. Kruger—"

"She stole it while my back was turned," Polly

said. "Stole it because she's jealous of my cooking."

Gladys planted her hands on her ample hips. "You're the jealous one. Jealous because everybody loves my roast chicken." Gladys turned to Jason. "She's been after my secret ingredients ever since I came here."

Polly gasped. "That's a lie!"

"It is not! You're the jealous one!"

Jason waved his arms. "All right, now, hold it down."

"It's my recipe! I tasted my special ingredients the minute it touched my lips! And Gladys stole it from me! Taste it for yourself, Mr. Kruger. You'll see." Polly shoved the pie toward him.

"Mr. Kruger doesn't want to taste your ol' pie!" Gladys reached for the pie, bumped the plate and jarred it from Polly's hand. It landed with a thud on Jason's desk. Apples splattered across his papers, over his shirt and down his trousers.

There was a collective gasp, then a tense silence filled the office. Jason looked down at the gooey pie clinging to his clothing.

"Where's my gun?" he asked softly.

Polly whimpered. Gladys groaned.

Duncan pushed his way between the two women. "Now, Mr. Kruger, think about what you're saying. You can't really shoot these women."

"I'm not going to shoot them." Jason lifted his head slowly. "I'm going to shoot *you!*"

Gladys burst into tears.

"Now, Mr. Kruger, you don't want to go and do that." Duncan wrung his hat fitfully.

"Get these women out of here!" Jason pointed toward the door. "I don't want to see another woman in my camp!"

"But Mr. Kruger—"

"No more women! Ever!"

The office door opened and Shady Harper ambled inside.

"What do you want, Shady?" Jason snarled.

Shady took in the office with squinted eyes. "I brung you back something from town, boss."

His face brightened. "My package?"

"Naw. Weren't no mail today."

Jason's frown returned. "Leave it outside, Shady."

"Don't think I'd better do that." Shady wiggled his fingers toward the door. "Come on in here."

A delicate fragrance drifted into the office seconds before a woman stepped inside, bringing a hush to the room and freezing Jason in place.

She blinked up at him with big blue eyes. "Mr. Kruger? I'm Miss Amanda Pierce from San Francisco."

He scowled at her. "Yeah?"

"I'm here at your request," she said.

"My request?"

"Yes, Mr. Kruger. Your request for a wife."

Chapter Two

"A wife!" Jason shouted.

Amanda glanced around the room at the faces staring at her. "Really, Mr. Kruger, there's no need to raise your voice."

"A *wife?*"

She was tired from her long journey and a headache threatened from the bone-rattling trip up the mountain. This Mr. Kruger was testing the limits of her good manners.

"Yes, Mr. Kruger, a—"

"What about my pie recipe?" Polly demanded.

"And what about her accusing me of stealing?" Gladys asked.

Duncan wrung his hat. "Mr. Kruger, you got to settle this once and for all."

"Now look, all of you," Jason said, "I don't—"

"Excuse me, Mr. Kruger." Amanda leaned closer and lowered her voice. "You've spilled a little pie on your shirt."

The words just hung there for a moment between the two of them.

"Thank you," he finally said, grinding out the words between clenched teeth as if he hadn't the least bit of appreciation for her helpful comment.

He turned to the other women. "Now look, I don't give a damn about whose pie recipe is whose, or who puts what into their roast chicken, or who stole what recipe. None of it amounts to a hill of ants and I don't want to hear another word about it."

Polly bristled. *"Well!"*

"I never...." Gladys put her nose in the air.

"Get out of my office," Jason said, "all of you. Come back when you've got a serious problem."

Duncan moaned. "But Mr. Kruger..."

"Excuse me, Mr. Kruger?" Amanda said. "If I may say so, what you have here is, indeed, a serious problem."

For a moment Jason Kruger looked as if he intended to toss her out of his office along with the others, but Amanda stood firm. He couldn't give her his full attention until the stolen pie recipe was dealt with, and since Jason wasn't taking it seriously, she would.

"If I may?" Amanda asked Jason.

He threw both hands up. "Have at it, lady."

Amanda turned to the women. "As I understand it, one of you thinks the other stole your recipe."

Polly jerked her head toward Gladys. "She stole my apple pie recipe."

"And she's after my roast chicken ingredients," Gladys said.

"A woman works for years perfecting a recipe. She certainly doesn't want another woman taking it, then passing it along for everyone to use." Amanda turned to Jason. "Are you following this, Mr. Kruger?"

He threw her a sour look. "Hanging on every word."

"Good," Amanda said. "As I see it, there's but one way to settle this issue. You ladies will exchange your pie and chicken recipes with each other. Only the two of you will have them. That way you can be assured neither recipe will be passed along to anyone else without fearing that your own recipe will then be passed on in retaliation. How does that sound?"

Gladys and Polly looked at each other, then finally nodded their agreement.

Duncan rushed forward and took Amanda's hand. "Thank you, ma'am, thank you kindly. This here is surely a load off of my mind."

He escorted the two women out of the office, then stuck his head back in. "Mr. Kruger, that little lady's going to make you a fine wife. A real fine wife."

The door closed, bringing a silence more uncomfortable than the shouting match that had gone on earlier. Jason stared at her, and Amanda found herself pulled into his gaze, held there against her will.

He was tall, with black hair and green eyes that unsettled her. He spent his days in the sunshine; it had deepened the color of his face and etched fine lines at his eyes. He worked hard, too. Thick muscles moved against the sleeves of his pale blue shirt. His shoulders were straight, his chest wide, his waist tight, and his—

Amanda pressed her lips together, containing the little gasp that threatened to fill the silent room. Her gaze collided with his and for a flash of a second he looked as naughty as she felt. Her cheeks warmed. What had *he* been thinking while staring at *her?*

Jason frowned. "Do you want to tell me just what the hell is going on here, Miss Pierce?"

"Ain't you even going to invite the lady to sit down?" Shady snorted.

Amanda had forgotten he was in the room. Jason Kruger seemed to take up all the space, breathe up all the air.

Shady dragged a chair across the room and plunked it down in front of Jason's desk. "Sit yourself down, ma'am."

Amanda smiled gratefully as she settled into the chair. In the hours she'd spent in the freight wagon with Shady she'd gotten to know him well and decided she liked him. Gruff and hard-edged on the outside, he was a softy inside.

"Thank you, Shady."

"Yes, ma'am." Shady looked at Jason. "Miss Pierce here has had a long, rough trip up the mountain. And she's only here 'cause you went and sent for her."

Jason lowered himself into the chair behind his desk and pushed his hand through his hair.

"I haven't been down off this mountain in months, Miss Pierce," he said. "There's no way in hell I could have asked you to marry me."

"She's got a letter," Shady said. "A letter writ by you."

"It's a request, actually," Amanda said, and pulled the letter from her handbag. "You see, Mr. Kruger, I'm here from the Becoming Brides Matrimonial Service."

Shady chuckled. "Well, I'll be damned—a catalog bride."

Jason leaned back in his chair. "Are you saying I *ordered* you?"

"It's all right here in your letter."

He snatched it from her hand. His eyes darted back and forth across the page, then cut over to Shady.

"Go find Ethan."

"Sure thing, boss." Shady headed out the door.

Amanda watched Jason read the letter again, then level his gaze at her across the desk.

"Looks like you came a long way for nothing, Miss Pierce," he said. "I didn't write this letter."

Amanda's stomach squeezed into a knot. He hadn't written the letter? She'd come all this way for nothing? Endured the hardships of the trip, spent her carefully budgeted money—for nothing?

Amanda shook her head. "Aren't you Jason Kruger? Isn't this the Kruger Brothers' Lumber and Milling Company?"

"Yes. But I'm telling you, Miss Pierce, I didn't write this letter. I never even heard of the Becoming Brides Matrimonial Service until just now."

"But…" Amanda sank back in her chair.

The door opened and a man walked inside. Tall, with dark hair and the same green eyes as Jason, they could only be brothers.

Except that this brother was grinning from ear to ear.

He pulled off his hat and nodded politely to Amanda.

"Pleased to meet you, Miss Pierce. I'm Ethan Kruger," he said. "Shady just told me he brought you up the mountain today."

"Nice to meet you, Mr. Kruger." Her manners were so deeply ingrained they sustained her even in this time of distress.

Ethan turned to Jason. "So, you sent off for a bride, huh? I should let you do the ordering all the time."

Jason, unamused, pushed himself to his feet. "I didn't order a bride."

Ethan frowned and gestured to Jason's shirt. "Eating at the trough with the pigs again, Jas?"

He looked down at the apple pie still stuck to his shirt and trousers, mumbled a curse, and headed for the washstand in the corner.

Ethan eased onto the corner of the desk. "Tell me, Miss Pierce, have you two set a date for the blessed event?"

"Just shut your mouth," Jason said, pointing a

dripping finger at his brother. "I'm not marrying her. This is all a mistake. Look at the letter."

Ethan grinned at Amanda, then picked up the letter and looked it over. "This isn't your handwriting."

"I know that." Jason wiped the last of the apple pie from his clothing and flung the rag into the basin.

"Can't say that I recognize whose it is." Ethan shook his head. "Must be some sort of a joke."

"A joke?" Amanda came to her feet.

Ethan chuckled. "It is sort of funny."

Funny? Amanda's temper rose. She'd traveled miles and miles from the safety and security of home to come here—and she wasn't exactly sure where *here* was—endured hardships, threats to her personal safety, bad manners and foul smells. And the Kruger brothers thought it was funny?

"Somebody made the whole thing up and forged my name," Jason said to Ethan.

"Who'd do a thing like that?" Ethan asked.

"I don't know, but I intend to find out." Jason walked back to his desk.

Ethan shrugged. "Why don't you just go ahead and marry her?"

Jason stopped short. "What the hell would I do with a wife?"

"If you have to ask that question, you *have* been up on this mountain too long," Ethan said with a grin.

Jason's gaze came up quickly and landed on Amanda. Her cheeks flushed, taking the edge off her anger and reminding her that she was here on business and she should stick to it, even if these two men wouldn't.

"Mr. Kruger," she said. "I believe you've misunderstood my intentions here. I only—"

"Look, Miss Pierce," Jason said. "I'm not looking for a wife now or anytime in the future."

"If you'd just let me explain."

"The last thing anybody here needs is a wife," Jason said.

"But—"

"This is a logging camp," Jason said. "My men work twelve hours a day, six days a week. It's dangerous work. Just a few seconds of lost concentration can cost a man his life—or the life of the men he's working with. I'm not having a bunch of women up here distracting my crew from their job. Nobody here wants a wife."

"Nobody?"

"Nobody."

Amanda drew in a deep breath. "I see...."

Bitter disappointment coursed through her. She'd pinned so much on this trip. All the plans she'd made—plans that had kept her going in the past few days—were gone. Along with her high hopes for the future.

Amanda swallowed hard, refusing to let her feelings overwhelm her. She'd come here to find out, to learn, to investigate. Now she had her answer.

She drew in a big breath, pumping up her courage. "Well...I suppose there's nothing left to do but...leave."

Ethan poked Jason in the arm. "You could at least tell her you're sorry she came all the way up here for nothing—on account of you."

"Oh, yeah." Jason shifted uncomfortably and turned to Amanda. "Look, Miss Pierce, I really am...sorry...you got dragged up here on some wild-goose chase."

"No you're not," Amanda said, her disappointment turning to anger. She'd had enough of the Kruger Brothers' Lumber and Milling Company, and enough of the Kruger brothers themselves. Jason had made it abundantly clear that he had no use for her whatsoever, and she was in no mood to be patronized.

"Well, look, Miss Pierce—"

"You're not the least bit sorry I wasted my time, so don't pretend otherwise," Amanda told him. "You, Mr. Kruger, are thoughtless, inconsiderate, and rude. Don't add lying to your list of faults."

Amanda put her nose in the air and sailed across the office, then looked back at him. "*And* you have horrible table manners!"

She gave the door a very unladylike slam on her way out.

Jason and Ethan just stood there staring at the closed door.

"Damn...." Jason mumbled.

Ethan grinned. "Yeah, bedding down with her would—"

"That's not what I was thinking," Jason said quickly.

"Like hell you weren't."

Jason turned away, pacing the width of the office, refusing to look at his brother.

"What are we going to do with her?" Ethan asked, as he pulled matches from the desk drawer and lit the lanterns on the walls.

Jason spun around. "Do with her? I'm not going to do anything with her."

"It's too late to get her down the mountain to-night," Ethan said. "Shady can't make that trip in the dark. The trail is dangerous enough in broad daylight."

"She can't stay here."

"What do you want to do, Jas? Give her a candle and a map and tell her to start walking?"

Jason grumbled under his breath. "This is why I don't want women up here. They're nothing but trouble."

"Maybe," Ethan said. "But she's here now. We've got to do something with her."

"You're right. I guess she'll have to stay." Jason paced a little more, thinking. "Take her over to Mrs. McGee's place and see if she'll put her up for the night."

"Meg…?"

"There's no other place for a decent woman to stay."

"Yeah, I know…but…"

"But what?"

"Nothing." Ethan shifted from one foot to the other. "I can take her over there…I reckon."

* * *

Outside, Amanda stood on the porch holding on to the rough support column and gazing around at the logging camp. What little she could see of it, at least. When she'd arrived earlier, she had only gotten a vague impression of the camp, and that wasn't much to go on now that it was dark.

Off in the distance a few windows glowed yellow with lantern light. She made out shadowy silhouettes of buildings and a couple of dark figures passing in front of them. A cool breeze blew. A dog barked somewhere.

If she had good sense she might be frightened, Amanda decided. But right now she was simply too tired, too angry, and too disappointed to feel anything else.

She needed to find Shady Harper and ask him to take her down the mountain tonight. But where was he? The freight wagon she'd arrived in was nowhere to be seen, and neither was Shady. She had no idea where to look for him.

The little cluster of buildings that Shady had called a town was only a short walk east. Maybe he was there. If not, surely she'd find a hotel where she could spend the night. All she had to do was get there without falling over something and killing herself stumbling along in the dark.

Amanda glanced back at the door of Jason Kruger's office that she had slammed so indignantly moments ago, and decided that she wasn't desperate enough to ask that man for help—not now or in the foreseeable future.

The door opened just then and he walked out, his tall, wide frame outlined by the lantern light behind him. Amanda's temper rose again.

His face was in shadows and when he stepped closer Amanda realized it wasn't Jason, but his brother. Her anger turned to something that for a flicker of a second seemed like disappointment. Amanda pushed it aside quickly. Certainly it couldn't be that.

"Miss Pierce?" Ethan said. "I'm going to take you some place to stay for the night."

"That won't be necessary, Mr. Kruger."

"Just call me Ethan. It can get kind of confusing around here, otherwise." He grinned and nodded toward the office. "Besides, I don't like being mistaken for my brother, if you get my meaning."

"I do indeed get your meaning." Amanda glared at the office door, then looked at Ethan. "But your help isn't necessary. I'm going to have Shady take me back to Beaumont."

"Not tonight, he can't." Ethan shook his head. "Shady can't make that trip after dark."

"Then I'll get a hotel room for the night."

"There is no hotel."

"No hotel?" Amanda asked. "But surely—"

"Just do like you're told." Jason walked up, his footsteps heavy on the wooden porch. Amanda sensed he'd been standing there, listening... watching.

Anger threaded through her again. "You may be in charge of the logging camp, Mr. Kruger, but you have no say over what I do. Now, I am going to find Shady Harper and arrange for transportation down the mountain tonight.''

''No, you're not.''

His big hand closed over her elbow. Long fingers exerted just enough pressure to keep her in place. She sensed incredible power in his grip, power barely under control.

Heat rushed up her arm, twined down her throat into the pit of her stomach causing her anger to bloom again.

And it *was* anger. What else could it be?

Amanda jerked her chin. ''I am not your concern, Mr. Kruger.''

He leaned closer. A raw physical energy radiated from him, engulfing Amanda with its potency.

''That's where you're wrong, Miss Pierce.'' His voice was deep, heavy with authority and determination. ''Everything and everybody on this mountain is my concern.''

''Including me?''

He tightened his grip and leaned closer. ''Especially you.''

Chapter Three

"Let me give you a hand, Miss Pierce."

Ethan's fingers closed around Amanda's elbow, steadying her over the uneven terrain. His grip was as strong as his brother's but not threatening in the least. In fact, Amanda barely noticed it.

But she had certainly noticed Jason when he'd stalked back into his office, leaving his brother to deliver her to a safe place for the night. And that suited Amanda just fine. Jason's mere presence rankled her.

"You'll like Mrs. McGee," Ethan said, holding the lantern higher to light their way. The road was rough and rutted, dangerous in the dark.

Amanda held up her skirt, picking her way along. "You're certain she won't mind if I stay the night with her? It's hardly proper to show up uninvited and ask such a favor. I can pay her, of course."

"Mrs. McGee could surely use the money, but I doubt she'll take it," Ethan said. "She'll probably

just be glad for the company. Meg works hard. Too
hard. Sometimes I worry that she's—''

Amanda dared to take her eyes from the road.
Ethan's expression was unreadable in the dark.

''I gather there aren't many women up here,'' she
said.

''Half-dozen or so,'' Ethan said.

''Your brother seems most adept at running them
off,'' Amanda said.

Ethan chuckled. ''This is Mrs. McGee's place.''

They both stood there for a moment gazing at the
little wood frame cabin with lantern light shining in
one window.

''Aren't we going to knock?'' Amanda asked,
when Ethan made no move toward the porch.

''Well, sure, I just...''

Ethan gave himself a little shake and placed the
lantern on the steps. He climbed onto the porch,
pulled off his hat, slicked back his hair, brushed at
his sleeves, and tugged down on his vest. Drawing
in a deep breath, Ethan studied the door for a moment, then finally knocked.

It opened and Mrs. McGee stepped into view.
Amanda had expected her to resemble the two
women she'd met in Jason Kruger's office, big
women capable of weathering life in the rugged logging camp.

But Mrs. McGee was delicate and shapely, about
the same age as Amanda. Her blond hair was twisted
neatly atop her head, and her dress, while service-
able, was flattering.

''Good evening, Mr. Kruger,'' she said.

"Mrs. McGee." Ethan twisted his hat, then plastered it against his chest. "I, uh, I'm sorry to bother you so late, but I'd like to ask a favor, if I can."

"What sort of favor?" she asked.

"Well…" Ethan seemed lost for a moment. He looked down at his feet, then back at her. "Well…"

At this rate they'd be standing here all night. Amanda climbed onto the porch. "Mrs. McGee, I'm Miss Amanda Pierce. I'm very sorry to disturb you, but I find myself stranded here on the mountain. Ethan felt I could impose on you for a night's lodging."

She turned a warm smile on Ethan. "How thoughtful of you…."

Ethan turned several shades of red. He seemed to stop breathing for a moment, as well.

"I hope it's not too much to ask, Mrs. McGee," Amanda said.

"Of course not. And please, call me Meg," she said.

Ethan nodded toward Amanda. "Miss Pierce was supposed to get married up here, but—"

Meg's eyes widened. "Married?"

"To Jason."

Meg smiled broadly at Amanda. "That's wonderful!"

"It's all a mistake," Amanda said. "I'm not marrying anyone."

"But…" Meg's shoulders slumped.

"I'll round up Shady and have him bring your bags over," Ethan said.

"Thank you very much, Ethan," Amanda said,

and stepped inside the house. "You've been very kind."

Ethan stood there on the porch for a moment, twisting his hat and shuffling his feet.

"Well...'night, Mrs. McGee," he said.

"Good night, Ethan." Meg paused for a moment, then closed the door softly.

Amanda was pleased to see that the McGee home looked comfortable and inviting. A big cookstove, a dining table and chairs, and a settee and rocker crowded the little room, decorated with lace doilies and a glowing lamp, all scrubbed clean and neat as a pin. Amanda felt herself relax for the first time since coming up the mountain.

"You must be starved," Meg said. "Let me get you something."

"I don't want to impose on you any further," Amanda said. "But I am quite hungry."

Meg smiled. "It's nothing fancy, just some chicken left from the supper I made for Todd and me."

"Todd is your husband?" Amanda asked.

Meg stopped suddenly and her face blanched. "No. Todd is my son. My husband is...gone."

Amanda cringed. Jason Kruger had told her about the dangerous work in the logging camp. She should have been more considerate about asking after Meg's husband.

"I'm sorry to be so thoughtless," Amanda said. "Please forgive me, and accept my condolences for your loss."

Meg shook her head. "My husband isn't dead. He's...gone."

There was surely more to the story than Meg was telling, but it was hardly any of Amanda's business so she didn't ask anything else.

Amanda didn't pry into other peoples' pasts because she knew—far too well—how hurtful that could be.

She slipped off her gloves and unpinned her hat while Meg moved around the kitchen. A knock sounded at the door, and when Meg answered it, Shady Harper ambled inside carrying Amanda's two carpetbags and satchel.

"So, when are you and ol' Jason gittin' hitched?" Shady asked.

"There will be no wedding," Amanda said. "It seems Mr. Kruger didn't write that letter after all."

Shady squinted hard at her. "And he's not marrying you? Not doing the right thing by you?"

"You see, Shady, I never intended to marry Mr. Kruger."

Shady tilted his head. "How's that?"

She'd tried to explain it to Jason Kruger in his office but he'd refused to listen. She may as well tell somebody in this logging camp.

"I'm the *owner* of the Becoming Brides Matrimonial Service, not a prospective bride," Amanda said. "My service is very selective. I don't accept just any woman as a bride, nor do I blindly fill a request from every man who makes one."

"So you come up here to have a look-see at Jason, after you got that letter from him asking for a wife?'' Shady asked.

"Yes," she said. "I came to determine if Mr. Kruger would be an acceptable Becoming Brides husband."

"And you come all the way up here just to find out?" Shady asked.

"No, not entirely." Amanda paused, reluctant to go into her real reason for being here. She already felt foolish enough in coming this far for nothing. But what damage could it do to talk about it now? She would leave in the morning and never see any of these people again.

"Actually, I'd hoped that other men here in the logging camp would want wives also," Amanda said.

"That's a wonderful idea," Meg said.

"Darn tootin'," Shady said.

"I didn't know Mr. Kruger had a rule about not allowing women here. It seems I've brought my catalog of brides all the way up here for nothing." Amanda gestured toward her satchel Shady had placed beside the stone fireplace.

"A catalog?" Shady asked. "Like a mail-order book? With pictures? Of women wanting to get hitched?"

Amanda nodded. "Dozens, actually. I offer brides of varying size, shape, hair color. All are educated and have excellent homemaking skills. Many are proficient in music and art, all sorts of things."

Shady nodded toward her satchel. "And you got all them women in that book of yourn?"

"And the women are willing to come up here to the mountain to live?" Meg asked.

"Willing and anxious," Amanda said. "I was disappointed, of course, when Mr. Kruger said no one here was interested in a wife."

"Jason said that?" Meg asked.

"Yes," Amanda said. "Several times—and not very pleasantly, I might add."

"Humph." Shady snorted and hitched up his trousers.

"There's nothing left for me to do here," Amanda said. "I'd like to ask you to take me back down the mountain in the morning, Shady."

"You're leaving?" Meg asked. "So soon?"

"I've no reason to stay."

"Maybe if you give Jason time to think it over he'll change his mind," Meg said.

Amanda shook her head. "He was adamant about not allowing other women up here, even without knowing I owned the matrimonial service. Can you imagine his reaction if he knew I wanted to bring a large number of brides to his logging camp?"

Jason stood on the porch outside his office soaking up the silence and the peace and solitude of the darkness. During the day the mountain roared with the buzzing of saws in the mill, the horses and oxen straining against their heavy loads, axes splitting wood, and the shouts of his men felling the timber.

At night it was quiet. Peaceful. Jason's mind could rest and his body could unwind. He treasured this time.

Except that tonight his thoughts hummed like a band saw and his body was wound tight enough to explode.

It was that woman's fault. That Miss Amanda Pierce. Sashaying into his office with her bustle bobbing and her skirts swaying. Batting her eyelashes at him. Poking her lip out in a pout.

Well, damn if she'd come prancing onto his mountain and change the way he did things. Jason had a business to run. A business he'd fought hard to get started, and fought even harder to keep going. Big things were on the horizon. He didn't need any distractions.

And Amanda Pierce was definitely a distraction.

Jason leaned his shoulder against the support column and gazed down the road toward town. He could still smell the scent of her lingering in the air. Sweet, delicate. Womanly.

He let his gaze wander to the McGee house. Shady Harper had gone inside a few minutes ago carrying her baggage. The whole house probably smelled like her by now.

The front door opened just then and Shady walked outside. A woman stepped into the doorway, outlined by the lantern light inside. Jason straightened and craned his neck. Was it her? Was it Amanda?

"Damn."

Jason turned away mumbling a curse into the darkness. Women were a distraction, all right, and he'd just proved it, lurking in the dark, hoping to catch a peek of one. Even if it had been a long time since he'd peeked at a woman—or done anything more pleasurable with one.

He swung around again watching Shady on the porch talking to the woman in the doorway. It was Amanda. He was sure of it now.

Maybe Ethan was right. Maybe he had been up on this mountain too long.

Amanda was a good-looking woman. All the right curves in all the right places. Done up proper, begging to be undone. A tight little package waiting to be opened.

He'd like to unravel that package, and take his time doing it. Slow, easy, until he'd—

Jason snorted another curse and pushed himself off the porch, angry at his thoughts and his body's reaction to them.

What the hell was he thinking? He didn't need or want a woman in his life. Especially this one, full of vinegar and sass, calling him names and insulting him to his face, right in his own office. Miss Amanda Pierce would be gone in the morning, and good riddance to her.

Jason stalked down the road away from his office. He was going home. He'd get a good night's sleep and set his mind back on work. He was expecting a package, and if Shady brought it up from Beaumont tomorrow he had to be ready to deal with it. He needed to keep his mind on business.

But a fragrance tickled Jason's nose, stopping him in his track. He turned, his gaze drawn once again to the McGee house just as Amanda stepped back inside. Jason stood there a moment longer staring at the closed door, sniffing the air for the scent of her.

"Hellfire...."

Jason stalked away.

The gray of dawn seeped into the house as Amanda opened her eyes to the little room she'd slept in. She'd fallen asleep as soon as her head had hit the feather pillow last night, then awakened this morning to the smell of something delicious cooking in the kitchen—and the certain knowledge that she wasn't in her own bed at home in San Francisco.

Amanda lay on the smooth cotton sheets for a few minutes, thinking. Here she was in a strange bed, a strange house, a strange place. The well-ordered life she'd left behind in San Francisco over a week ago seemed very dear to her right now.

Her father had been a successful merchant, and had left Amanda and her mother financially comfortable upon his death. But her mother wasn't very wise in business and it hadn't taken long before most of the money was gone.

Her mother was gone now, too. Amanda had used what money was left to start her Becoming Brides Matrimonial Service. The business filled several of the empty spots in her life.

Amanda pushed back the coverlet and sat up. The air in the little house was cool. She rose and dressed quickly.

Meg stood at the cookstove and Todd, her son, sat at the table. Amanda had seen the boy last night when Meg had roused him out of his bed and given it to Amanda. Todd was eight years old with blond hair, like his mother. His looks came from his father, Amanda guessed. His father who was...gone.

"Good morning," Meg said, and smiled. "You're just in time."

"Can I help?" Amanda asked.

"No, thanks, all done." Meg turned a pan of scrambled eggs into a bowl and set it on the table alongside a stack of biscuits. "Sit down."

Todd dug in before Amanda and Meg got seated and finished before they got started.

"Can I go outside, Mama?" Todd asked.

"Yes, but don't go far," Meg said. "And don't go near the mill."

Todd rolled his eyes as if he'd heard those instructions before and darted out the front door. Amanda watched him go, watched the love in Meg's gaze follow the boy outside.

"He's a sweet child," Amanda said.

Meg's smile faded. "It's been hard for him since his father...left."

"Is he away on business?" Amanda asked.

"No." Meg sipped her coffee.

"Sorry," Amanda said. "I didn't mean to pry."

Meg sighed. "The whole mountain knows, so I suppose there's no reason you shouldn't. I woke one morning to find a note from Gerald saying he couldn't live here any longer. He was moving on. He was sorry that he couldn't take Todd and me with him, but he had to go find his own way."

"And he left? Just like that?"

"Gerald was never the stable type," Meg said.

"We always moved from place to place, job to job."

"That's how you ended up here?"

"Gerald started a business in town. It failed. He tried again, then again, never with much luck. Then finally, he simply left."

"How awful."

"Yes, it was awful at first." Meg managed a smile. "But Todd and I have a roof over our heads and I find enough work to keep us fed. We're doing all right."

"Why don't you leave?"

"I have no family now, except for Todd," Meg said. "Where would I go?"

"Do you like living here?" Amanda asked. She managed to keep from sounding judgmental. Though the mountain was foreign to her, that didn't mean others wouldn't like it.

"Yes," Meg said, "but it is a little lonely without other women around."

"Thanks to Mr. Kruger," Amanda grumbled.

"Jason let Duncan's wife come here because he was injured in an accident a few months back and she nursed him back to health. There's no doctor in camp, you know. The few other women who live here work in town."

"Does Mr. Kruger own the town as well?"

"The land under the town, but not the businesses," Meg said. "He has a lot of influence over what goes on there. Why shouldn't he? He owns the mountain."

Amanda's eyes widened. "He *owns* it?"

"Yes, he does."

Amanda sat back, disturbed, but not knowing why exactly. There was something very powerful about a man who owned an entire mountain.

"The rules he has," Meg said, "like no drinking and no smoking in camp, are for the safety and well-being of the loggers. He's very concerned about his men. Jason is actually a very good boss."

"You'll forgive me if I differ with you on that."

Meg smiled. "I've heard about other logging and milling companies from the men who work here. Most of them pay in script and the only place to shop is the company store, where prices are ridiculously high. Sometimes when the lumber market isn't good, the owners refuse to redeem the script. The crews are stuck with no money and no way to get any. All they can do is keep working for the same owner."

"That's terrible," Amanda said.

Meg nodded. "But Jason pays his crew in cash. Since he doesn't own any of the businesses in town, his men can shop wherever they want."

Amanda pushed her plate aside. "Still, to be so controlling…."

"Jason's no saint," Meg said. "But he is fair. That's why I think you should go to him again this morning and explain about your plan to bring brides up here."

Amanda remembered the look on Jason Kruger's face last night and shook her head. "He seemed adamant."

"But it's a wonderful idea. You've come this far,

Amanda, you can't just leave without giving it one more try," Meg said. "All the women here would be so grateful."

Amanda mulled it over. She had come a long way and she deserved another chance. Maybe Jason would see things differently in the light of day. Once he heard her plan he might welcome the idea of brides on his mountain, as long as he didn't have to marry one of them himself.

She'd been so determined, so anxious when she left San Francisco. Making the difficult trip, waiting in Beaumont two long days hadn't deterred her. Even the rough trip up the mountain wasn't enough to make her lose the enthusiasm for her plan. Nothing was, except meeting Jason Kruger.

Something about that man unsettled her. What was it?

Amanda didn't want to think too hard on that notion. "All right," she said. "I'll give it another try."

She rose from the table filled with determination and purpose once again. She'd talk to Jason Kruger.

What could he do but say *no?*

Chapter Four

The gray dawn clung to the treetops as Amanda left Meg McGee's house carrying her satchel and her hopes for the future, in search of Jason Kruger.

It didn't seem quite fair that her dreams hinged on that particular man. Amanda had run the Becoming Brides Matrimonial Service for a little more than a year and she had plans for her business, for herself.

And for her prospective brides. They'd come to her with hopes and dreams of their own. A family, a husband, children, a home. All were things she could provide, with the right contacts.

Amanda picked her way along the rutted road. No, being dependent on the whim of Jason Kruger for her success and the happiness of her brides was not desirable at all. But at the moment, she had no choice.

What Amanda hadn't seen last night when she arrived in the dark took her by surprise as she made her way down the road. The logging camp and town had been quite literally carved out of the mountain.

A wall of thick trees towering two hundred feet in the air surrounded a large clearing. Inside lay the town, which was behind Amanda as she headed west, and in front of her was the logging camp. Off to her right was the sawmill and millpond.

The bone-rattling road that had brought her up from Beaumont last night separated the camp from the town, then continued on, winding its way up the mountain. The bunkhouse, storehouse and cook-house lay ahead of her in the heart of the camp. A few smaller buildings were scattered between them, including barns and animal pens where horses and oxen stood, waiting to start their day of toil.

Across the road was Jason Kruger's office. A house sat behind it; she guessed it belonged to the Kruger brothers. Absently, Amanda wondered what it looked like inside. Probably not one doily or lace cloth in the place.

There was wood everywhere. Amanda had never seen so much wood. Wooden houses, wooden shingles, wooden furniture. Stumps, slivers and shavings of wood, broken boards, sawdust. The air smelled of trees, sweet sawdust and sap.

The camp had the feel of hasty construction about it, as if it had been thrown together out of necessity in a rush to get on to more important matters.

No one was out at this hour. Meg had told Amanda she would find the men in the cookhouse before heading up the mountain for the day. Jason would be there, too.

A rumble of voices drew Amanda to the large building Meg had described. Delicious scents drifted

on the air. Amanda paused outside the door, straightened her skirt and touched her hand to her hat.
While the other women she'd met in camp dressed
more simply, Amanda was here to conduct business,
and it was important that her appearance reflect that.

She started inside, then stopped. She wasn't all
that anxious to meet Jason Kruger again.

Or was she?

He'd been on her mind all morning, even before
Meg had suggested she talk with him again. She
remembered last night and how irritating he'd been.
How demanding. How arrogant.

How she'd called him those terrible names.

Amanda wasn't all that experienced at business,
but it probably wasn't good to call your prospective
customer thoughtless, inconsiderate and rude, and
still expect him to do business with you. Even if he
deserved to be called all those names.

As Jason Kruger did.

There was nothing she could do but continue on.
Talk to Jason, present her plan, and hope for the
best. Though he'd probably be less than happy to
see her again, Amanda consoled herself with the
thought that the worst he could do was say no. He
certainly wouldn't toss her over his shoulder, lash
her to the wagon, and send the team careening down
his mountain, back to Beaumont.

Amanda shifted her satchel from one hand to the
other. Her future lay inside this cookhouse, in the
hands of Jason Kruger. She drew in a deep breath
and walked inside.

Rows of long tables holding platters of food filled

the room. Men crowded the benches eating from tin
plates, drinking steaming coffee from tin cups. The
cook, a round-bellied man in a soiled apron, stood
in the corner. The men kept their heads down, eating
and talking while young boys, the cook's helpers,
scurried down the aisles refilling cups, bringing
more platters of food.

Amanda raised on tiptoes looking over the sea of
bobbing heads. There must have been fifty men here
and she wasn't sure how she'd find Jason among
them.

A man seated at the table nearest Amanda noticed
her. He did a double take, elbowed the man beside
him, and pointed.

That man looked, then the one seated beside him
looked, until the whole table was staring. Their
hands stilled halfway to their mouths.

The table beside those men noticed Amanda, then
the next table, and the next.

Silence crossed the cookhouse like ripples in a
pond. No metal forks clicked against tin plates. No
coffee slurped from cups. The cook's helpers
stopped between the tables. The room froze in reverent silence.

Fifty faces turned to Amanda. Fifty pairs of eyes
widened. Fifty jaws sagged.

The thought that she was glad she'd dressed for
the moment skittered through Amanda's head.

Across the room, in the far corner, one man rose
from the table. Tall. Wide chest. Straight shoulders.

Thoughtless, inconsiderate, rude.

Handsome.

Jason Kruger.

Amanda's heart sped up urging her to run. Toward him, or away from him? She wasn't sure.

Jason charged across the room frowning and scowling even more than last night. For an instant Amanda wondered if she'd been wrong. Might he do something worse than simply say *no?* Being lashed to a wagon careening down the mountain didn't seem outside of the realm of possibility at the moment.

Jason stopped in front of her, towering over her, crowding her. His glare gave off heat. It ensnared Amanda, refusing to let her back away.

She gazed up at his hard, angry face. "Good morning, Mr. Kruger."

"What the hell are you—"

Jason stopped and glanced back at the men sitting like fifty statues at the tables. He lowered his voice.

"What are you doing in here?"

"I have a business proposition to discuss with you, Mr. Kruger."

He nodded toward the door. "Get outside."

Amanda's spine stiffened and her chin went up. "Mr. Kruger, I will not be ordered about like a servant."

Jason pressed his lips together, holding in his simmering anger. "Miss Pierce, would you kindly step outside? Before you get yourself mauled by fifty men?"

Amanda peeked around Jason at the men staring at her. "They seem harmless to me."

"Some of these men haven't laid eyes on a woman like you in months."

"A woman like me?" Amanda asked. "And what sort of woman would that be?"

Jason faltered. His angry expression collapsed as his gaze raked her from head to toe. His lips twitched as if he wanted to spit out a mouthful of words, but he held them in.

"Would you just go outside?" Jason glared down at her. "Please?"

The morning sunlight crept over the treetops as Amanda stepped out of the cookhouse. Before she could pause, Jason clamped onto her elbow and propelled her across the road. The chatter inside the cookhouse started up again.

Jason stared at her and tugged down on his hat brim, bringing it lower over his eyes.

"Look, Miss Pierce, I haven't got a lot of time. I've got a business to run. I'm sorry you got hauled up here for nothing, but I'm not going to marry you and that's all there is to it."

"As it happens, Mr. Kruger, I have no desire to marry you," Amanda said.

He looked offended now. "How's that?"

"As you said last night, the letter I received was a mistake," Amanda said. "But that doesn't mean we can't work out a mutually beneficial arrangement."

"You don't want to marry me, but you think we could work out some sort of arrangement?" Jason looked hard at her and dragged the back of his hand across his mouth. His lips twitched again. "What, exactly, did you have in mind, Miss Pierce?"

"I think my services are exactly what you need, Mr. Kruger."

He shifted from one foot to the other. "Your *services?*"

"Yes," Amanda said. "Your logging camp is a long way from Beaumont and even there you'll find few women to choose from. The proper kind of woman, if you get my meaning."

He scratched his chin. "I think I do."

"Life up here on the mountain must get very lonely at times. The work is hard. A certain amount of comfort in the evening would go a long way toward making life more enjoyable. Wouldn't you agree, Mr. Kruger?"

He nodded. "Oh, yeah. I'd agree with that, all right."

Amanda had rehearsed her sales pitch on the way from Meg's house this morning hoping Jason would go along with her idea to bring brides onto his mountain. And he seemed to be quite taken with the idea, so much so that he was starting to perspire.

"Perhaps we should go into your office and get down to business?" she asked.

"Now?" His eyes widened. "Right now? You and me? In my office? Now?"

"If you're not too busy, that is."

"Too busy?"

Voices carried across the road as the loggers streamed out of the cookhouse. The men filed past, some tipping their hats to Amanda, some simply staring.

Amanda lifted her satchel. ''Should I approach the men now while they're assembled? I have pictures.''

''*Pictures?*'' Jason reeled back.

''Certainly,'' she said. ''Or would you like to go into your office first? Send for your brother, perhaps?''

His eyes widened. ''My brother?''

She gazed up at him. ''Wouldn't you like to have him involved in this with us?''

Jason looked horrified. ''Miss Pierce, what the *hell* are you talking about?''

''Brides.''

''Brides!''

''Yes, brides.''

Gracious, was this man soft in the head? How much more plain could she say it?

''I'm the owner of the Becoming Brides Matrimonial Service, Mr. Kruger. That's why I came here in the first place.''

He pulled off his hat and dragged his sleeve over his forehead. ''That's what this is all about? Bringing brides up here?''

''Certainly. What did you think I meant?''

''Well—'' Jason ran his finger around his shirt collar. ''Never mind what I thought.''

Jason yanked on his hat again. ''So you're saying you didn't come up here thinking I was going to marry you?''

''No, not me personally,'' Amanda explained.

"In fact, under normal circumstances I would have disregarded your request for a Becoming Bride immediately."

His lines in his forehead deepened. "Are you saying I'm not good enough for your brides?"

"Well, Mr. Kruger, we do have standards," Amanda said. "But when I read how miserably alone you were, you sounded so pathetic I had to come up and investigate."

Jason pointed his finger at her. "It wasn't me that wrote that letter."

"Last night you made it abundantly clear that you weren't interested in a bride for yourself, and I do understand your rule about no women in the camp," Amanda said. "But I couldn't leave this morning without discussing it once more with you."

Jason sighed impatiently. "Look, Miss Pierce, I have a business to run and I don't have time to—"

"I have a business to run also, Mr. Kruger," Amanda said. "The happiness of my potential brides is my business. I don't understand why you won't at least give my idea some consideration. It's not like it wouldn't benefit you as well."

"And just how is this supposed to benefit me?" He folded his arms across his chest, challenging her.

"Several ways. First of all—"

Amanda stopped as she noticed the loggers milling around the cookhouse door staring at her in silence. Jason saw them also.

"Let's talk inside." Jason caught her elbow and steered her toward his office.

Inside, Amanda dropped her satchel by the door.

The room seemed smaller than it had last night. Quieter. More secluded. Jason seemed taller, wider, more rugged. She suddenly became conscious of the dress she wore, how it fit snug against her breasts, the fabric clinging to her skin.

"Sit down?" Jason asked.

The blustery anger she'd seen in him moments ago was gone now. He tossed his hat aside and gestured to the chair she'd sat in last night.

She sat, and he eased himself into his chair behind his desk, leaned back and steepled his fingers in front of him.

"You were about to tell me all the reasons I needed brides on my mountain, Miss Pierce."

His intense gaze riveted her to her chair, making it difficult to breathe. Amanda gave herself a mental shake. This was her chance. Her future—and that of her brides—depended on the outcome of this conversation.

Amanda drew herself up a little straighter in the chair.

"First of all, Mr. Kruger, there's the stability of your crew," she said. "Married men are more stable, therefore, you'd have less turnover among your men. It's more difficult for a man to pick up and move if he's got a wife and a home to take with him, so he'd be more likely to stay put."

Except for Gerald McGee, who'd left Meg and Todd with only a goodbye letter. Amanda didn't want Jason bringing up that example so she pushed on.

"Then there's the safety issue," Amanda said.

"I'm sure it's of concern to you when your men have time off. How safety conscious can they be returning from Beaumont after several days of drinking and—"

Amanda clamped her lips together. Goodness, she'd almost said the word aloud.

Jason's eyebrows raised. "And what?"

He watched her like a cat studying a cornered mouse. Amanda clung to her dignity, refusing to let her cheeks flood with color.

"Another reason brides would—"

"Hold on a minute," Jason said. "You were talking about safety. Days of drinking and…what?"

He was enjoying her discomfort. It showed in his eyes, plain as day. Amanda drew herself up with what she hoped was regal aplomb.

"Socializing," she said.

"Socializing?"

Jason Kruger knew what she meant, what she'd nearly said aloud. He was toying with her for his own pleasure, and Amanda was tired of it.

"Yes, Mr. Kruger. Socializing. Mindless socializing. Days and days on end of nothing but thoughtless, incoherent, continuous socializing. Hour after hour of—"

"All right, I got it." Jason sat forward suddenly and squirmed in his chair.

Amanda drew in a breath, calming herself, focusing her thoughts. "Next, there's the financial matters."

Jason rose from his chair and stalked across the room. He flung the window open wide. Amanda was glad. The room had grown awfully hot. He kept his back to her and didn't say anything, so she continued on.

"As I understand it, you own the mountain. Married couples will need a place to live. You can lease or sell homesites to them. The town will expand, offering another opportunity to profit from your land. And, of course, all of this will create a local market for your lumber."

He stood with his back to her for a long time, gazing out the window.

Amanda stood. "Mr. Kruger, have you heard one word I've said?"

He looked back over his shoulder. "Every word. And the answer is still no."

She crossed the room and stopped behind him. "I've just given you several excellent reasons why brides would be of great benefit to your logging camp. I don't understand why—"

"Then I'll tell you why." Jason swung around. "If I let women up here, first thing you know there will be lines at the barber shop. Men will ask to be let off early to take a bath."

"What's so wrong with that?"

"Next thing you know, they get married. Then curtains start going up in the windows. When my men ought to be resting up for the next day's work, they're busy fixing things up, making them look pretty."

Amanda rolled her eyes. "Well, we certainly wouldn't want *that* to happen."

Jason edged closer. "Then my crews aren't concentrating on their jobs because their women are mad at them. Or because they're anxious to get home. Either way, my men aren't thinking about work.''

Amanda felt heat roll off of Jason. It soaked into her.

He leaned his head down. ''And a year from now I'll have babies up here because of all the *socializing* going on.''

Amanda's cheeks flamed. How dare he say such a thing to her? She should have slapped his face. And she would have if she hadn't been so hopelessly caught in the molten aura he gave off.

He came nearer. She wanted to back away— should back away. Then his mouth clamped over hers, and she wanted desperately to stay right where she was.

Jason looped his arm around her waist and pressed himself against her. Heat flamed between them. His lips moved against hers, plying, wanting, asking. He splayed his hand over her back.

A thousand explosions pierced her body. She'd never been kissed before—not like this. Never been touched as Jason touched her now. It wasn't proper. It certainly wasn't dignified.

But it was wonderful.

Amanda swayed against Jason. She grabbed his shoulders to keep from falling and parted her lips ever so slightly.

He slipped inside her at once, tasting her, exploring her. Luring her, tempting her until she did the same.

A groan rattled in his mouth as Amanda pressed deep, matching his movements. He pulled her tighter against him.

Amanda was lost in the feel of him, the taste of him. Hopelessly lost in the decadent moment of their mouths blending together.

Until he suddenly yanked his mouth from her and looked up.

A voice intruded into the fog clouding Amanda's mind. She turned. Ethan stood in the open doorway.

Chapter Five

Ethan froze in midstride. "Uh...sorry." He backed outside and closed the door.

Jason clung to Amanda, holding her against him. She was soft and warm. She smelled better than anything on his entire mountain. He didn't want to let her go.

Her lips were wet and her cheeks pink. He'd done that to her. Done it and enjoyed it.

Her eyes were wide with embarrassment. He'd done that, too.

Jason eased his grip on her. She looked so vulnerable, so confounded, that he wanted to keep her in his arms and hold her, comfort her, and make everything all right for her.

But she pushed away from him, drew herself upright, and spun away. She rushed to the door, then stopped, as if unsure which was more embarrassing—going outside and confronting Ethan, or staying inside with him.

"Miss Pierce, wait—"

His words spurred her into action. Amanda yanked open the door and fled, leaving Jason staring after her.

"Dammit...."

Jason raked his hands through his hair and stared at the still open door. He wanted to go after her. He wanted her back. He wanted to hold her, and smell her, and kiss her, and...

And what? Jason grumbled another curse into the quiet office. He knew what he wanted to do. His body had already made it perfectly clear.

The office door opened wider and Ethan stepped inside. "Did you and Miss Pierce kiss and make up? Or just kiss?"

Jason cursed again and waved toward the door Amanda had just disappeared through. "That's another reason I don't want women up here."

Ethan pushed the door closed and dropped into the chair in front of the desk. "Have you something against kissing all of a sudden?"

Jason glared at him. "No."

"Then what the hell are you talking about?"

"Women gussied up in city clothes, all proper and dignified, getting flustered by a simple kiss," Jason said. "What kind of wife would that be?"

Ethan grinned. "In the case of Amanda Pierce, a pretty good one."

Jason cursed again.

"She's got spirit," Ethan said. "Determination, drive. If you ask me—"

"Nobody asked you." Jason grabbed his hat off

his desk and stalked to the door. "We've got work to do."

"Jason, hold up a minute." Ethan rose from the chair. "You work harder than any man on this mountain. You ought to take some time off, go down to Beaumont for a few days."

"I've got a business to run."

Ethan touched his shoulder. "Working yourself into the ground isn't going to make up for Pa."

"That's not what I'm doing," Jason said. He stalked outside, slamming the door behind him.

Bad enough that he'd gone and kissed Amanda Pierce, that she'd set his body on fire and sent his mind churning. Ethan didn't have to bring up their father as well.

Jason stood on the porch of the office looking at his logging camp, his mountain. He'd bought it with his own money. He'd designed the layout of the camp and put the crew together. He'd built it himself and he was proud of it.

Ethan had come along later with the idea for the sawmill and put up the money for the new equipment. Since then they'd worked together, planned together.

For most of their lives, wherever Jason went, Ethan was seldom far behind. Ethan was only a year younger. They were closer than most brothers. That suited Jason just fine because the rest of the family was scattered. They drifted in and out of his life with an occasional letter. Thanks to their Ma and Pa.

Jason didn't like being reminded of their father. And he sure as hell didn't need to be reminded of how long it had been since he'd left his mountain. Miss Amanda Pierce and her kiss had done that—with predictable results.

Jason walked off the porch. He needed to get his mind on work, and off Miss Amanda Pierce. She was leaving today, anyway. And good riddance to her. Her and her brides…her sweet smell…her kiss.

Jason hiked to the skid road that led up the mountain. To his surprise he found his crew congregated there loaded down with their axes, saws, canteens and cans of pitch. The bull whackers had two teams of sixteen oxen harnessed, ready to head up the mountain. But they were all standing around talking when they should have been working already.

"What's going on?" Jason demanded. His first thought was that there'd been an accident, someone had gotten hurt. But the men were too noisy for anything serious to have happened.

Buck Johansen, a big round-chested man, made his way from the center of the gathering. Buck was in charge of the lumberjacks. He was the boss logger, the bull of the woods, who ran the daily operation on the mountain. It was his responsibility to decide which trees to fell, how they should fall, and where cuts for logs should be made once the trees were down. There could be only one bull of the woods, and Buck was it.

"There's talk going around," Buck said, stopping in front of Jason. "Talk about you getting married."

Jason's gaze landed squarely on Duncan in the center of the crew and knew where that piece of gossip had come from.

"I'm not getting married," Jason barked.

"But what about that pretty little lady in your office last night?" Duncan called out. "We all saw her this morning at breakfast."

"Get to work, all of you," Jason said, "before I dock you a day's pay."

A grumble went through the men, but they turned and headed up the mountain.

Buck Johansen stayed behind. "Some of the men were wondering—"

Jason cursed. "If you can't keep these men's minds on work I'll find somebody who can."

Buck just looked at him, and Jason regretted his words. Buck was one of the best, and Jason counted himself lucky to have him on his mountain. He shouldn't have lashed out at Buck when it was really himself he was mad at.

"Look," Jason said, softening his stance, "I've got no time for this kind of problem."

Buck nodded his understanding, then gestured toward the crew hiking up the mountain. "I know. But I've got these men who are wondering what's going on around here."

"Nothing's going on."

"Some say maybe you ought to get married," Buck said. "Take the edge off."

Jason bit back a retort, then looked away because he couldn't disagree with Buck.

"I've got a lot on my mind," Jason said. "This deal I'm waiting to hear on, for one."

"There's been deals before."

Jason pulled on his neck. "Keep the men working. Keep their minds on their jobs. I don't want anybody getting hurt today.''

Buck hesitated a moment, then nodded and headed up the road behind the men.

Most days Jason would have gone up with them. Today, though, he stood where he was, looking at the towering trees, feeling the early morning sun on his face, and decided not to go up yet. He had some business to attend to in camp.

Jason hiked over to the sawmill. Work was underway on the logs that had come down from the two sections of the mountain his men were working. About half floated down river to the millpond, and the rest were dragged down the skid road by teams of oxen.

Just outside the sawmill, a conveyor belt brought logs out of the millpond with the help of the river pigs, the sure-footed loggers who leapt from log to log guiding them and breaking up jams.

Inside the sawmill a steam engine powered the band saw that cut through the massive logs. Two men rode the carriage back and forth, holding the log in place with a series of levers. Another crew of men stacked the cut lumber and prepared it for shipment down the mountain.

Ethan was busy overseeing the work. Jason waved to him. They walked outside, away from the relentless whine of the saw.

''Talk to Shady before he heads down to Beaumont today,'' Jason said. ''Be sure he checks the mail while he's there.''

''Shady knows we're looking for that packet from

San Bernardino,'' Ethan said. ''He won't head home until he's checked on it.''

''Remind him, just the same.''

''Don't know if I can.''

Jason's brows drew together. ''He's left already?''

''Does that bother you?'' Ethan grinned. ''Maybe you're sorry to see Miss Pierce leave after all.''

''You see? This is what I'm talking about.'' Jason threw out both hands. ''A woman—one single woman—shows up in camp and the whole place is thrown into an uproar.''

''Seems like you're the one in an uproar,'' Ethan said. ''Everybody else is doing fine.''

Jason grumbled under his breath and stalked away.

There was nothing like a brisk walk to take the edge off of one's emotions, Amanda decided as she made her way toward town. Particularly a walk over a road as rough as this one, where a lady might easily fall on her bustle and embarrass herself in front of anyone and everyone passing by.

Amanda stopped and caught her breath. Which was worse? Being embarrassed by total strangers, or being embarrassed by the two Kruger brothers?

One of whom she'd kissed. Hard. On the mouth. With her lips opened.

Amanda's cheeks flamed again, churning up her emotions once more. At this rate she'd have to hike all the way to Beaumont to burn off the sting of that

memory. Such wanton behavior. What had pos-
sessed her to do such a thing?

Jason Kruger. Amanda was tempted to curse
aloud. The words burned her tongue. Jason had
caused her to act in such an unladylike fashion.

He was no gentleman, she decided. A gentleman
didn't have big hulking muscles. A rock-hard chest.
A hot mouth. A gentleman didn't lock a lady in his
arms and pull their bodies together so that they
touched. He didn't allow a lady to feel his thighs,
his belly, his—

Amanda gasped aloud, and plastered her fingers
to her lips. She glanced around quickly. A man she
didn't recognize sauntered toward the animal pens
on the other side of camp.

Had he seen her? Did he suspect what she'd been
thinking? Not to mention what she'd been *doing.*

Amanda hiked up her skirt and hurried toward
town.

She was short-winded by the time she reached
Meg's house and went inside. One of the ways Meg
made money to feed herself and Todd was by doing
mending for the loggers. She was hard at work sew-
ing on missing buttons, closing ripped seams and
patching holes when Amanda sat down on the settee.

''Has Shady come by?'' Amanda asked.

Meg lowered the worn shirt. ''Does this mean Jason turned you down again?''

''I'm afraid so.''

''Even after you explained about your brides?''

Even after she'd kissed him.

Amanda shifted on the settee, anxious to change

the subject. "If you won't let me pay you for a night's lodging, the least I can do is help with your mending."

"Don't be silly," Meg insisted. "I was glad to have you here. You can't imagine how lonely this mountain gets without another woman to talk to."

They spent the next several hours working their way to the bottom of the mending basket. Meg talked nonstop, and Amanda realized that she was indeed lonely for female conversation. Her heart sank a little. Another reason she was sorry to leave with her mission unfulfilled.

"Gracious, it's late." Amanda looked out the window and saw that the sun was high overhead now. "I can't imagine where Shady is."

"Shady operates on a timetable of his own," Meg said.

"Maybe I should look for him." She didn't want to wait until it was too late to go down the mountain and risk not finding a hotel room in Beaumont.

"The crews will be down from the mountain soon to eat," Meg said. "The smell of the food will draw Shady out, if nothing else."

"I think I'll go look for him," Amanda said. She pinned her hat in place, and headed out the door.

Though she tried to resist, her gaze turned to Jason's office just down the road. A strange quivering sensation passed through Amanda. Her lips twitched suddenly at the memory of the kiss they'd shared. Why couldn't she forget?

Amanda turned quickly and walked the other way.

By the time she reached the barber shop in town, Amanda had decided it was simply this place that made her act so wanton in Jason's office. The isolation. The wild, rugged mountain. The lack of anything resembling the civility of the city.

After all, what else could it be?

Amanda strolled through the town. It seemed to have grown up on the edge of the logging camp as an afterthought. There was no boardwalk in front of the few businesses that were open. Most of their trade came from the loggers, Amanda guessed, because only a few patrons were on the street.

The town had a temporary feel to it. The buildings looked hastily thrown together with little concern for appearance or appeal. There was debris and clutter outside the stores as if the owners had no one to impress but the loggers, and the loggers weren't there to be impressed.

It was all so different from the shops she was used to. The magnificent stores, restaurants, the streets crowded with carriages and people. Amanda hadn't expected this place to look like San Francisco, but still….

After peering into shop windows and down tiny alleyways, Amanda didn't find Shady. She sighed and headed out of town. Shady knew he had to take her down to Beaumont and would find her soon enough. Maybe Meg was right, that he'd come for her after he'd eaten. She'd get her things together and wait at Meg's house until he arrived.

A shudder passed through her so violently she

stopped dead in her tracks. Her satchel. She'd left her satchel in Jason Kruger's office.

Amanda pinched the bridge of her nose, thinking hard about what to do. She had to get it back, of course. She couldn't possibly leave it.

Meg had told her this morning that Jason usually went up to the mountain with the logging crews, so it was probably safe to go to his office and retrieve her satchel. Probably.

Amanda drew in a heavy breath and started walking again. How did she keep ending up in so many awkward situations on this mountain?

Amanda knocked on the closed office door hoping she'd get no response. She glanced around. This part of the camp was nearly deserted during the day. She heard the whine of the sawmill in the distance.

She knocked again, then opened the door and stepped inside. No one was there.

When she'd been in the office before she'd noticed little more than Jason himself. He seemed to take up the entire room.

Now she had a chance to look the place over. Jason's desk and another one, presumably Ethan's, sat at right angles, with Jason's facing the door. Maps and charts were tacked to the wall. Ledgers, papers, more maps and charts were stacked haphazardly on the desktops and on shelves. Sawdust had been tracked across the floor.

The office was still. Amanda walked through the room. She touched the ledgers, flipped one open and saw heavy, straight figures entered in neat columns.

She ran her hand over the back of Jason's chair, felt the smooth grain of the wood. On his desk a technical journal lay open.

For all his faults—and Amanda had counted many—Jason Kruger had to be admired for what he'd accomplished. When she first received the letter requesting one of her brides, the letter she'd thought came from Jason, she'd asked around.

Logging was backbreaking work, she'd learned, requiring tireless energy and strength. New, inventive techniques had to be devised to get the huge trees out of the forests. The size of the trees here in these woods presented problems unheard of by loggers on the east coast. She'd been told that any man who could harvest the big trees in the Sierra Nevada would find fortune greater than the West's silver and gold.

Amanda sighed in the silent office. Too bad Jason didn't want to share that wealth with anyone. Or that life. She picked up her satchel where she'd left it beside his desk and headed for the door.

It swung open as she reached for it. The doorway filled with Jason Kruger. Amanda reeled back.

He stopped short, as stunned as she by the unexpected meeting. They both stared. The room shrank again, closing in on Amanda, robbing her of an easy breath.

"I thought you'd gone," Jason said.

"I—I left my satchel." She hefted it higher, offering it as evidence that she was still here for a good reason. "And I'll be leaving shortly."

He stood in the doorway, blocking her way. "Just

as long as you understand that this brides notion is over with.''

''What I understand, Mr. Kruger, is that you're a stubborn man.'' Amanda nearly gasped aloud when she heard the words slip through her lips. Good gracious, she'd called him another name. What came over her when she got around this man?

''Stubborn? Me?'' Jason stepped inside and pushed the door shut. ''You're the most hardheaded woman I've ever met. And pushy, too.''

''Pushy!''

''Yeah, pushy. You keep sticking your nose in where it doesn't belong and isn't wanted.''

Amanda drew herself up to her greatest height, though it was woefully short of his. ''Somebody on this mountain wrote that letter to me, Mr. Kruger. Somebody wants brides up here. You'd better face that fact.''

He pointed his finger at her. ''I can tell you this, Miss Pierce, when I find out who wrote that letter I'm going to fire that man so fast he won't know what hit him.''

''Oh! You pigheaded man!'' Amanda jerked her chin. ''Don't worry. I'm leaving for good. I won't be back, and you'll never hear from me again. You'll have your precious mountain all to yourself. I hope it keeps you warm at night.''

A little mewl slipped from Amanda's lips as she realized what she'd said. Her gaze locked with Jason's. He gulped.

They both stood motionless for a long moment,

visions of heating up the nights on the mountain spinning between them.

Jason inched forward. Amanda backed up. He had that same fiery look in his eye he'd had earlier when he'd kissed her. Was he going to kiss her again? Should she let him?

Jason stopped. Amanda stepped toward him.

The door burst open behind them and a breathless young man rushed into the room.

"Mr. Kruger! Mr. Kruger!" The tall, skinny boy pressed one hand to his heaving chest.

Jason caught his arm. "What's wrong with you, boy?"

"My pa...my pa's the postmaster down in Beaumont. He said you'd been expecting this." The boy waved a large, rumpled envelope. "He told me to get up the mountain with it right away. I rode fast as I could."

Jason pulled the envelope from the boy's hand. "Go get my brother. He's at the sawmill."

"Yes, sir." Chest still heaving, the boy ran out the door.

Jason tore the envelope open and yanked out its contents. He scanned it, then clenched his fist. A smile bloomed on his face. Not a grin or a snicker, but a genuine smile so wide it showed his teeth.

He whirled toward Amanda. "I got it!"

His happiness overwhelmed her. She smiled, too, infused with his enthusiasm.

"Got what?"

"The contract!" He shoved the thick packet of papers toward her.

"That's wonderful!" She had no idea what the contract was for or what it meant, but she couldn't hold herself back in the face of his excitement. "What sort of contract?"

He eased beside her, pointing to the papers. "It's from the Santa Fe railroad down in San Bernardino. They're expanding. They need cross-ties. Do you know what kind of trees make the best cross-ties?"

Amanda shook her head quickly. "No."

"Douglas fir. And do you know what kind of trees I've got all over this mountain?"

"Douglas fir?"

"Douglas fir!" Jason threw back his head and howled with delight. He shook the contract at Amanda again. "See this? An order in writing. A big order. Do you know what this means?"

She could only guess. "You'll make lots of money?"

"Not just that." Jason shook his head slowly and gazed down at her. "The railroad doesn't deal with just anybody who comes down the pike. This means respectability, Amanda."

He'd never used her first name before, and the word flew like an arrow straight through her chest. Amanda put her hand on his arm. "Oh, Jason. That's wonderful."

He looked down at her delicate fingers clutching his arm, then lifted his gaze to her face. "Nothing can stop me now, Amanda. Nothing."

"Nothing *should* stop you...."

Jason lowered his head toward her.

"Mr. Kruger! Mr. Kruger!"

The messenger boy from Beaumont charged into the room again, panting worse than when he'd left.

Jason pulled away from Amanda. "Did you find Ethan?"

"Yes, sir, I did. But he ain't coming over here. He says for you to come over there. Right now."

"What's wrong?"

"I don't know, exactly." The boy shook his head. "All he said was come over there. Something happened with the crew."

Chapter Six

An odd feeling of disappointment lingered in Amanda's chest as Jason hurried away from his office, the messenger boy at his heels. And why she felt disappointed she wasn't sure, exactly. Disappointed that he'd taken off so quickly? That his life was so full there was no room for anything else...or anyone else?

Or that he'd almost kissed her again, but hadn't?

Amanda left the office, hauling her satchel with her. Inside it were the women who wanted to be kissed, wanted to be loved, wanted to make a home for themselves and a family. Amanda wasn't one of them.

At least, not anymore.

Those women—her brides—were her priority. She'd be better off putting everything else out of her mind and concentrating on work. That's what Jason Kruger was doing.

He'd taken off for the sawmill when the messenger boy had told him there was a problem with the crew. He'd taken off and not looked back. Amanda knew she should do the same.

But her footsteps slowed on the road as she watched Jason disappear from sight. What sort of emergency with the crew? Had someone been hurt? Killed?

Amanda looked around at the huge trees, the wooden buildings, the little town and logging camp so far from civilization. So isolated. So desolate. There wasn't even a doctor here, according to Meg.

For a moment she was tempted to run after Jason, to find out what had happened, to help, if she could. But she didn't. Jason wouldn't want her there. He didn't need her.

For all his other faults—and she'd recognized many—Jason Kruger was a capable man. Strong, determined, smart. He didn't need help from anybody.

Amanda drew in a breath, resigning herself to the fact that her trip to the Kruger Brothers' Lumber and Milling Company had been a mistake. Her brides didn't belong here, and neither did she.

A little knot squeezed in her chest, quite unexpectedly, at the realization.

Amanda headed for Meg's house. She would pack her few belongings and wait for Shady to take her back down the mountain.

Back home. Back where she belonged.

Jason squeezed his hands into fists trying to keep his anger under control as he faced his logging crew on the skid road near the sawmill. The midday sun shone bright in the clear sky. Leaves rustled in the breeze.

Ethan was beside him, but hadn't said much. Buck Johansen was trying to play pacemaker; it wasn't helping.

His crew stood in front of him, bunched together. About half had a genuine interest in this standoff. The other half were waiting to see what would happen. All of them should have been at the cookhouse for their noon meal.

"It ain't so unreasonable," one of the men called out.

"They got 'em at other camps," another said.

"If you can have one for yourself, Mr. Kruger, why can't we have one, too?" a brave soul called out from the rear of the gathering.

A chorus of hoots and yelps rose from the men.

"I'm not getting one!" Jason shouted. "I'm not getting married!"

"Just 'cause you don't want a wife, don't mean we don't," a man called.

"Shady says that Miss Pierce's got a book full of women wanting to get hitched," someone else said. "We can pick out what we want and have 'em shipped right here to the camp."

Another round of agreement rumbled through the group.

Jason swore under his breath and glanced at Ethan. He didn't say anything. Buck stepped closer and lowered his voice.

"That's all the crew's been talking about this

morning,'' Buck said. ''Talk's turning ugly, Jason.
You'd better think long and hard about this.''

Jason swore again. He glared at his men, trying
to keep his anger under control.

But it wasn't them he was mad at.

''Get down to the cookhouse, then get back to
work,'' Jason said to his men.

Buck turned to the crew. ''Move along, boys.
Give Mr. Kruger some time to think this through.''

The men headed down the skid road toward the
cookhouse, mumbling and talking among themselves, chancing a glance or two at Jason. When
they were gone, Buck spoke again.

''You can't blame them, Jason. It's only right that
a man wants a wife waiting for him at the end of
the day, wants sons to follow in his footsteps.''

Jason glared at him, but didn't say anything.

Buck went on. ''Other camps let the loggers have
wives with them. Some of the men are saying maybe
they ought to move along, get jobs some place else.
In fact, a whole lot of them are saying that.''

''Dammit....''

''They don't mean it as a threat,'' Buck said. ''It's
just a fact. And this isn't the first time something
like this has come up, Jason.''

Jason stomped away, down the skid road. Ethan
fell in step beside him. Neither spoke until they were
inside the office.

''Damn that woman, this is all her fault,'' Jason
said, and threw his hat onto his desk.

Ethan closed the door and dropped into the chair
in front of Jason's desk.

"Like Buck said, it's been coming for a while now," Ethan said. "Ever since Duncan's wife got here there's been talk. Amanda and her brides finally tipped the scales."

Jason paced back and forth across the office. "I can't afford this problem. Not now." He picked up the rumpled envelope from his desk and tossed it to Ethan.

"What's this?" Ethan asked, pulling out the contents.

"Messenger brought it up from Beaumont," Jason said and started pacing again.

Ethan looked at the contract and grinned. "Well, hot damn!"

A minute passed while Ethan flipped through the pages.

"We can't fill this order on time if half the crew walks off the job," he said.

"Let them leave," Jason said, and flung his hand out. "I'll hire more. There's plenty of men where they came from. I'll pay higher wages, get them up here quick."

Ethan shook his head. "You can't get a whole new crew—or even half a crew—up here in time. You're already paying good wages. Any more will be cutting into profits."

Jason mumbled another curse and kept pacing. He couldn't deny the truth in what Ethan was saying. That's why his brother was good for the business, good to have as his partner. Ethan's was the voice of reason.

Even though Jason was fighting it like hell right now.

"Of course," Ethan said, "you could always—"

"Don't say it." Jason whirled to face his brother. "I am not changing my mind about having women up here."

Ethan rose from his chair. "Then you risk losing this railroad contract."

Jason glared at him and started pacing again. He knew Ethan was right. Knew it in his gut. He just didn't want to admit it.

"What's so wrong with having a few women up here?" Ethan asked. "If it keeps us from losing this contract?"

"You know how I feel about having women around," Jason said. "And you know why."

"Yeah, I know why," Ethan said. "But this hasn't got anything to do with Ma—or Pa either, for that matter. We haven't seen or heard from them in nearly a year now."

"Thank God for that," Jason muttered.

"We've both worked hard to build up this company," Ethan said. "So what other choice do you have?"

"No." Jason shook his head. "There's another way."

"Okay. What?" Ethan asked. "What other way?"

Jason rubbed his forehead, thinking hard. There had to be another way. There just had to.

He'd carved his lumber company out of this

mountain, built it from nothing. And now, just when things were looking up, this had to happen.

Above all, he couldn't lose that railroad contract. He had a few contracts now, but they were small. The rest of his lumber was shipped off to market and sold to whoever needed it.

But this railroad contract was the key to bigger and better opportunities. A contract with the railroad was not to be taken lightly. Word would get out. Other companies would come to him wanting to buy his lumber. His company would grow. His future would be secure. It would be everything he'd hoped for, everything he'd dreamed of, everything he'd worked for.

But to fill the requirements of that contract Jason needed a full crew to deliver the lumber. An experienced crew who knew how to work together. He needed the crew he had in place right now.

Ethan sighed. "Look, Jas, I just don't see any way around this."

Jason stopped pacing and cursed again. No matter how he looked at it, or how much he thought about it, he couldn't come up with anything else.

"Yeah, you're right," Jason said.

A few minutes passed while the finality of the decision sank in. Jason folded his arms across his chest and stared out the window. Finally, he shook his head and turned back to his brother, accepting the decision.

"Let's go tell Miss Pierce to bring her brides up here." Ethan said. "She can probably get them here in a few days, don't you think?"

Jason mumbled another curse.

Ethan slapped him on the back as they headed for the door. "Don't look so down. It might not be so bad," Ethan said. "How much trouble can a few women cause, anyway?"

Jason cringed at the thought. He already knew how much trouble *one* woman had caused him.

Meg had talked almost nonstop since Amanda had met her last night, but Amanda enjoyed her company. They sat together in Meg's little cabin, sipping coffee, waiting for Shady to show up and take her back down the mountain.

Back to Beaumont, back to San Francisco, back home. Amanda set her coffee cup aside, half listening to Meg, half thinking about the journey that lay ahead. Amanda dreaded the thought of making the long, arduous trip.

But was that the only reason she was reluctant to leave? Of course, she told herself.

"You're the talk of the mountain this morning," Meg said. "Everyone is saying how smart you were to solve the problem between Gladys Duncan and Polly Minton."

"Yes, their recipe dilemma."

Meg leaned forward. "I can't believe you actually made peace between those two. They've been at each other's throats since the day they met."

"At least my coming here wasn't a complete waste."

"I wish you'd stay awhile longer," Meg said.

"I can't. I have to get home, back to my business." Amanda shook her head. "I wish I knew who'd written me that letter, pretending to be Jason Kruger asking for a wife."

"Maybe you should stay and find out?" Meg suggested.

Amanda considered it for a moment, a fleeting moment, then thought better of it. The farther she got away from Jason and his mountain, the better off she'd be.

"It's a mystery that will have to remain unsolved," Amanda said.

A knock sounded at the door and when Meg answered it, Shady stepped into the room.

"You ready to head down the mountain, Miss Pierce?" he asked, squinting at her.

A little knot tightened in Amanda's chest as she rose from the table.

"All set," she said, and pinned her hat in place.

Shady picked up her satchel and two carpetbags, and followed Amanda and Meg outside. He loaded her belongings into the freight wagon, then busied himself checking the horses' harness.

"I'll miss you," Meg said.

Amanda took a final glance around the logging camp, and it occurred to her that she might miss this place.

"You'll write?" Meg asked.

"Of course." Amanda sensed the loneliness Meg felt, as one of the few women here in the camp. But without a husband, Meg's isolation ran deeper.

"Maybe you'll come to San Francisco?" Amanda suggested.

Meg smiled gently, but shook her head. "I don't see how I could ever do that."

Amanda knew she was asking much from a woman who could barely keep herself and her child fed, but she'd wanted to ask, just the same.

"Well, good luck," Meg said.

"You, too."

Shady ambled over to them. "Ready to head out?"

Amanda and Meg hugged briefly, and as Amanda turned to climb into the wagon, Shady gazed off toward the camp.

"Hold up just a minute, Miss Pierce," he said.

Amanda turned and saw Jason and Ethan walking their way.

Her heart fluttered for a second or two. She hadn't expected Jason to come wish her a fond farewell, yet he was definitely walking toward her.

Amanda took that moment, the last one she had, to look at him. Tall, strong. Handsome. He fit his surroundings. He belonged on this mountain. Jason Kruger was one of those rare men with the tenacity and strength to forge a living out of the wilderness.

"Afternoon," Ethan said, and tipped his hat to Meg when the two men stopped beside the wagon.

Little patches of pink colored her cheeks and she dipped her lashes. "Good afternoon, Ethan."

Their gazes met for a few seconds, then they both looked away, their conversation drying up.

Jason filled the silence.

"You got your way," he told Amanda, none too happily. "Get your brides up here."

Amanda looked back and forth between the two men.

"What are you saying?" she asked.

Jason glared at her. Clearly, he didn't want to repeat himself; it was painful enough the first time.

"I decided you can bring your brides up here for my crew," he said. "So get them up here. Now."

Amanda could only stare at him. This should have been the happiest moment of her business career. She'd traveled a long way, endured hardships, all in the hopes of hearing the words Jason Kruger had just uttered.

But Amanda wasn't happy. Not at all.

And she was about to make Jason Kruger just as unhappy.

"I'm afraid that's not possible," she said.

Twin frown lines creased Jason's forehead. "What?"

"I cannot, under any circumstances, bring my Becoming Brides up to your mountain, Mr. Kruger," Amanda said. "And that's final."

Chapter Seven

"What the hell?" Jason glared down at her in disbelief. "What do you mean you can't bring your brides here?"

Amanda straightened her shoulders. "It's just as I've said, Mr. Kruger. I can't bring them."

"Well, why the hell not?" he shouted.

Ethan poked him in the side. "Calm down. You won't get anywhere yelling at her."

Jason pulled in a breath, visibly calming himself. He pushed his hat back on his head.

"Look, Miss Pierce, ever since you got here last night you've done nothing but ask about bringing your brides up here. Now you're telling me you can't. What the hell happened?"

"Your language, for one thing," she told him.

Jason glared at her. "If you think I'm going to say 'pretty please' you can forget it."

"Mr. Kruger, you can say 'pretty please' until your face turns blue, for all I care, but the fact remains that I am not bringing my brides here."

Amanda turned to Shady. "Mr. Harper, I'm ready to leave now."

Shady pulled on his beard. "Well, okay, I reckon."

Amanda put her nose in the air and walked over to the freight wagon. Jason went after her.

"Hold on," Jason said, and planted himself in front of her. "You're not going anywhere until I say you can."

Amanda glared up at him. "I will not be bullied, Mr. Kruger."

Jason pulled in a deep breath, trying to calm himself. "Look, Miss Pierce, I want those brides of yours up here—"

Amanda skirted around him. "Shady, would you help me into the wagon, please?"

"Sure thing, ma'am," Shady said and hurried over to her.

Jason caught Shady's shoulder and held him back.

"You're not going anywhere until we get this thing settled," he said and blocked her path once more. "Now look here, Miss Pierce—"

"Jason." Ethan stepped between the two of them. "Maybe you should ask Miss Pierce the reason she won't bring her brides up here?"

"Oh," Jason said, as if that idea hadn't occurred to him.

Amanda didn't wait for his question. "My coming here was a mistake, for numerous reasons. Bringing my brides here is out of the question."

Jason gritted his teeth. "Now, look here—"

"No, you look—"

"Hold on now," Ethan said, easing between them. "Just wait a minute, before one of you says something you'll regret."

Amanda glared at Jason, her temper still running high. Jason glared right back at her.

"Now, the truth is, Miss Pierce," Ethan said, "that you really want to find husbands for those brides of yours. Right?"

"Well, yes," Amanda admitted.

"And Jason, you need those brides up here for your crew," Ethan said. "Right?"

"Yeah, you know I do."

"Okay, then," Ethan said. "You two need to find a way to come to some sort of agreement. Now, why don't both of you go down to the office and talk this thing out?"

Amanda's temper was winding down, but only marginally. She glanced at Jason. His was still simmering, too.

But what Ethan had said made sense. In fact, at the moment, Ethan was the only one making sense.

A low hum of chatter and footsteps in the dirt turned Amanda's attention to the loggers heading up the mountain, back to work for the afternoon.

They all wore caulked boots, boots with little spikes in the soles to help keep their footing on the logs. Their trousers were either short or stuffed into their boots to prevent them from being snagged by exposed roots or fallen branches. Most had beards or mustaches that were untrimmed. The odor of seldom washed bodies trailed after the group.

Some of the men nodded politely and tipped their

hats. Others nudged each other in the side and pointed. Frowns rippled through the group. Some of them stopped, causing a pileup behind them. A murmur went through the crowd. After a moment, they'd all stopped and were staring.

Amanda had nothing against any of the men, personally. In fact, deep down they were just the sort of men many of her prospective brides wanted. But on the surface, it was an entirely different matter.

Buck Johansen conferred with the loggers, then walked over to Amanda. He touched the brim of his battered hat respectfully.

"Miss Pierce, the men are asking if they can have a look at that catalog of yours," Buck said.

Amanda glanced at Jason, then back to Buck.

"Actually, it hasn't been decided whether my brides will come to the mountain, or not," she said.

"I know," Buck said. "But my men would appreciate it if they could just look at the pictures."

It was a simple request, one Amanda could not refuse.

She fetched her catalog from her satchel and carried it to where the loggers were gathered. She smiled, and opened the book displaying rows and rows of pictures of her Becoming Brides.

The men crowded close, elbowing each other, craning their necks to see. Amanda held the pages open as they looked, their eyes moving from one picture to another in reverent appreciation. The loggers went past in a long procession, some of them tipping their hats politely, a few mumbling their thanks.

When they were all gone, Buck took a long look at the pictures, sighed, then thanked Amanda and headed up the skid road with his crew.

Amanda closed the catalog, touched by the look on some of the men's faces. She'd thought before how lonely it was on the mountain for the few women who lived here. Now she realized that the loggers were just as lonely.

A little lump of sadness settled in her chest. Wasn't this why she'd started the Becoming Brides Matrimonial Service in the first place? To find partners for people? To make families? To keep others from being so lonely?

Amanda walked back to the freight wagon. Jason was still there, staring at her. Meg was watching her, too. Ethan had eased a little closer to Meg, fascinated, it seemed, by little strands of her hair blowing across her cheek.

Shady took the catalog from her. "So, are we getting brides up here, or ain't we?"

Amanda turned to Jason. "I'm willing to discuss the matter."

Jason gestured toward his office across the camp. "After you, Miss Pierce."

They walked down the road, side by side. Halfway to the office, Jason caught Amanda's arm, steadying her over the roughest terrain. Warmth spread up her arm, tingling at his gentle touch. She glanced up at him, but he kept his gaze focused on the office.

They walked inside together and Jason pushed the door shut. He tossed his hat on the desk.

Amanda was a little uncomfortable being in Jason's office again. The last time she was here she'd thought he was going to kiss her. And the time before that he had, in fact, kissed her. Would he do the same now?

Gracious, such thoughts, Amanda decided. She was here to discuss her brides. Nothing more. Determinedly, she focused on the business at hand.

Jason seemed lost himself, for a moment or two. Finally, he turned to her.

"Let me say right off, Miss Pierce, that I don't think too highly of you for coming here, getting my men all stirred up, then refusing to bring your brides," Jason said. "You shouldn't have started this if you didn't intend to follow it through."

"I came here to investigate a business opportunity," Amanda said. "Don't tell me you've never done that, then decided it wasn't right for you."

"Well, yes, I've done that," Jason admitted. "But this is different. You're fooling around with peoples' feelings. It's just not right."

"It was never my intention to hurt anyone," Amanda said.

Jason watched her closely for a few minutes and Amanda's skin warmed under his gaze. Was he deciding if she was telling the truth? she wondered. Was he wondering if he could trust her?

Or was he thinking about kissing her again?

Abruptly, Jason sat down behind his desk.

"Let's get down to business. I've got things to do," he said. "Why don't you want to bring your brides up here?"

"I think the first issue we should discuss is why *you* don't want them here," Amanda said, and sat down in the chair in front of his desk.

"I already explained that," Jason said.

Amanda shook her head. "You gave me a few reasons, but I think there's more to it than that. Something deeper."

Jason shifted in his chair. "I asked my question first."

"So you did." Amanda thought for a moment, trying to come up with a delicate way to phrase her objections.

"Just spit it out, Miss Pierce, whatever it is," Jason said.

It disturbed her that he frequently seemed to know what she was thinking.

"All right," Amanda said. "Frankly, Mr. Kruger, your men smell bad."

He raised an eyebrow at her. "They do?"

"Don't tell me you haven't noticed."

Jason shrugged noncommittally.

"Well, they do," Amanda said. "I couldn't hazard a guess on when any of them last bathed, not to mention had a haircut, or a shave. Really, Mr. Kruger, can you imagine a wagonload of women arriving and finding your men as their intended husbands? They'd stampede back down the mountain."

Jason pulled on his chin. "Well, you've got a point there."

"And there are no facilities here for my brides," Amanda said. "No place for them to live."

"Won't they be living with their husbands?"

"Not immediately," Amanda said. "You didn't think we'd have weddings performed as the brides climb off the wagon, did you?"

Jason shrugged as if he didn't see anything wrong with that.

"Aside from no place for the brides to live, there's no school, and no church," Amanda said, "And your men have no sense of decorum."

Jason leaned closer. "Decorum?"

"Yes, it means—"

"I know what it means," Jason said. "But what do you expect from lumberjacks?"

"I expect them to behave exactly as they do," Amanda said. "And that's just the reason they are unacceptable for my brides."

Jason studied her. "So that's it? Those are your reasons? You're saying that if my men get cleaned up and learn some manners, you'll bring your brides up here?"

"No, there's still one thing I need," Amanda said. "I need an answer to the question I asked you a few minutes ago, Mr. Kruger. Why don't you want my brides here?"

Jason sat back in his chair. "It's enough that I changed my mind and I want your brides now. Let's just leave it at that."

"I find that unsatisfactory," Amanda said.

Jason reared back farther in his chair and glared at her, unaccustomed to having anyone on his mountain disagree with him. Amanda could see Jason Kruger was a man used to getting his own way.

She folded her hands in her lap. "I don't see how

we can make this project work if you're not willing to be honest with me.''

Jason got up from his desk and walked to the window. He kept his back to her as he stared outside.

''Mr. Kruger?''

He didn't answer, leading Amanda to believe that her hunch had been right. Jason did have other reasons for not wanting brides on his mountain, other than the ones he'd laid out for her earlier.

''Are you married?'' Amanda asked.

He glanced back at her. ''Hell, no.''

''Were you ever married?''

''No.''

''Engaged?'' Amanda asked. ''Hurt by a woman you loved? Have your marriage proposal turned down?''

Jason turned to her, frowning. ''Miss Pierce, I just don't like having women around. I don't like the way they take over, how men turn to a bowl of mush and do whatever they want.''

''What woman turned you into a bowl of mush?''

''Nobody,'' he told her.

''It must have been someone,'' Amanda said. ''Someone who hurt you.''

Jason paced across the room, waving the idea away with his hands. ''It was nobody.''

''Mr. Kruger, we're never going to work out this situation if you won't tell me the truth.''

He stopped and stared at her for a moment.

''My mama,'' he finally said. ''She had us moving from one end of the country to the other, then back to the other again. Wanting to live here, then there, then someplace else. Looking for a business one place, a way to make more money some other place.''

Amanda was stunned by the bitterness in his words. What he was telling her was personal, highly personal. She hadn't meant to pry, hadn't expected to discover a spot so raw. Still, it touched her that Jason was sharing this with her. She knew he was a man unlikely to do such a thing.

''And your father went along with that?'' she asked gently.

''Never opened his mouth,'' Jason said. ''Whatever she wanted to do, that was just fine and dandy with him. I don't even know how many different places we lived. How many relatives I got dumped off on.''

''That must have been difficult for you,'' Amanda said.

Jason flung out his hand. ''I've got brothers and sisters scattered everywhere. Hell, some of them I wouldn't recognize if they walked through the door right now.''

''And you blame your father for not stopping your mother?'' Amanda said.

''He let her walk all over him. Whatever made her happy was all right with him,'' Jason said.

''Your childhood must have been very painful.''

Jason didn't answer. He walked to the window and stared out again.

His reasons for not wanting her brides on his mountain were very clear to Amanda now. And, really, given what he'd been through, she couldn't blame him. His feelings were genuine.

Amanda crossed the room and stood at his side, gazing up at his profile as he continued to look out the window.

"You're right," she said softly. "Things do change when women are involved."

Jason glanced down at her, but didn't say anything.

"Yet change is exactly what your men want," Amanda said. "If you expect me to bring my brides up here, Mr. Kruger, you'll have to accept that things on your mountain will change, too."

"Maybe they'll have to change," Jason said, "but that doesn't mean I have to like it."

"You don't have to like it, but you do have to cooperate."

He didn't like being told what to do. Amanda saw it in the tightening of his jaw and the squaring of his shoulders. Jason Kruger was a man used to giving orders, not taking them.

"Just so we're clear on one thing," Jason said. "Work comes first around here. Nothing is more important than meeting that railroad contract. Understand?"

"Perfectly," Amanda said.

Jason's expression hardened a little more. "I won't have you taking advantage of my men."

"I assure you, Mr. Kruger, that won't happen."

Jason studied her, as if once again determining whether or not he could trust her. From his expression, Amanda could tell what he'd decided.

"I'll pull some men off the crew and get them started on a place for your brides to live," Jason said. "I want those brides up here as soon as it's ready."

Amanda's chin went up a notch. "You just be sure the dormitory is ready by the time I get my brides here."

She'd had enough of Jason Kruger and his high-handed ways. Amanda turned to leave, but he caught her arm with the slightest of touches. It stopped Amanda cold in her tracks.

Deep lines cut into his forehead, and his green eyes had turned a hard gray. She imagined that look frightened every logger he turned it on. It made her heart beat faster and her breath come quicker, but not from fear.

"I don't want any problems with my men because of your brides," Jason told her.

Amanda pulled her arm from his grasp. "If you think that is within anyone's control, Mr. Kruger, you really have been on this mountain too long."

Chapter Eight

The cookhouse was crowded when Jason walked in. The morning air held a chill, but it was warm inside. The aroma of breakfast and the chatter of his men drifted through the room.

A workday, just like every other day. Jason liked the sameness. He liked waking up in his bed, looking out at his mountain, knowing what lay ahead. Sure, there were problems and challenges he faced regularly, but they were all similar in nature, and he could handle them.

But this morning, things felt different.

Jason sat down at a table beside his brother at the back of the cookhouse. One of the cook's helpers poured him a cup of coffee. Jason drank a sip.

"You look like hell," Ethan said, around a mouthful of scrambled eggs.

"I feel like hell," Jason mumbled, and rubbed his eyes.

"Up all night having sweet dreams about Miss Pierce?" Ethan asked.

"No," Jason said quickly. Too quickly.

"I heard she's staying," Ethan said.

Since talking to Amanda yesterday afternoon, Jason hadn't seen Ethan to let him know they'd come to an agreement. Ethan had been busy all evening with a problem at the sawmill. But, somehow, word had gotten out and had spread all over the mountain that the brides were coming.

"It will be good," Ethan said. "You'll be glad you agreed, Jason."

"All I'm glad about is that we can get to work on that railroad contract," Jason said.

He filled his plate from the platters on the table and ate rather than discuss the matter with Ethan any further. Jason still had his doubts about the women coming up to his mountain. But because of the railroad contract, he'd had to go along with it.

But he hadn't had to tell Amanda about his mother and father.

Jason cringed at the memory of how easily he'd poured out his personal problems to Amanda yesterday afternoon. He'd said things to her he'd never said to another person. She knew things about him no one else on the mountain knew.

And he'd just spewed them out. Opened his mouth and out they poured, as if she were his dearest friend, his closest confidant. Jason didn't even like talking to Ethan about their parents. Yet he'd talked to Amanda about them.

Jason sipped his coffee trying to clear his thoughts. Women. This was just the kind of problem they created.

Determined to get down to business, Jason turned to his brother.

"This morning I want you to…"

Jason's voice trailed off as a wave of silence crossed the cookhouse. He saw Amanda standing at the door.

She was a pretty woman, no doubt about it. This morning she was all done up in pink, looking fresh and clean, all proper and dignified. Like a fine lady ought to look.

Along with every other man in the cookhouse, Jason just stared. He got lost in the vision of Amanda outlined by the morning sun streaming in around her, until Ethan elbowed him in the side.

"If nothing else," Ethan said, "the scenery sure has improved around here."

Jarred out of his stupor, Jason left the table and crossed the cookhouse. Amanda waited by the door, serene, aware that every eye in the place was trained on her, and smiled pleasantly at his men.

Then she turned that smile on Jason. His knees weakened for a fraction of a second and he felt his chest tighten just a bit, which irritated him.

"Step outside, Miss Pierce," he said.

"I'll just wait here until you finish eating," Amanda said. "That way I won't disturb you."

She'd already done that, in more ways than she would ever know.

"Outside." Jason jerked his chin toward the door, then remembered himself. "If you please, Miss Pierce."

She gave a pleasant little nod to the loggers seated

at the tables, then walked out the door. Jason trailed after her swaying bustle.

"I thought this morning after breakfast might be a good time to discuss the brides with your crew," Amanda said when they stopped outside the cookhouse. "I need an exact count of how many men are interested in acquiring brides, so plans can be made accordingly."

"Plans?"

"Yes, plans," Amanda said. "How many brides I must arrange for, how much housing they'll require, furnishings they'll need, additional supplies."

"Well, sure," Jason said, a little surprised Amanda had put so much thought into the situation.

"This might be a good opportunity for the men to understand what's expected of them, as well," Amanda said.

"You mean about how they stink and don't have any manners?"

"I'd planned to put it a little more delicately than that," Amanda said, and gave him a small smile.

Jason wished she hadn't smiled at him. It made him smile back, and he didn't want to.

"That's why I'd better talk to them about it," he said.

They went back inside. Only one or two loggers were still eating, but none had left his seat. They were all staring at Amanda, and it bothered Jason. He stepped in front of her.

"All right, listen up," Jason said, his voice carrying through the cookhouse. "Any man wanting to hear what Miss Pierce has to say about finding a bride, wait here. The rest of you head out.''

Slowly, some of the men got to their feet and made their way out the door, but not without craning their necks for a better view of Amanda. About half the crew remained seated at the trestle tables.

She smiled easily at the men and stepped from behind Jason.

''I'm pleased to see so many of you are interested in my brides,'' Amanda said. ''Let's get down to business. First of all, the usual price for acquiring a Becoming Bride is two hundred dollars. However, since there are so many of you interested, I can reduce that to one hundred fifty.''

Amanda felt Jason's gaze on her and hoped he was pleased by the reduction in her fee. She'd stayed up late last night talking to Meg, discussing the situation, figuring out expenses.

''I'll conduct interviews this evening after supper,'' Amanda said. ''All of you who are interested, please see me then.''

She glanced at Jason, gave the crew a final smile, then left the cookhouse.

She was glad Jason had offered to discuss the hygiene issue with the men himself. But even outside, she heard Jason's strong voice telling the men in no uncertain terms that they stunk and needed to learn some manners if they expected anybody to marry them.

At times Amanda envied men their freedom. They could do and say almost anything and get away with it, simply because they were men. No one expected

them to behave in a certain way, to be demure, sub-
missive, gentle and dignified. They could be irre-
sponsible and footloose, if they chose, and not worry
about their reputation. Something few women could
do.

A few minutes later, the logging crew left the
cookhouse and headed up the mountain. Jason followed them outside.

"How many bolted at the thought of bathing and
manners?" Amanda asked.

Jason shook his head. "Not a one."

"Good. That means I'll need twenty-three wives.
I'll get to work immediately."

Amanda started to leave, but turned back. "Oh,
Mr. Kruger, one more thing. I'll need a place to live,
since it seems I'll be here for a while now."

"What's wrong with Meg's place?"

"It's a little cramped. And it's really not fair that
I should disrupt her and Todd's living arrange-
ments." Amanda pointed to the cabins scattered
across the hillside behind Meg's house. "I noted one
of those little houses is empty. Would it be all right
if I moved in?"

Jason shook his head. "Miss Pierce, I already told
you work comes first around here. Nobody has lived
in that cabin for months. I can't spare any of my
crew to help you."

Amanda's shoulders squared. "Did I ask you for
any help, Mr. Kruger?"

"Well, no. But that cabin is filthy. You can't—"

"It's not up to you to tell me what I can or can't

do, Mr. Kruger. You may own this mountain, but you don't own me.''

The little challenge in her upturned face sent a charge through Jason. Nobody defied him on his mountain. Nobody. And here was Miss Amanda Pierce doing just that—again. His whole body crackled with a strange heat.

''All I want to know, Mr. Kruger, is whether or not I can move into the cabin.''

He wanted to kiss her. His whole body came alive with the desire to wrap his arms around her, to smother her against him. To run his hands—

''Mr. Kruger?'' Amanda shifted impatiently. ''Are you paying even the slightest bit of attention to me?''

Jason yanked his hat lower on his forehead. ''Yeah, you can move in. But I'm telling you that cabin is filthy. It's going to need—''

''Thank you. That's all I need to know.'' Amanda gave him a brisk nod and headed off.

Jason stared at her delicious little bustle, too stunned for a moment to move. Then he went after her. He didn't like Amanda—or anybody—*handling* things. It was his mountain. *He'd* handle them.

Jason planted himself in front of her, stopping her short. ''I'm not having you running all over this mountain, doing whatever suits you. I make the decisions around here.''

Amanda rolled her eyes and threw out her hands. ''First, you tell me you don't want me interfering with you, your crew or their work schedule. Then, you insist that I do exactly that. You can't have it both ways, Mr. Kruger.''

He took a step closer and leaned down. ''Yes, I can. This is my mountain. I can have things anyway I want.''

Amanda stretched her nose up to meet his. ''And these are my brides. It's my responsibility to get them here, and that's what I intend to do. Whether it suits you or not.''

She yanked her skirt up, circled around him, and marched up the mountain.

Jason stared after her, his whole body humming. Damn, she was an irritating woman. Hardheaded, stubborn, pushy.

He pulled off his hat and dragged his sleeve across his forehead. He was annoyed with her, but he was more annoyed with himself. Because despite everything, he still wanted to kiss her.

For the second day in a row, Jason didn't go up the mountain with his crew. Instead, he spent the morning in his office doing paperwork.

Or trying to, anyway.

His desk chair sat at just the right angle to see across the camp to the little cabins that were scattered up the hillside. And, if he leaned to the left, he could see the exact cabin that Amanda was moving into this morning.

Jason grumbled under his breath and pulled his gaze from the mountainside back to his ledgers again. His neck was starting to hurt. Determinedly, he stared at the pages of columns and the figures, refusing to look out the window.

The dozen or so cabins were occupied by the merchants who ran businesses in town, and by some of the loggers. Jason didn't care where his men lived, provided they lived near the camp. Some of them disliked the bunkhouse and had built their own cabins. That was all right with Jason, too, as long as they did it on their own time and with their own money.

The abandoned cabin Amanda had selected for herself had belonged to one of his men who'd left the camp months ago. It was situated the farthest up the hillside, nestled among the trees. Built for one man, it was small and isolated so no one else had wanted it.

But this morning Amanda was cleaning the place as if the Queen of England intended to take up residence there. Jason had seen Amanda and Meg make trip after trip to the little cabin, carrying buckets, brooms, mops, boxes of cleaning supplies. They'd spent hours in the place.

And Jason had spent almost as much time leaning to his left, watching them out his window.

He cursed under his breath again, realizing that he was doing just that once more. Still, he couldn't stop himself.

Cleaning a place as dirty as that little cabin was hard work. Amanda was a proper lady. She probably had maids and housekeepers who'd done that sort of work for her all her life. She wasn't accustomed to doing heavy cleaning. She might hurt herself.

Jason flipped a page in his ledger. It would serve her right if she did get hurt, he decided. The way she'd insisted on doing everything herself and ignored his good advice. Stubborn woman....

Of course, to do that cleaning she'd put on a different dress. Jason had noticed that first thing. Or rather, he'd noticed that she wasn't wearing a bustle. Which meant she probably wasn't wearing all the other underthings women wore.

Tension hummed in Jason's veins. Determinedly, he kept his gaze on the column of figures in front of him, trying to concentrate. It didn't work. The figures all swarmed together. He slammed the book closed.

This was just the sort of thing he didn't want to have happen. He hadn't been able to get any work done because of a woman in the camp.

Jason let his thoughts sink even deeper. It wasn't just *any* woman, it was Amanda Pierce.

He adjusted his thinking back to his original concern for Amanda. She wasn't used to doing heavy work. She was too headstrong to admit she needed help. She might hurt herself. And he didn't need anybody getting hurt in his camp.

He was in charge of this mountain. It was up to him to make sure his rules were followed. He'd march right up there and tell Miss Amanda Pierce just that. Again.

Jason pushed to his feet, grabbed his hat and left the office.

The buzz of the sawmill sounded across the camp as Jason walked toward the little gathering of cabins.

Few people were in camp at this time of the day, a couple of the town merchants' kids, a dog running free. The cook and his helpers were busy working on the next meal.

Jason hiked up the hill, past the occupied cabins, farther into the woods to the cabin Amanda had chosen. Sunshine filtered through the canopy of leaves above, warming the air. It was nearly noon and the day had grown hot. He stopped at the front steps.

The cabin didn't look like much. Just one room, a pitched roof, a front porch. But it was solid and sturdy. The logger who'd built it knew what he was doing. The door stood open a crack but Jason heard no voices.

He climbed the porch and poked his head inside. The few pieces of furniture that had been left behind by the now departed logger had been pushed to one side of the room, the side that still needed cleaning. The area where the kitchen was located had been scrubbed already.

No sign of Amanda or Meg.

He hadn't seen either of them leave, but maybe they'd left during one of the few moments he'd actually been concentrating on his ledgers.

Jason jumped from the porch and circled the little cabin. At the back corner, he froze. His breath caught.

Amanda was on the tiny back porch. She'd changed from the pink dress he'd seen her in earlier to a simple green gingham print that she must have borrowed from Meg. A yellow scarf was wrapped around her hair.

She sat on the porch, leaning against the back door, her eyes closed, her legs—her bare legs—stretched out in front of her.

Jason's gut tightened as he stood at the corner of the house, staring. She'd pulled up her dress to her knees, exposing her slender, shapely legs and tiny bare feet.

Heat bloomed in Jason's belly and shot downward.

Idly, eyes still shut tight, Amanda lifted a handkerchief from a pan of cool, clear water beside her. She popped open the top two buttons of her dress and leaned her head back. She squeezed the handkerchief. Droplets fell on her throat, drizzled down her chest, and disappeared under the fabric of her dress.

Jason pressed his mouth closed to keep from moaning aloud. That didn't keep the rest of his body from reacting, however.

Mesmerized, he stared at Amanda. Gone was the prim and proper lady he'd seen sashaying around his camp. Here was a woman, a real woman. Relaxed, unrestrained, uninhibited.

Touchable.

Yes, touchable. The notion surged through Jason's body. And at that moment, he wanted to touch her like he'd never wanted anything in his life. Desire clawed at him.

He watched Amanda, caught in the spell she didn't know she'd cast over him. His insides tugged at him. His imagination flew at a wild gallop.

How he'd like to lick his tongue against those

little rivers of water rolling down her chest. Press his lips against her damp skin. Mold her flesh with his big hands.

Jason watched her, lost—happily lost—until, finally, his conscience kicked in.

He was reluctant to end this private moment with her, when she was there just for him to see, but he knew he had to.

Jason moved back around the corner and called out her name. He gave her a few seconds, then stepped forward again. When he rounded the corner of the cabin Amanda had recovered, but he hadn't.

She was sitting up now, buttons fastened, her skirt pulled down, her knees drawn up, her arms folded around them. But having her look all proper now only reminded Jason of what he'd just seen…and how much he'd like to see it again.

To his surprise, Amanda didn't look frazzled or panicked that she'd almost been caught in an unguarded moment. "What are you doing up here?" Amanda asked. A little frown creased her forehead.

Jason walked over to the edge of the porch, gazing down at her.

"Don't tell me I've disturbed work on the mountain, somehow," she said.

Jason dropped to the porch, sitting a few feet from her, fighting the urge to answer her question truthfully, and tell her that the only thing she'd disturbed on his mountain this morning was him. The words would have slipped out easily. Jason didn't like that.

"How's the work coming?" he asked and nodded toward the house.

"About half done," Amanda said. "Meg's gone to get us some lemonade. I don't know what I'd have done without her this morning."

Jason nodded, but really, he hadn't heard half of what she said. He caught a glimpse of her white petticoat. That caused him to realize how naked she was under her dress, without her bustle, corset and all the other underthings women wore.

"It's very different up here," Amanda said softly, gazing up the mountain at the towering trees, the wildflowers, the underbrush.

Jason's gaze followed hers and he shrugged. "Different from San Francisco, you mean? Yes, I'd say it is."

"You've been to San Francisco?" she asked.

"I've been lots of places."

"But you like it here best?"

Jason shrugged easily. "It suits me."

"This mountain is so wild. Untamed. Almost exotic." Amanda's gaze moved from the trees and settled on Jason. "Is that why you like it?"

"Is that why you *don't* like it?" he countered.

Amanda looked slightly offended. "I can be wild...sometimes."

Jason grunted. "Like what? Not putting up your pinky at a tea party?"

"I've done that twice, I'll have you know," she informed him.

A little grin tugged at the corner of her mouth and Jason realized she was teasing. He grinned, too, even though he hadn't expected to.

"So what about you?" Amanda asked. "Have you ever been wild?"

"I've had my moments," Jason said, and eased closer.

"I doubt that," Amanda said.

Jason scooted a little closer and grinned. "I might surprise you."

"You're always working," Amanda said. "Ethan said you haven't been off this mountain in months."

"I didn't have a good reason to leave," Jason said, and almost added that now he had none at all.

"See? That's exactly what I mean. You're always working."

Her words didn't sound critical, just conversational. Jason couldn't remember the last time he'd simply talked to a woman. He remembered the last time he'd bedded down with one, though her face wasn't clear in his mind. He remembered casual conversations, but nothing meaningful. No woman had ever held his attention long enough for anything like that.

And he couldn't even say it was the conversation that fascinated him at this moment. Because right now, he was having a hell of a good time just watching Amanda's toes peeking out from under her skirt. Just why he was so enthralled with ten little pink toes, he didn't have any idea.

Jason rolled his shoulders to ease the tension in his neck. Maybe he should get off this mountain of his more often.

He glanced at Amanda beside him, feeling the

urge to lean against her, capture her cheek in his hand, kiss her hard on the mouth.

Jason looked away. Maybe he'd better get off this mountain soon.

Chapter Nine

Voices intruded, then Todd raced around the corner of the cabin, his blond hair bouncing. A moment later, Meg followed. Like Amanda, she wore a plain dress and scarf wrapped around her hair. Ethan walked beside her carrying a pitcher of lemonade.

Jason shot to his feet. Ethan stopped at the porch steps.

''You're supposed to be at the sawmill,'' Jason told him.

''You're supposed to be doing the books,'' Ethan countered.

They eyed each other for a moment, then Meg spoke up.

''Ethan helped me with the lemonade,'' she said.

Amanda pulled on her slippers and rose, feeling a little emptiness inside that she and Jason didn't have the porch to themselves now.

They moved into the house and settled in the half of the room that had been cleaned already, the kitchen area. Amanda dried several tin cups she'd washed earlier. Meg poured the lemonade.

"Place is shaping up. You got a lot done this morning," Ethan said, looking around. "Maybe we ought to put you ladies on the logging crew."

Everybody laughed. Todd raced into the house through the back door.

"Slow down, partner," Ethan said, and caught the boy before he crashed into Amanda.

Todd tugged on his mother's sleeve. "Ethan said me and him could go fishing on Sunday."

Meg turned to Ethan. "Really? Are you sure you can spare the time?"

Ethan shrugged. "Sure. I like fishing, and Todd is a good fishing buddy."

Todd wiped his sweaty forehead with the back of his hand. "Me and Ethan have been fishing lots of times."

Meg touched her son's head lovingly and passed him her cup of lemonade.

Ethan nodded toward the other half of the cabin, still filthy and cluttered with the rough furniture.

"Did you two women move that stuff yourself?" he asked.

"Of course we did," Amanda said.

Ethan and Jason exchanged a wary look.

"Some of this furniture is heavy," Ethan said.

"We can manage," Amanda said.

Jason frowned at her. "Look, Miss Pierce, I know you're used to having maids and butlers do things like this for you. But you've got to realize that doing all this heavy cleaning is hard work."

"Maids? Butlers?" Amanda tensed. "I wouldn't know what to do with either, even if I had one."

Jason's frown deepened. "But I thought—"

"Exactly." Briskly, Amanda took the empty cup from his hand and set it aside. "If you two gentlemen will run along we have a lot to do this afternoon."

Neither Ethan nor Jason moved.

"I don't like the idea of you two moving all this furniture," Jason said.

"We've already moved it once," Amanda said. "All we have to do now is push it on the porch, do our cleaning, and put it back inside again. We'll be fine."

Jason and Ethan looked at each other, the furniture, then at the two women.

Ethan shook his head. "I'll stay and help."

"No, I'll stay," Jason said.

"You're supposed to be doing the ledgers," Ethan said.

"And you're supposed to be working at the sawmill."

The two men glared at each other for a moment.

"The sawmill can run without me for a while," Ethan told him.

"And those ledgers will be there when I get back," Jason said.

"Neither of you is helping," Amanda declared.

She stepped between the two men, caught each of their arms, and escorted them to the door of the cabin.

"Good day, gentlemen," Amanda said.

Both men stopped, shrugged out of her grasp and walked back into the cabin.

"Grab that other end," Jason said to Ethan. They picked up the kitchen table and carried it outside.

Amanda opened her mouth to protest, but changed her mind. Jason had that determined look on his face she'd seen so many times before, so she knew anything she said would fall on deaf ears. Stubborn man.

The men made quick work of moving the table, chairs, bed, mattress, bureau and settee out to the porch. Amanda hadn't wanted their help. She'd wanted to prove to Jason that she could prepare his mountain for her brides all on her own. But seeing how easily the men handled the heavy furniture, she was glad for their assistance.

When everything was sitting on the front porch, Ethan called Todd over.

"You come get me when these things need to be moved inside," he said to the boy.

He nodded eagerly. "I will."

Ethan smiled and ruffled his hair. "I'm counting on you, Todd."

Amanda stepped outside. Jason was on the porch.

"I didn't want you to do that," she said. "But thank you."

Jason pulled off his hat and wiped his forehead with his shirtsleeve.

"I did it so you wouldn't get hurt," he said. "I can't waste a day sending a man down the mountain for a doctor. Business comes—"

"—first around here. Yes, you've made that perfectly clear, Mr. Kruger."

Jason pressed his lips together, fighting off a smile, and pulled his hat on. "Just be careful."

Ethan came outside. He and Jason stood around for another moment or two, then left. Amanda and Meg waited on the porch, watching them hike down the hillside. Ethan glanced back and waved.

"He's a nice man," Amanda said.

"Yes, he is," Meg said softly.

To Amanda's surprise, Jason looked back. He didn't wave, just took a quick peek and kept walking. Still, Amanda's heart did an unexpected little flip.

"I guess we'd better get started again," Amanda said, still watching the men.

"Yes, we should," Meg said, still rooted beside her.

A few minutes passed and neither of them moved.

"You like him, don't you?" Amanda asked softly.

Meg turned to her then, a denial on her lips ready to be spoken. Instead she sighed. "Yes...for all the good it does me."

"Your husband?"

"Yes. I'm still married," Meg said. "And no matter what I feel for Ethan, that won't change."

"Have you considered divorcing Gerald?"

Meg shook her head. "I have no idea where he is."

"Ethan could find him," Amanda said, and she knew he would. He'd track down Gerald McGee, secure a divorce for Meg. The Kruger brothers were alike in that way. They got what they went after.

"I've thought of that." Meg twisted her fingers together. "Ethan has never done one thing inappropriate. I'm still married and he respects that. But there's been something between us for some time now."

"He's never said anything?"

"No." Meg shook her head. "He wouldn't. Not until I'm…free."

"But you're not ready for that yet?"

"I can divorce Gerald legally, but what about morally? He's my husband. I took vows before God." Meg gazed off into the trees. "And he will always be Todd's father."

"Todd is crazy about Ethan."

"I know. Ethan has spent a lot of time with him," Meg said. "It's helped Todd deal with things since Gerald left."

Amanda sighed heavily. This really was a difficult dilemma. Meg and Ethan were attracted to each other, maybe on the verge of falling in love—yet separated by a man who wasn't even there.

Meg gave herself a little shake and forced a smile. "We'd better get back to work."

The next hour passed with Amanda and Meg knocking down cobwebs, washing walls and windows, scrubbing things off the floor that Amanda didn't care to identify. It was hard work but Amanda was glad to do it. Having a place to live was just another step in the process of bringing her brides to the mountain. And nothing was more important to her than that.

"Hey, y'all."

Amanda's back ached as she turned, mop in hand, to find a young woman standing in her doorway.

She waved and smiled broadly as she walked inside. Her gaze settled on Amanda. "You must be that Miss Amanda Pierce. Gracious, Miss Pierce, you've got this mountain buzzing like a hive of honeybees."

Meg stopped scrubbing a window. "Amanda, this is Becky. She's Polly Minton's niece. Becky just moved here from Georgia."

Becky made a face and rolled her eyes. "Just got sentenced here, more like it."

The girl was about sixteen, Amanda guessed, with corn-silk hair and blue eyes.

"This mountain is about as exciting as a Quaker meeting," Becky lamented. She propped her hands on her hips and drew in a big breath. "So, I figured I'd come on over here and see if I could lend a hand."

"Doesn't your Aunt Polly need you for anything?" Meg asked.

"Shoot, Aunt Polly works like a field hand at harvesttime," Becky said. "She doesn't hardly let me do nothing."

"Then by all means, grab a bucket and rag," Amanda said, and smiled. "I'd appreciate your help."

By late afternoon the three women pronounced

the little cabin livable, then moved out onto the porch and gave the furniture a thorough cleaning.

Todd, who was playing in the trees nearby, called, "You want me to go get Ethan and Mr. Kruger to move the furniture, Mama?"

"Shoot, we don't need men to move this stuff," Becky declared, pushing away a stray lock of hair. "Men are slower than cold molasses running uphill. And they're grumpy as all get-out when it comes to moving furniture."

Neither Amanda nor Meg could disagree with Becky's assessment. They started moving furniture. Between the three of them they got it situated just the way Amanda wanted it, then hung the curtains that Meg had loaned her.

Amanda pressed her hand to her back. "You're a godsend, Becky. How can I thank you for all your hard work?"

"I didn't come over here expecting no money," Becky said. "I just came to do the neighborly thing."

"Well, thank you very much," Amanda said. "I really appreciate it."

"See y'all later." Becky gave a friendly wave and headed out the door.

"Is there anything else I can do?" Meg asked.

Amanda couldn't imagine asking her for anything more. She'd already loaned her curtains, linens, kitchen utensils and food. Not to mention all the backbreaking labor she'd performed.

"I can't think of a thing," Amanda said. "I'll

return your things as soon as I get down to Beaumont to do some shopping.''

''No rush.'' Meg smiled warmly. ''I'm glad you're here.''

Meg left, leaving Amanda alone in the cabin. Alone in her new home. It wasn't much to look at, just a single room with a bed, bureau and washstand and lamp in another corner sectioned off by a curtain, a settee, table and lamp in another corner, and a cookstove, cupboards, table and chair at the rear.

Drawing in a determined breath, Amanda renewed her commitment to her purpose here. Here in the cabin, on the mountain, in the timber country. The first step had been completed, and she was warmed by her accomplishment.

Now, on to the next.

The loggers would be down from the mountain soon to have their supper. Amanda would meet with each of the prospective husbands and determine which brides to send for. She smiled to herself, standing alone in her silent cabin.

This was the part of her business she liked best. Determining what each man and woman was looking for in a spouse. Finding a compatible mate. Bringing two people together for a lifetime of happiness.

A lifetime of happiness....

Amanda turned away abruptly and busied herself pumping water into the washbasin. Just because it hadn't happened for her didn't mean it couldn't happen for her brides. That was why finding the right husband was so important. Very important, as Amanda well knew.

Amanda pushed the thought aside, focusing on what lay ahead. Meeting with the loggers.

Her breath caught. That meant she'd have to see Jason Kruger again. Could they possibly have another moment together without arguing?

Or kissing?

Chapter Ten

If Amanda had thought things could go smoothly between Jason and herself later that afternoon, she was quickly disappointed when she walked into his office.

Jason sat at his desk, head bent, studying a ledger. He looked up when she stepped inside, his forehead creasing and his brows pulling together. Amanda's steps faltered. Her first inclination was to ask if she was disturbing him. But she already knew the answer.

"Good," she said briskly walking to his desk. "You're here. I'd like to discuss a few things with you."

Jason's frown deepened as he took in her appearance from head to toe. Amanda, dressed now in her pink skirt with print overskirt and matching blouse, knew she looked more presentable than when he'd last seen her cleaning her cabin, but didn't think she warranted this much attention.

"Did Ethan move your furniture?" Jason asked.

"It wasn't necessary," Amanda replied, stopping in front of his desk. "I took care of it."

"I told you not to move that furniture."

His words came out as a command, which did not sit particularly well with Amanda. Still, she forced away her anger, not wanting to waste time on something that was of so little consequence. She ignored his comment.

"The first thing I'd like to discuss with you, Mr. Kruger, is—"

"Now, look, Miss Pierce," Jason said, coming out of his chair, "when I tell you something ought to be handled a particular way, that's what I mean to have happen."

Amanda gazed up at him. "Are you still talking about the furniture?"

"Yes."

"Well, I'm not." Amanda opened her satchel. "Now, first of all—"

"Hold on—"

"No, you hold on." Amanda stopped, her breath catching in her throat at Jason's low, determined tone. Across the desk, he towered over her. Somehow he looked taller, his chest wider. But it wasn't fear his physique evoked in Amanda. It was something else. Something that sent a warm rush zinging through her, urging her to circle the desk and get closer to him.

Though just what she'd do once she got there she wasn't sure.

Amanda huffed, willing away whatever it was that she felt.

"Very well, Mr. Kruger, you've made your point," she said. "Can we move on now?"

He seemed reluctant to let it go but relaxed his stance and did just that.

"What do you want to talk about?" he asked.

"The brides' dormitory."

"Oh, yeah. I've got plans here," Jason said, and ambled to a cabinet along the back wall of the office.

Amanda smiled. Plans? He'd drawn up plans? He'd put thought into what the women would need and gone to the trouble of preparing a formal plan? She relaxed a little. Maybe this project wouldn't be an uphill battle after all.

Jason rummaged through the cabinet for a few minutes, came up with a roll of paper, then spread it out across his desk, securing each end with his ledgers. He picked up a pencil and pointed.

"This will house twenty-four men—uh, women, that is." He glanced up at Amanda briefly before turning back to the diagram. "Six rows, four bunks each. Three rows on each wall. That makes twenty-four bunks."

"Bunks?" Amanda asked, looking at the plans from the opposite side of the desk.

Jason nodded, then pointed to the other end of the diagram. "Down here there's a cupboard for each woman."

"A cupboard?" Amanda asked, turning her head one way, then the other.

"Yeah. See? Right here," Jason said, tapping the pencil against the paper. "To put their things in."

"Well, yes, I see it," Amanda said, twisting her

head far to the left. "But, well, frankly, Mr. Kruger, I don't understand."

He looked up at her. "What's not to understand? It's twenty-four bunk beds, and twenty-four cupboards all in one room."

"That part is clear," Amanda said. "What isn't clear is how you could possibly think my brides would live this way?"

Jason dropped the pencil on the plans. "These are the same plans I used to build the bunkhouse for the loggers. What's wrong with them?"

"Nothing, if it's for your men. But my brides can't live in these conditions." Amanda waved her hands over the plans. "There's not enough space between the rows of bunks for the brides to dress, to say nothing of the privacy issue. And what woman could possibly get by with one small cupboard for her belongings?"

Jason drew in a resolved breath. "And I guess you've got a better idea?"

"Well, as a matter of fact I do." Amanda drew a sheet of paper from her satchel, unfolded it and laid it atop the bunkhouse plans.

Jason looked at her for a moment, then propped his hand on his hip and stared down at the paper.

"It's just a sketch I made," Amanda said apologetically. "Not as complete as your bunkhouse plans, of course."

He rubbed his chin thoughtfully and turned his head from side to side, silently studying the plans in front of him.

"This is a two-story building," Jason said, still not looking up at her.

"Yes," Amanda said and smiled, pleased her drawing was readable.

"Twelve rooms upstairs."

"All good-sized rooms."

Jason grunted. "And there's a kitchen."

Amanda tapped the plans. "With a pantry, of course."

"Of course."

"And storage rooms," Amanda said.

"Yep. I see that."

"The best part of the whole dormitory is this large room downstairs," Amanda said, pointing. "It can be used for many, many things."

Jason nodded. "It's a big room, all right."

Pleased, Amanda asked, "Well, what do you think?"

Slowly he lifted his gaze from the plans to her face. "I think, Miss Pierce, that you're crazy as hell if you think I'm going to spend the kind of money it will take to build a monstrosity like this."

A few seconds passed before his words sank in. He'd said them so nicely, Amanda missed his meaning at first. Then her spine stiffened.

"A monstrosity?" Amanda's temper rose along with the color in her cheeks. "You have the nerve to call my plan a monstrosity—when your own plan is *idiotic?*"

Jason yanked his bunkhouse plans off the desk. "This is a workable plan. I've built it already, and

I can tell you for a fact, Miss Pierce, that it works just fine.''

Amanda's chin went up. ''You have no foresight, Mr. Kruger.''

That made him mad. His nostrils flared, his chest swelled and his shoulders widened.

''No foresight?'' He bellowed the words across the desk at her.

''Exactly.'' Amanda grabbed up her plan and waved it in the air. ''My idea could earn you back every penny you spend. And I'm not even going to insist on a share of the profit.''

''A share of the profit!''

''Would you stop shouting at me?''

''I'm not—!'' Jason clamped his mouth shut and glared at her.

Amanda glared right back.

Minutes crawled by as they stared at each other across the desk.

''You are so stubborn,'' Amanda said.

''And you aren't?''

She tossed her head. ''I never said I wasn't stubborn.''

''But you're convinced you're right?''

''Exactly.''

Jason pressed his lips together. ''I hate to break the news to you, Miss Pierce, but that's exactly what being stubborn is all about.''

She thought for a moment. ''I don't see it that way.''

Jason shrugged, then plucked her dormitory plan

from her hand and slapped it down on the desk. "Okay, Miss Pierce. Convince me."

Amanda circled the desk as Jason dropped into his chair.

"First of all," Amanda said, pointing to the plans, "the brides will live in the upstairs rooms until they're all married, which should happen very soon after their arrival. As newlyweds, they'll need a place to live, giving you the opportunity to rent out the rooms."

She glanced down at Jason. He kept his eyes on the plans and didn't say anything. Taking that as a good sign, Amanda kept going.

"Now, this large room on the main floor can be used for many things. We'll hold dances, we can—"

"Dances?" He glanced up at her.

"I'm planning a get-acquainted social as soon as the brides arrive," Amanda said. "Church services can be held there. It can also serve as the school. So instead of having to construct three buildings, this one will serve for everything."

Jason studied the plans, thinking.

"So, actually, Mr. Kruger, I'm saving you a lot of money."

He glanced up at her then, his face tense.

Amanda ventured a small smile. "You can thank me now."

Jason made a little grumbling noise and rose from his chair, forcing Amanda back a step. He walked to the window and stared out for a moment.

As much as he hated to admit it, she'd come up with a good idea. If he hadn't been so befuddled by the sight and smell of her, he'd have seen it for himself. Probably.

Jason rubbed his neck. The woman was too pretty to be this smart. Or too smart to be this pretty. He wasn't sure which. Either way, it was a combination to be wary of.

And want to roll around in bed with.

He leaned forward and rested his head against the glass panes of the window as his body reacted to the thought that had bounced around in his head so much of the time lately. That woman brought out strong feelings in him. Anger, annoyance, surprise. And they all led to the same place. And left him in the same condition.

"Mr. Kruger?"

He looked back over his shoulder at Amanda, her gaze on him, her eyes wide, her head tilted slightly. The simmering heat in his body grew hotter. Jason knew he'd better stick to business. Before he kissed her. Or did something better.

"All right, Miss Pierce," he said. "You can have your dormitory."

She smiled, a big full smile. Jason's chest tightened, inordinately pleased that he had made her happy.

"Thank you, Mr. Kruger," she said, closing her satchel. "My brides will be so much happier this way. And you'll profit from it, too."

"I'll get a crew on it."

"Thank you," she said again, and gave him another smile. "Oh, there's one more thing."

"Just *one* more?"

"I'm meeting with the prospective husbands tonight after supper and I'll need a place to work. Will the cookhouse be satisfactory?"

Jason shook his head. "You can work here."

She stopped and looked around the office. "Here? I thought you didn't want me disturbing your work?"

"I don't want you making promises to my men that you can't keep," Jason said. "I'm keeping a close eye on this whole thing, Miss Pierce."

"Very well." Amanda headed for the door, then stopped. "Oh, there's something else."

"Now why doesn't that surprise me?"

"At supper tonight, could you seat the husbands at the same tables? I'd like to observe their manners so I'll know where to start for their etiquette classes."

"You want to eat with the men?" Jason asked. "Don't you think you're rushing things a little?"

Amanda gave him a small smile. "If you'll remember, I've seen the men at mealtime. Getting *too* early a start isn't possible."

Jason shook his head. "I don't think that's such a good idea. Supper time is when the men relax after a hard day. Having a woman at their table can cause all sorts of problems."

Amanda drew in a breath. "Mr. Kruger, are we going to argue over every decision that needs to be made?"

He looked at her. "Probably."

She sighed. "Well, at least we agree on that."

Jason watched her open the door and step outside. "Amanda?"

She turned in the doorway, looking back at him with an expectant look on her face. Jason didn't know why he'd called her name. He hadn't really meant to.

But there she stood, pretty, fresh and so very feminine, waiting for him to say something. He could have looked at her all night.

"You can eat with the men tonight, if you want," Jason said. "But I still don't think it's a good idea."

Another big smile came over her face, and Jason felt it down to his toes. Pleasing another person had never mattered to him before. Now, pleasing Amanda meant everything.

"Thank you," she said.

Amanda lingered in the doorway for a few seconds longer, then left. Jason stood rooted to the spot, savoring the sight of her bustle as she swayed from view.

And he couldn't help but wonder just how agreeable Miss Amanda Pierce would be in bed.

Chapter Eleven

Supper that evening consisted of big platters of ham, hot biscuits, bowls of peas, yams and corn. Amanda stood at the front of the cookhouse near the doorway, savoring the aroma. The food smelled delicious. Life on the mountain might be rough, but the lumberjacks ate well.

She heard the loggers' chatter as they washed their faces and hands at the water trough outside after their hard day's work bringing down the timber. Their talk died down and she heard only one voice, Jason's, advising the prospective husbands to sit together at the first two tables.

A moment later when the men filed inside, Amanda smiled and nodded pleasantly. Some of the loggers nodded back, some tipped their hats, others just stared. All of which resulted in some pushing from the men at the back of the line to get inside. Gradually, all the loggers filed around the tables and sat down.

Amanda kept her smile in place as she approached the table closest to the door. "I hope you gentlemen don't mind if I join you this evening?"

A strange hush fell over the whole cookhouse as heads turned to stare. Elbows punched ribs. Fingers pointed, and whispers rose.

The ten men seated on the benches at Amanda's table froze. They looked at each other. Finally, a young man halfway down the bench dragged his hat off and pressed it to his chest.

"Why, yes ma'am, Miss Pierce," he said. "We'd be proud to have you eating with us."

Head nodding and a general grumble of agreement rose from the rest of the men seated at the table.

"Thank you," Amanda said, then turned to the table beside her where the other prospective husbands were seated. "Good evening, gentlemen."

A chorus of "howdy, ma'am" and "evening, ma'am" answered her.

Standing at the head of the table, Amanda suddenly realized she'd gotten herself into something of a dilemma. She had no place to sit—at least not properly. Long benches ran the length of the tables, and she certainly couldn't climb over one of those— not if she wanted to keep her dignity.

She looked around, wondering what she should do, then saw Jason. He stalked toward her carrying a straight-backed chair.

Amanda smiled her gratitude and stepped away from the table.

He didn't look any too pleased to come to her rescue. Jason scowled and plunked the chair down at the head of the table. Then he glared at the loggers.

"You're supposed to stand until the lady is seated," he barked.

The loggers scrambled to their feet. In the commotion, three men from the adjoining table squeezed onto the already crowded benches at Amanda's table. A shoving match broke out. One of the benches turned over. Curses flew. Then fists started to flail.

Amanda gasped. Gracious! A fight had broken out! She'd never seen a fight in her entire life. All she could do was stand there and stare.

Suddenly an arm circled her waist and jerked her off her feet. A little scream slipped from her lips. Her hands grabbed the arm holding her captive, ready to dig her nails in. She froze. That muscled arm felt familiar. She glanced over her shoulder and saw that it was Jason.

He whisked her out of harm's way and plopped her down—rather unceremoniously—in the doorway. She barely got her feet under her and he was gone, wading into the thick of the fight.

Jason grabbed two men by their collars and yanked them away from the table. Ethan appeared out of nowhere and jumped into the melee. Amanda plastered her hands over her mouth.

The Kruger brothers made quick work of breaking up the fight. Jason stepped up onto the bench that hadn't overturned.

"Everybody sit down and shut up!" he shouted. The men got to their feet brushing off their clothes, finding their hats. Two of them righted the other bench.

"Hey, how come we don't get no woman at our table?" someone called from the back of the cook-house.

"Yeah, how come?" another man shouted.

"Shut up!" Jason shouted again. He flung his hand at Amanda. "She's not some sideshow freak for you to gawk at! Sit down and eat your supper, or else get out of here!"

A low rumble of complaints went through the cookhouse. Jason stood on the bench glaring at the men, then stepped down.

Amanda's heart already beat fast, but when Jason turned his scowl on her it started to race. He stalked toward her, closing the distance with long, striding steps.

She wanted to run. In fact, it seemed like the best idea she'd had since she arrived on this mountain.

He bore down on her, scowling. Amanda gulped.

A wave of guilt washed over Amanda. She'd caused that fight to break out. Caused it by simply being a woman.

Amanda braced herself, ready for whatever Jason chose to let loose on her.

Instead, he gently took her elbow and urged her toward the table. Amanda didn't move at first, just stared up at him, unsure of his intentions. Was he about to haul her to Shady's freight wagon? Run her off of his mountain once and for all?

Jason increased the pressure on her elbow ever so slightly and walked her to the chair he'd placed at the head of the table. He held it for her. Amanda primly lowered herself into the chair.

"Sit down," Jason snarled at the lumberjacks at the table. The loggers sat.

Jason went to the opposite end of the bench, yanked the young man off his seat, then sat down himself.

Obviously, he intended to stand—or sit—and guard over her table for the duration of the meal. Amanda was glad to have him there.

One of the cook's helpers brought Amanda a plate, cup and utensils, and scurried away. The loggers dug into the food, spearing big slices of ham, grabbing for bowls of vegetables. Across the table of elbows and flying forks, Amanda caught Jason's gaze. She gave him a grateful smile. He glared at her, then glanced away.

Well, she supposed she deserved that, for all the trouble she'd caused.

At the other tables, conversation slowly resumed. No one spoke at Amanda's table. She wasn't sure if the men were uncomfortable because of her presence, or Jason's.

She dared not look at him again. He ate, but at the same time kept a watchful eye on the men around him. At their table, at all the tables.

Amanda had never known a man like Jason. Strong. Smart. So utterly in control of everything around him. Her stomach did a strange flip as she recalled how he'd jumped into the fight with no thought for himself. He'd just waded in, broken it up. But first, he'd made sure she was safe.

Another little jolt warmed Amanda's stomach. How easily he'd lifted her—with only one arm. No man had dared to put his hands on her before. But Jason had done it without even asking.

She'd felt so powerless in his grip. Yet at the same time a feeling of power had hummed through her veins. How odd. She wasn't sure what it was, but knew it was something Jason had caused.

That man was responsible for all sorts of feelings in her since the moment she'd arrived on his mountain. New feelings, certainly. Strange feelings, of course. Bad feelings? No, being on Jason's mountain hadn't caused her to feel bad about anything.

Except maybe the fight she'd caused. She'd been responsible for it, although technically she hadn't actually done anything.

She doubted Jason would see it that way.

Halfway through the meal, Amanda had had enough of her own thoughts and the silence.

"I'm planning a get-acquainted social when the brides arrive," she said.

The ten men seated at her table froze, forks halfway to their mouths, in midchew, midswallow. They all shifted uncomfortably, glanced at each other, then at Jason. He kept eating. No one responded.

Amanda tried again. "Do any of you gentlemen dance?"

After more squirming and furtive glances, one young man spoke up.

"Well, I do. Some, ma'am."

"Wonderful." Amanda smiled. "What's your name?"

Beneath his tanned face, red showed through. He was barely in his twenties, with a slight build and a shock of unruly brown hair.

"Henry, ma'am. Henry Jasper," he said, his cheeks turning a deeper red with each word he spoke. "My ma, she made me learn."

"What about you other gentlemen?" Amanda asked. She glanced around the table.

Jason's gaze bored into her, expressing his displeasure with her in no uncertain terms. No doubt he feared another fight would break out, and wanted to finish his supper in peace.

But she'd started this conversation, she couldn't let it go. Amanda eyed the man directly to her right. "What about you?"

He rolled his shoulders around, then cleared his throat, and drew in a breath. "Well, ma'am, no. Sorry to say I don't dance a lick."

"And you other men?" she asked the table in general.

The loggers looked at each other, then at her, all shaking their heads.

"Does that mean we can't have the social?" Henry asked, sounding a little worried.

"No, of course not," Amanda said. "I'll just have to teach you all how to dance."

At the far end of the table Amanda saw Jason roll his eyes, and she could have sworn she heard him moan.

Amanda managed to keep a conversation going and by the end of supper the men didn't seem so reluctant to talk to her. That pleased her. After all, teaching the loggers proper manners and dancing would require a great deal of time together. It would go better if she'd established some sort of relationship with them.

"I'll be in Mr. Kruger's office after supper to discuss your preferences for a bride. So if you gentlemen will excuse me?" Amanda said and rose to leave.

Jason rose from the bench. The loggers took their cue from him and clattered to their feet. Amanda smiled and walked out of the cookhouse.

She could have sworn she heard a sigh of relief when she left.

At the cabin that was now her home, Amanda freshened up after supper, picked up her satchel and headed for Jason's office. The sun dipped below the treetops dappling the ground with patches of light. The air had grown cooler.

Amanda's steps slowed as she saw her twenty-three prospective husbands crowded around the porch of Jason's office. Men. All men.

She understood how isolated the women felt on the mountain. No wonder Meg had been so happy when she'd arrived, and so disappointed when initially she'd changed her mind about bringing her brides here. In Meg's place, she'd have done most anything to get more women onto Jason's mountain.

Amanda drew in a deep breath, put on a smile, and kept walking.

"Good evening, gentlemen," she called.

They murmured greetings, nodded politely and opened a path so she could get onto the porch.

Shady stepped in front of her and tipped his battered hat. "Howdy, Miss Pierce."

She smiled, genuinely glad to see him. "I didn't realize you were looking for a wife."

"Shucks, no. What would an old dog like me do with a wife?" Shady chuckled. "Nope. I just come by to see what was a-goin' on."

"I'm glad you're here," Amanda said. "Would you mind giving me a hand?"

"Be proud to."

Amanda opened her satchel and passed Shady a handful of folded papers. "These are numbered, one through twenty-three," she said, speaking loudly enough that all the men could hear her. "Each man will take a number determining in what order he can request his bride. It's the only fair way."

The men nodded in agreement and crowded closer as Shady passed out the numbers.

"Can I put you in charge of the catalog?" Amanda asked.

"Them pictures of your brides?" Shady nodded broadly. "Yes, ma'am."

Amanda pulled the catalog from her satchel and gave it to Shady. The men pushed closer.

"Take some time to look at the brides," she said, "so when you're called inside you'll know what type of wife you're interested in. I can't guarantee that I can get the women who are pictured. There's always a chance they've already found a husband on their own. But I'll try the very best I can. Either

way, I'm sure I can find each of you the kind of
wife you're looking for.''

She wasn't sure the men heard her as they pushed
closer to Shady, who jealously guarded the catalog,
reveling in the authority he'd been given. She went
inside the office.

Jason was already there seated at his desk.
Amanda expected him to say something about the
fight that had broken out at supper, but he didn't.
Still, he didn't look all that happy to see her.

''I fixed you a place to work,'' Jason said, and
waved his hand.

Amanda turned. ''Oh…''

Situated across the office were two sawhorses
with a couple of rough planks stretched between
them. A chair sat behind them, making a desk of
sorts.

It was the most dismal looking thing Amanda had
ever seen. She didn't want to work there.

But she was tired. She'd already had a long, hard
day cleaning the cabin, moving the furniture, incit-
ing a near riot at supper. It had all taken its toll.

Pushing on, Amanda spread out her papers and
pencils on the makeshift desk. She felt Jason's gaze
on her, even after he'd sat down in his desk chair
and turned his attention to his ledgers.

He'd told her he intended to keep an eye on her,
make sure she didn't cheat his men. Apparently, he
intended to do just that.

Amanda called Shady into the office.

''Would you please let the men know I'll have

time to take only five applications tonight?'' she said. ''The rest will be done tomorrow.''

''Sure thing, Miss Pierce,'' Shady said.

''Send in the first prospective husband.''

Amanda waited by the doorway and listened as Shady passed along her instructions. She'd expected some complaints, but heard only a little grumbling. None of the men left, though. As she headed to her desk she saw them still crowded around the catalog.

The first prospective husband ambled into the office. He gave a nod to Jason, then sat down in the chair in front of what passed for Amanda's desk. Bill Braddock didn't seem to notice that it was planks and sawhorses as he gave his name when Amanda asked for it.

''Now, Mr. Braddock, could you tell me a little about yourself?'' Amanda asked.

All muscles and brawn, Bill looked like the lumberjack that he was. Big, sturdy, deeply tanned face and unkempt beard.

He squinted at her. ''Whatcha want to know that fer?''

From the corner of her eye, Amanda saw Jason glance up at her. She pretended not to notice him.

''So I can match you up with a wife who will share your same interests and beliefs,'' Amanda explained.

Bill thought that over for a moment, then gave Amanda a rundown of his life, where he was born, his education, his religious beliefs, his family, the jobs he'd worked. Amanda nodded pleasantly, asked a few questions to draw him out, and noted everything on the paper in front of her.

"Now," she said, "tell me what sort of wife you're looking for."

"I'll take number six."

"Number six in the catalog?" Amanda asked.

The brides' pictures were numbered, no names given. Amanda kept most of the women's personal information separate. That way the slots in the catalog could be used over again, and the women's names weren't available to the public in general.

"Yeah, that's the one I want," Bill said. He reared back in his chair and crossed his ankle casually over his knee. "That there catalog of yours says she's a widow. That's the one I want. One that's already broke in."

Jason came out of his chair and circled the desk before Bill Braddock had time to uncross his leg, towering over him, clenching his fists.

"Shut your filthy mouth," Jason snarled. "That's a lady you're talking to."

Bill's eyes got big as he slouched farther in the chair, gazing up at Jason.

Amanda's face turned bright red.

"No, Mr. Kruger, you got me all wrong," Bill said, holding up his palms. "I just meant I wanted a wife who was used to cooking and cleaning and knew how to wash clothes. That's all. I didn't mean nothing else. I swear."

Jason glared down at him for another moment, curling and uncurling his fists, then backed off. He glanced at Amanda and her scarlet face.

"Just watch what you say," Jason told Bill, then went back to his desk.

An extremely awkward moment passed while Amanda pretended her face wasn't red and that another fight hadn't almost broken out. Finally she concluded her interview with Bill Braddock. He paid her fee, then left.

A tense silence filled the office. Jason turned the pages in his ledger, nearly ripping them out. Amanda stacked her papers with a vengeance.

"Any more trouble you can cause for one day?" Jason asked.

"Me?" Amanda sat straighter in her chair. "I didn't cause that. I didn't do anything. You're the one who tried to start a fight."

"What the hell did you expect me to do, sit here and let Braddock talk to you like that?"

"No," Amanda told him. "I expected you to sit there and mind your own business."

Jason came to his feet. "This is my business. Everything on this mountain is my business."

Angry, Amanda opened her mouth, but no words came out. Exhaustion overwhelmed her. She didn't have it in her for another battle with Jason tonight.

"Since you want to be in charge of everything," Amanda said, "would you ask Shady to send in the next man?"

He looked at her, then stomped over to the door. Amanda was certain she heard him say something to the next man who came in, but she couldn't tell what it was. She decided it was just as well.

The evening wore on and Amanda got all five

interviews completed. Shady brought her catalog inside and she packed it into her satchel along with her orders and other supplies.

Neither she nor Jason had said a word to each other since Bill Braddock left the office.

"You want to put that cash in the safe?"

Jason's words jarred Amanda out of her thoughts. She looked up at him, then down at the money she'd collected, and was about to stuff into her satchel.

"Everybody in camp knows you've got it," Jason said, waving toward the money. "Those locks on your cabin doors won't keep anybody out if they're determined to get in."

Amanda blanched. She hadn't thought she wouldn't be safe in her cabin, on Jason's mountain. The feeling that she was vulnerable troubled her.

"Do you think I'm going to lock it in my safe and not give it back to you?" Jason asked, a tinge of annoyance in his voice. "I'm not going to steal it from you."

He'd steal her heart, but never her money.

That thought ricocheted through her mind. Gracious, why had such a notion come to her?

"I trust you," Amanda said, and held out the cash. "With my money, anyway."

Jason paused a moment before he took it from her. When he did, their fingers brushed. Both pretended it didn't happen.

"Well, good night," Amanda said, picking up her satchel.

He glanced back over his shoulder as he headed

for the big, black safe sitting in the back corner of the office.

"You're leaving?" he asked.

She paused. "It's late. We both should get into—"

Bed.

The unspoken word hung between them, charging the air and causing Amanda's spine to prickle. Jason's eyes seemed to see right through her to her pounding heart. It was as if he could read the naughty thoughts racing through her mind.

Amanda grabbed her satchel and hurried out of the office.

Chapter Twelve

What was happening to her?

Amanda trudged up the mountain toward her cabin—at least in the direction she thought her cabin was in. She couldn't be certain in the dark.

Since coming to this mountain, she wasn't certain of anything anymore.

The satchel Amanda carried dragged like a boat anchor, slowing her pace further over the rough terrain. She was tired, nearly exhausted. The tiniest pain throbbed in her head. Her arm muscles hurt from moving furniture and scrubbing, and her face muscles ached from smiling through supper.

In general, she was a mess. And Amanda was never a mess. At least, she'd never been one until she came to the lumber camp. Now, nothing was the same. Certainly not herself.

Through the shadows and the trees, Amanda made out the outline of her little cabin. Her home. Such as it was.

Another thing that was different.

Visions of her home in San Francisco played in Amanda's mind as she climbed the porch, found the lock with the key she kept in her pocket, and went inside.

She stood in the doorway for a moment. If she tried hard, could she imagine she was about to step into her neat little parlor back home, with her doilies, lace and china figurines?

Amanda felt her way inside, found the lantern on the wall beside the door, located the matches and struck one. Sulphur burned her nose as it sparked to life. She touched it to the lantern's wick, then lowered the glass chimney.

Slowly, Amanda turned. Her shoulders slumped. The little cabin looked just as she remembered. And nothing like her home in San Francisco.

In the silence, Amanda closed the door, undressed and slipped into her pink nightgown. The air in the cabin was stuffy from being closed all day. She pushed two of the windows open, letting in the cool night air.

Standing in the middle of her little cabin, the silence roaring in her ears, reality hit Amanda square on the chin. Jason had been right. This mountain wasn't a place for women.

The fight in the cookhouse tonight served up proof of that. Jason's attitude toward her confirmed it.

Maybe he was right about everything, Amanda mused. She didn't belong here. Going home suddenly seemed like a very good idea.

Loneliness and sadness overwhelmed Amanda.

Tears stung her eyes. She sniffed them back, put on her robe and went out onto the back porch. It was quiet, so very quiet. All she saw from her little porch was darkness. Not a single light shone anywhere up the mountain. There were none of the sights or sounds of the city she was used to.

Slowly, Amanda sat down on the steps. Through the canopy of leaves, a thousand stars winked down at her. She leaned her head back, bracing her elbows on the step behind her, and searched the night sky.

She'd already promised she'd stay. She'd given her word that she'd bring her brides here. The loggers were anxious for them. But Jason...

Tears swelled in Amanda's eyes once more. Jason didn't want her brides here. He'd only agreed to the whole thing because he needed to keep his crew happy while he filled the railroad contract.

A tear rolled down Amanda's cheek. More than that, Jason didn't want *her* here.

Hurt coiled deep in her belly. Amanda crossed her arms in front of her, holding the ache inside. A tear trickled down her cheek.

Maybe she should give Jason what he wanted, she thought. Maybe she should leave.

Jason hadn't liked supper tonight one bit. All those other men staring at Amanda. Her sitting right there at the table for all of them to look at, ogle, think all sorts of things about.

Never mind that he'd been thinking those same things.

Jason closed his ledgers and stacked them on the

corner of his desk. Without wanting to, he glanced at the chair Amanda had sat in tonight.

As if supper hadn't been enough to endure, he'd had to listen while she talked to his loggers. That hadn't suited him either. He'd had to sit there while she asked them questions, smiled at them, made pleasant remarks about their pasts, inquired what sort of wife they wanted—smelling good the whole time.

Jason shoved the ledgers into one of the cupboards. That had been the last straw. He'd nearly come to blows with one of his men, breaking his own rule about no fighting in camp.

Amanda Pierce had turned everything upside down. Including him.

The door swung open and Ethan strode into the office, smiling.

"Miss Pierce left already?" he asked.

"Yeah," Jason grumbled, slamming the cupboard door.

Ethan eyed the makeshift desk. "Is this what you gave her to do her work on?"

"What's wrong with it?" Jason demanded.

"It's just so damn warm and inviting I'm surprised she's not spending the night down here," Ethan told him.

"What the hell is that supposed to mean?"

"You know what I mean," Ethan told him. He shook his head. "Why don't you relax and enjoy her company, Jas? It won't last forever."

Jason snorted. "Won't last forever? In another

few weeks there'll be women swarming all over this mountain.''

"Yeah," Ethan said. "But Amanda won't be one of them."

Jason stopped suddenly, then turned to his brother, his brows drawn together, his face pale.

Ethan shook his head. "You didn't think Amanda would stay here, did you?"

"Well..."

"Once the brides are married off and settled, Amanda's job will be done. She'll be gone."

"I know that," Jason insisted.

"Then how come you've got that stupid look on your face?"

Jason brushed by his brother. "Lock up, will you? I'm going home."

Closing the office door behind him, Jason stopped at the edge of his porch and drew in a breath of fresh air. The camp was settling in for the night. It was cool. A few lights burned in the bunkhouse and in the building in town.

He liked this time of day. Evening, when things quieted down, the men and their problems were out of his hair and he could relax.

His gaze wandered to the cabins scattered on the hillside, to the smallest cabin, the one farthest up the mountain.

Amanda's cabin.

He'd known she wouldn't be on his mountain forever. Really, he'd known that.

But Amanda had held such a presence since coming here, and occupied so much of his time, he couldn't imagine her not being around. She seemed to belong here as much as anyone did—as much as he did.

Jason grumbled a curse at himself under his breath. What the hell was he thinking? Amanda didn't belong here. She was a city woman. A refined, proper lady. She didn't have what it took to live on his mountain.

His gaze traveled to Amanda's cabin again. A soft yellow light glowed through the window. She was still awake.

What was she doing? Jason watched the window but saw no shadows move across them. Was she having something to eat? Getting ready for bed? Undressing? Bathing?

Maybe she was already in bed, snuggled under the coverlet. In a nightgown? Naked?

Buck naked, maybe. Her supple body spread out on the—

"Hellfire!"

Jason stomped off the porch and headed toward home. Just like Ethan said, in a few weeks Amanda Pierce would be gone. And that suited him fine. The woman was nothing but one problem after another. He'd be glad to see her off his mountain.

Wouldn't he?

Jason stopped. He squinted in the darkness at the outline of his own house tucked into the shadows.

He turned, gazing up the mountain. Though he knew better, Jason hiked toward Amanda's cabin.

It wouldn't do her reputation any good if he was seen there at this time of the night. Above all,

Amanda was a lady. She wouldn't appreciate him putting her in a compromising situation.

Jason didn't stop, though. He kept going.

This was his mountain, he decided. And he could hike up to anybody's cabin, anytime he saw fit. Including Miss Amanda Pierce.

His mountain or not, Jason came to his senses as he made his way up the hillside. He swung left in the general direction of the sawmill. Though it was doubtful anyone would see him tramping through the dark woods at this time of night, he wasn't about to set tongues wagging. He circled through the trees and came up on Amanda's cabin from the rear.

Light still shone from the windows so he knew she was awake. Twigs snapped under his feet as he crept closer. A shadow formed out of the darkness of the back porch and Jason realized that Amanda was outside, sitting on the steps.

Jason's feet dragged to a halt and he swallowed hard. She had on a nightgown and robe. The cool mountain air heated up a little as Jason stood there watching her.

He couldn't make out her face. Her hands covered it. She leaned forward, resting her elbows on her knees.

Jason turned his head, listening.

Sobs. He heard sobs.

Amanda was crying.

Thunderstruck, Jason charged out of the woods toward the cabin. Vivid images of what may have happened to her flooded his mind, filling him with a fear that cut him in half.

He raced up to her and dropped to his knees in front of her.

"What's wrong?"

Amanda's head came up quickly. Startled, she yelped and leaned away from him.

"No, it's okay," Jason said, and caught her arms. His gaze searched the length of her in the dim light. Tears stained her cheeks. Her eyes were wide with fright.

"What happened?" he demanded.

Amanda jerked her arms out of his grasp. "Nothing happened. Except that you nearly scared me to death."

"You're all right?" he asked, his gaze still searching her.

"I'm fine."

Jason frowned. "Then why are you crying?"

"Because I feel like it," Amanda told him, and swiped at her tears with the back of her hands.

"Oh." Jason looked closer at her. "You're sure nobody did anything to hurt you?"

"No."

"Or said anything?"

"No."

Jason rose from his knees and stared down at her. Towering above her she looked small and weak. He couldn't help but wonder if he was responsible for her tears. The idea didn't make him feel so good.

With a sigh, Jason sat down on the wooden step beside her and pulled his handkerchief from his hip pocket.

"I don't usually allow crying in my lumber camp," he said softly.

"Then I guess we're even," Amanda said, "because I don't usually cry."

She took the handkerchief from him and wiped her eyes, sniffed, crossed her arms in front of her and scooted to the right, far enough away to ensure they didn't touch.

In the dim light Jason watched her, feeling the pull to move with her, to get close enough that they did touch. He sat still, though.

Jason turned sideways on the step facing Amanda. "It's different here. Not like the city. People are different. They have to be tough to survive this place."

She jerked her chin. "Thank you very much for making me feel even worse about coming here."

"I didn't mean it like that," Jason said. "You're from the city. You can't help what you're like."

"Mr. Kruger, you don't know me well enough to determine what I'm like," Amanda said, then sniffed and wiped her nose with his handkerchief.

Jason gazed at her for a moment. Even with her cheeks still damp with tears, she held her nose in the air, her chin up. Lord, she was a stubborn woman. He knew that much about her.

A few minutes passed with only the sounds of the forest breaking the silence.

"It's pretty up here in winter," Jason said and nodded toward the trees. "Snow blankets the ground, and icicles hang from every branch of every tree. And in the spring the wildflowers bloom."

"I didn't think you noticed things like that," Amanda said, wiping away her last tear.

Jason shrugged his wide shoulders. "Not much to do up here after work but look at the scenery."

Amanda smiled and felt herself relax a little. "You like it here, don't you?"

"Yep. I do," Jason said, gazing off into the woods.

"It suits you," Amanda agreed.

He turned back to her. "You like your job, too."

Amanda nodded. "Yes, very much."

"How come you're always hunting down husbands for other women, but never found one for yourself?"

Amanda shrugged uneasily. "Well…"

"Don't you like the idea of being married?" Jason asked.

"I have no objection to it."

Jason leaned a little closer. "Then is there something about marriage that you do object to?"

A warmth spun between them, pulling Amanda closer to Jason. She knew what he meant, what he was asking about. And she should have been insulted, but wasn't. Still, she knew better than to answer his question.

"I started my business because I like to see people happily married," Amanda said. "Like your brother, for instance."

"Ethan?" Jason frowned. "What are you talking about?"

"He's in love with Meg."

"What? No, he's not." Jason shook his head,

then paused and turned back to Amanda. "Do you think he is?"

Amanda rolled her eyes. "You mean you never noticed?"

Jason shrugged helplessly.

"Yes, he loves her," Amanda said. "And Meg loves him, too."

"Then why don't they do something about it?"

"She's still married, remember?"

"Oh, yeah." Jason sighed thoughtfully, then stretched out his arm along the step behind Amanda's back. "Seems like a damn shame, if you ask me. Two people in love, but can't do anything about it."

"That's why my business is so..." Words failed Amanda as Jason leaned closer. He gave off a heat that pulled her toward him.

Jason closed his arms around her and Amanda let him. He lowered his head until his lips brushed hers. Amanda didn't resist. He felt warm, comfortable. As if she were...home.

With a little mewl of surrender, Amanda leaned into his familiar strength. She threaded her arms around his neck and held on while his mouth moved over hers. Leaning her head back seemed like the most natural thing to do. As did parting her lips for him. She welcomed the warmth of his tongue against hers.

Jason tightened his arms around Amanda and pulled her closer until her breasts brushed his chest. Heat rose in his belly, pumping his blood faster. She tasted sweet…so sweet. He kissed her until tasting wasn't enough.

Slowly, he traced his hand down her back and around her waist. Beneath her gown and robe, she wore nothing else, and that realization made his heart race faster. He marveled at the curve of her hip, her fine bones as he lifted his hand to capture her breast.

She gasped, but didn't pull away. Instead, she arched against him. Jason squeezed her ever so gently, and stroked his thumb until he felt her breast tighten at his touch. She gasped again, and so did he.

Jason moaned her name and buried his mouth in the sweet hollow of her throat. He tasted her flesh, felt the rhythm of her pulse beating against his lips. He slid his hand inside her robe and gown, pushing deeper until his fingers spread around her bare breast.

Desire flamed into passion. He'd never held anything so wonderful in his life. He wanted her. All of her. Now.

His body throbbed with need. Lifting his head, he saw her eyes closed. Her breath came in quick gasps, hot against his cheek. She was lost in the same desire as he—and all he'd done was kiss her and touch her breast. He knew he could have her. Here. Now.

Temptation nearly overcame him. But that nagging voice in the back of his head grew from a whisper to a scream. He eased away slightly, letting cool air swirl between them.

He'd found her sitting on her steps, crying. He wouldn't take advantage of that. No matter how badly he wanted to.

A little groan rattled in his chest as he withdrew his hand from her nightgown and pulled the fabric together. Amanda opened her eyes then and gazed up at him. She was a beautiful woman and he wanted her as he'd wanted no other. But not like this.

Jason pressed his forehead against hers and pecked tiny kisses on her face. She leaned closer and settled her head against his chest. It wasn't what he really wanted, but he'd take it.

After a few minutes Jason rose, pulling Amanda up with him. He walked her to her back door and guided her inside. They stood there, the threshold separating them, looking at each other.

After a few minutes, Jason said, "You never did tell me why you were crying tonight."

She touched her forehead, as if trying to recall a distant memory.

"It was because I decided to give you what you wanted," Amanda said.

Jason tensed. If Amanda knew what he really wanted, she'd likely slap his face.

Then she said, "I decided to leave."

Chapter Thirteen

"But don't get your hopes up. I changed my mind. I'm staying."

Amanda had said those words to him last night, gazing out her back door, while he still tasted her kiss on his lips and his fingers burned with the feel of her breast.

At the time, Jason had been relieved she wasn't leaving. Now, striding toward the cookhouse at sunrise, he wasn't so sure.

Up ahead stood Amanda, dressed in a pale green dress that hugged her waist and outlined her breasts. One of the breasts he'd held in the palm of his hand last night.

Without all the trappings of women's underclothing she usually wore, he'd discovered just how magnificent her breast was. And had been surprised at its fullness.

The ease with which she'd lost herself in what they were doing last night had surprised him, too.

Amanda was a proper lady. Proper ladies didn't throw their heads back and moan and writhe.

He'd only touched her. Briefly. With just his fingertips. If he did more, Amanda would—

Heat, want and desire converged behind the fly of Jason's trousers, slowing his steps. Annoyed, he cursed himself. He'd been this way most of the night.

Amanda wasn't the only one nearly out of control.

But he was the one who had a lumber camp to run. He joined the stream of men heading for the cookhouse, determined to focus his thought on business and not Amanda. Or her breasts.

That proved more difficult than he thought as he walked into the cookhouse past Amanda, who was smiling and nodding to the loggers. His gaze honed in on her bosom. The right one. The one he'd held. What did the left one feel like?

Jason growled under his breath and gritted his teeth as his condition worsened.

"Mr. Kruger?"

He heard Amanda's voice above the chatter of his men and glanced over at her, looking at her face this time. If she was embarrassed at seeing him this morning, after what had happened at her cabin last night, Amanda gave no indication. Except that she seemed to be looking at the top button on his shirt instead of his face.

Jason made his way through the crowd of loggers to where Amanda stood. He didn't get too close.

"I'd like to begin the etiquette instruction this morning," Amanda said. "Would it be too disruptive to pull two of the tables together so all the husbands can sit together?''

Jason turned and saw that the table Amanda had sat at yesterday already had sixteen men squeezed onto the benches meant for ten.

''No more disruptive than having another fight break out,'' he said.

Amanda kept out of the way as Jason had the men move the two tables together and arrange the benches around three sides. She wished she could avoid him altogether today. Things done in the dark took on a whole different meaning in the light of day. She didn't know what to do, what to say to him. How should a lady react upon seeing the gentleman whom she'd allowed to caress her breast the night before?

The quivering in her stomach started again. She'd lain awake most of the night thinking about it, then awakened this morning remembering.

She should have been ashamed by her unseemly behavior. The way she'd carried on—like a strumpet.

But she wasn't embarrassed and she didn't feel like a strumpet at all. Last night, with Jason, had felt right. Which just added to her confusion.

Amanda watched Jason as he fetched the straight-backed chair from the corner and situated it at the head of the now double-sized table. He didn't appear to be any different for their encounter. Except that he seemed to keep glancing at her left breast.

Amanda dismissed it as her imagination as she lowered herself into the chair.

The loggers clattered onto the benches and dived for the plates of sausages, bacon, flapjacks, eggs and biscuits on the table.

"Hold up!" Jason said, as he took a seat at the end of the table opposite Amanda. "You're going to learn some manners this morning."

The men looked none too happy at the prospect, but stopped reaching for the food and sat still.

"Good morning, gentlemen," Amanda said, smiling. "We'll make this as painless as possible. I know you're all hungry and need to get off to work. So we'll start with something simple this morning, and improve your skills with each meal. Is that agreeable with everyone?"

They fidgeted on the benches, eyeing the food.

"First of all, your napkin belongs in your lap. Not in your collar." Amanda made a show of unfolding her napkin and placing it on her lap.

"And unless you're cutting meat," Amanda said, "the hand you are not eating with belongs in your lap."

This instruction caused some confusion among the loggers as they shifted knives and forks and awkwardly placed their hands in their laps.

"You're doing fine," Amanda said, and smiled with encouragement. "Remember that eating should be silent. No slurping or gulping."

The men began eating their breakfast but looked uncomfortable. Amanda expected them to end up with indigestion before breakfast was concluded.

She tried to start a conversation, but the loggers' attention was taken up trying to hold their napkins on their laps and keeping their hands where they belonged, so she gave up.

"I'll be at Mr. Kruger's office to take the next five applications as soon as you're finished," Amanda said, and rose from the table.

Jason got to his feet. "Stand up," he barked, and the loggers scrambled to their feet, nodding politely at Amanda. She couldn't help noting they all looked relieved when she left. And really, she was a little relieved herself.

When Jason left the cookhouse after breakfast and went into his office, he thought he'd find Amanda there ready to take orders for her brides. Instead he found Ethan, and something he wasn't expecting.

"What the...?" Jason mumbled as he closed the door behind him.

Ethan, seated at his desk with his feet propped on the corner, grinned. "Nice, huh?"

Jason planted his fists at his waist and glared at the work area he'd put together for Amanda. Now, the sawhorses and rough planks were covered by a pink linen cloth. In the center stood a glass jar with a yellow scarf tied around it and filled with wild-flowers.

"Amanda did that, didn't she?" Jason said.

"Well, it sure as hell wasn't me."

"How am I supposed to work with this in here?" Jason asked.

"Same way as me." Ethan reared back in the chair and cupped his hands behind his head. "Just sit back and enjoy it."

"This is supposed to be a lumber camp," Jason said. "Whoever heard of a pink tablecloth in a lumber camp?"

"You're the one who moved her in here," Ethan pointed out. "What did you expect would happen?"

Jason plopped into his desk chair. "So all of a sudden you're an expert on women?"

"Just stating a fact," Ethan said.

"Like with Meg McGee?"

Ethan pulled his feet from the corner of the desk. They hit the floor with a thud.

"What about Meg?" he asked, growing serious.

"Why didn't you tell me you had designs on her?" Jason asked.

Ethan fiddled with a pencil on his desk and shrugged without answering.

"She's a married woman," Jason said.

Ethan looked up at him then. "Her husband's been gone nearly a year."

"That doesn't mean she's not married."

"I know." Ethan sighed heavily.

"Have you told her how you feel?"

Ethan shook his head. "Didn't seem like the right time."

"If you decide to make your move, let me know," Jason said. "We'll track down that bastard who deserted her and do whatever we have to do. You just say the word."

Ethan nodded thoughtfully and rose from his chair. "I'd better get to the mill. You going up the mountain today?"

"Yes, I'm going," Jason said. He needed to go.

He needed a hard day's work in the timber to get his mind off Miss Amanda Pierce.

The door swung open just then and Amanda walked in, reminding Jason of exactly what he'd been trying not to think about since last night. Her breasts. Only now he wasn't sure which one occupied his thoughts the most. The right one, which he'd touched, or the left one, which he had yet to sample. Either way, both were there, hugged by her dress, in all their glory, bringing on the same reaction in him. Jason was glad he was already seated.

"Good morning," Amanda said briskly as she straightened her work area and laid out her pencils and papers.

"Morning," Ethan said as he headed for the door. "I'm on my way up to the mill."

"Be safe," Amanda called as he walked out the door.

Jason struggled to keep his mind on the dormitory plans he pulled out of his desk drawer as Amanda sat down and took orders from five more prospective husbands. It wasn't easy. Not with her looking so fresh and smelling so sweet. It was all he could do to stay in his chair.

Grateful that the last interview was completed for the morning, Jason locked her fees up in his safe and headed up the mountain as quickly as he could.

Striding up the skid road into the high timber with his logging crew, Jason breathed in the fresh air. His body was wound tight. He needed a day of work. A day with his men. A day away from Amanda and all thoughts of women, brides and breasts.

He didn't get much of a respite. Where the men usually talked about the job, told tall tales and fishing stories, today they talked about the brides that were coming. They talked about Amanda. About their etiquette lesson this morning. Their upcoming dance lessons. The get-acquainted social. Three of the men realized they all wanted bride number nine in the catalog and a fight nearly broke out.

At noon, Jason hiked back to the cookhouse with his men feeling as grouchy as when he left. To his relief, Amanda wasn't there for another etiquette lesson. He thought he could eat his meal in peace until half the men at the husbands' table accused the other half of eating like pigs and ignoring Amanda's instructions. This time a fight did break out.

The afternoon on the mountain wasn't any better. Jason sought Buck Johansen and found him in the shade of a stand of towering Douglas fir.

"Yep," Buck said. "The men have been at each other's throats. They're afraid something will happen and Miss Pierce won't be able to bring her brides up here."

Buck went on. "Better get those women up here quick. And somebody better decide who's getting bride number nine."

"Hell...." Jason mumbled.

"It's just going to get worse as the time gets closer," Buck predicted. "Knowing they'll be bedding down with wives, tempers will get shorter. And the men who aren't getting wives? What kind of shape do you think they'll be in?"

Jason looked at Buck and knew he was right. He

was already antsy and short-tempered himself, just from having Amanda around. Amanda and her full, ripe breasts.

Pulling off his hat, Jason wiped the sweat from his forehead and mumbled a curse under his breath. To be so intrigued by a woman's breasts was loco. Just plain crazy. He'd been working and sweating all day and still that was all he could think about.

Jason plopped his hat on his head and decided it was high time he did something about it. Amanda wasn't likely to let him touch her breasts again, but there were plenty of other breasts he could fondle. And lots of other things he could do, too. Things he needed to do before he exploded.

He was going down to Beaumont to spend the day—hell, maybe two days—rolling around with a pretty whore in the town. Come tomorrow morning, Jason was leaving his mountain.

Chapter Fourteen

"Come on. Hurry up. Let's go," Jason said, pulling his brother off the bench in the cookhouse.

"What's the rush?" Ethan asked, shoving a last bite of flapjacks in his mouth. "Why are you in such a damn hurry to get to Beaumont?"

"Supplies," Jason said, striding past his men still eating their breakfast.

"Beaumont's not going anywhere," Ethan said, hurrying to catch up. "Those supplies will be there when we get there."

"Looks like it might storm." Jason waved his hand toward the western horizon as they walked out of the cookhouse. "Don't want to get caught in the rain."

"Since when?"

"Will you just come on?"

Jason had thought of nothing but this trip to Beaumont since yesterday afternoon. He'd left Buck Johansen in charge of the men with explicit instructions. He'd had Ethan put Rory Connor in charge of the sawmill. And above all, he'd stayed away from Amanda—and her breasts.

That had been no easy task. Especially since around midnight it had occurred to him how isolated her cabin was. Located farthest up the hillside, he could come and go as he pleased and nobody would see him. He could stay as long as he wanted, too. All night, even, if Amanda would let him.

But he didn't need that now. He was going to Beaumont. He had a wallet full of cash, and when they got to town he would tell Ethan how he intended for the Kruger brothers to spend the day— his treat.

As they approached the freight wagon waiting outside his office, Jason's steps slowed. He caught a glimpse of lace and pale blue on the other side of the wagon.

No.

Jason rounded the wagon and found Amanda, Meg and Todd waiting there.

"What's going on?" he demanded.

Both the women looked at each other and smiled.

"We're going shopping in Beaumont," Amanda said.

Meg giggled. "We saw that Shady had the wagon hitched and ready, so we thought, why not?"

Ethan beamed. "Great."

"No!" Jason shouted. "You can't go."

"Why not?" Amanda asked.

"Yeah," Ethan said. "Why not?"

"Because Shady's not going," Jason told him. "Ethan and I are taking the wagon."

Todd pulled on his mother's arm. "Ma, I don't want to go."

Amanda peered into the wagon. "Why can't we go, too? There's plenty of room."

"We've got business to take care of," Jason said, and tried to make it sound important.

"I have business, too." Amanda held up her leather satchel. "All the bride orders are complete. I have to send them off."

"I'll do that." Jason grabbed for the satchel.

Amanda pulled it away. "I'd rather do it myself. Besides, I have things to purchase."

"Ma, can't I stay here?" Todd asked. "I don't want to go shopping."

"Ethan and I can buy what you need," Jason told her, searching his pockets and coming up with paper and a nub of a pencil. "Write it down. We'll get it."

"Ma," Todd whined. "I don't want to go. Can't I stay here? I'll be all right."

Meg turned to her son. "No, Todd, I can't leave you here by yourself all day. I won't be back until late."

"Mr. Kruger," Amanda said, "what I need you can't possibly pick out."

"Sure I can," he said, and thrust the paper and pencil at her.

Meg turned to Amanda and glanced down at Todd. "Maybe I shouldn't go."

Amanda's disappointment showed. "But we were both looking forward to it."

"Yes, but Todd. He—"

"I'll stay here and watch out for him," Ethan said.

"You will?" Todd exclaimed.

"You will?" Meg asked.

"Like hell you will," Jason said. "Now look, Ethan and I have got important business to attend to today."

"I thought we were just buying supplies," Ethan said.

"Yeah, well, they're important supplies," Jason insisted.

Amanda gazed up at him. "Is there a reason you can't buy these supplies with Meg and me along for the ride?"

"Well..." Jason looked from Amanda's expectant face, to Meg's, to Ethan's.

"Sure he can buy supplies with you two along," Ethan said, looking at Jason as if he'd lost his mind. "You two women climb on up in the wagon. Go buy something pretty, and have a good time. Todd and I will be all right."

"Yeah!" Todd bounced on his toes.

Meg looked at her son, then at Ethan. "All right. If you're sure."

"You need some time off from being a mama," Ethan said.

She smiled. "Thank you, Ethan. That's one of the nicest things anyone has ever done for me."

"You deserve nice things to happen to you," he said.

"All right then, let's go," Amanda said.

Ethan assisted Meg, then Amanda up onto the

wagon seat amid a flurry of skirts and petticoats. He looked back toward the horizon, then turned to Jason.

"I think you're right. It might rain today. Better not stay too long," Ethan said.

Jason gritted his teeth. "Don't worry. I intend to do what needs doing, then get the hell out of there."

He vaulted into the wagon. His weight caused the seat to dip as he sat down. Amanda fell against him. She pushed away quickly, dragging her right breast across his arm.

His lips clamped together, holding in the groan that pushed up from his belly. Jason sighed heavily. It was going to be a long damn day.

Jason pulled the team to a halt on the edge of Beaumont outside the livery stable, set the brake, tied off the reins and jumped to the ground. He'd never been so glad the trip down the mountain was over.

Amanda had sat on the seat beside him, bumping and swaying with the rhythm of the wagon, their thighs brushing every once in a while. Flashes of white petticoat. Womanly smells.

Jason wiped his brow. It was damn near more than he could stand.

"Morning," the blacksmith called as he came through the double doors of the stable.

"Morning," Jason said to the burly, bearded man. "Take care of my team, will you? I'll be in town most of the day."

"Sure thing," he answered.

Jason flipped him a coin and headed toward town.

The blacksmith turned his attention to Amanda and Meg still on the wagon seat. "Morning, ladies. Let me give you a hand down from there."

Jason spun around as the blacksmith reached up to assist Amanda from the seat. He pushed in front of the man, got a face full of her bustle, then caught her waist and eased her onto the ground.

Amanda turned in his arms, surprised. She dipped her lashes. "Thank you," she whispered.

His palms stung, resting on her hips. Even though he couldn't feel anything but the fabric of her dress, he knew what was under there.

Meg cleared her throat and Jason helped her to the ground with much less fanfare. He stepped back as the women headed toward town.

They were both pretty women, Jason observed, watching them walk ahead of him. The two prettiest likely to be seen on the streets of this town today. He couldn't fault Ethan for having designs on Meg. She was smart, a good mother to Todd and she knew how to take care of herself.

Jason's brow drew together. That's what made Amanda and Meg appear so different, he decided, watching as they neared town. Amanda didn't look as if she belonged here on the rough and rugged streets of Beaumont. Her dress was a little fancier. She carried herself a bit differently. In short, Amanda looked like the proper city woman that she was.

And that made her easy prey on the streets of Beaumont. The notion startled Jason. He hadn't wanted to be saddled with the two of them today. He had other plans. But concern for their safety caused him to hurry after them.

"Hold up," he called, and stepped up onto the boardwalk behind them.

The women, who'd had their heads together talking, stopped and turned to him.

"Yes?" Amanda asked, gazing up at him with those big blue eyes of hers.

For a minute, Jason forgot what he wanted to tell them. It was hard to remember things when she gazed at him that way.

"Uh, look," he said, "when you buy something today tell the shopkeeper to hold on to it. We'll pick everything up on the way out of town so you don't have to carry heavy packages around all day."

"Fine," Amanda said, and turned to leave.

"And watch your money," Jason said.

She glanced back. "We will."

"You two should stay together," he said.

"We'd planned to."

"Don't be too friendly," Jason cautioned.

"We won't," Amanda said.

"You don't want anybody getting the wrong idea," Jason explained.

Amanda huffed and turned to face him. "I thought you were anxious to take care of your business here."

"Oh. Well, yeah, I am." Jason backed away a step. "I just want you to be careful."

"I promise." Amanda drew a little *X* on her chest with her fingertip.

Jason glanced at her bosom—the one part of her he'd tried desperately to avoid—and his gut knotted. He spun away.

"Mr. Kruger?"

Amanda's voice called him back.

"I'd like to thank you properly for allowing my brides on your mountain," Amanda said. "Would you care to eat together today?"

"Sure," he said, without even thinking.

Amanda smiled. "Good. We'll meet you at the restaurant beside the hotel at noon."

"I'll be there," Jason promised.

With a pleasant little nod, Amanda headed off down the street again talking to Meg.

Jason just stood there watching them. Two women—one from the city—alone on the streets of Beaumont. It didn't sit right with him.

For a minute he considered following them again, staying close to keep an eye on them. Anything could happen.

He shook off the notion. Following the two of them around all day was the very last thing he needed to do. And it was definitely not the reason he'd come to Beaumont. The urgency behind his real reason for coming to town was increasing with each passing hour. It was high time he did something about it.

Jason spun around toward the parlor house, which was situated just past the saloons on the other end of town. He'd come here to spend the entire day rolling around in bed and that's exactly what he intended to do.

Jason stopped short, nearly colliding with an elderly lady exiting the general store. How could he spend the day in bed when he'd promised to have lunch with Amanda?

A string of curses tumbled from his lips. Why had he said he'd meet her? She'd offered and he'd jumped at the chance without even thinking.

Jason heaved a sigh. Well, he was stuck now. He couldn't not show up to eat. How would he explain where he'd been? Not that it was any of her business—and he was under no obligation to explain himself to her—but still, he'd have to tell her *something* if he didn't appear at the restaurant.

Jason blew out a heavy breath, thinking. He really did need to pick up supplies in Beaumont today. He'd do that first, he decided, then meet Amanda and Meg to eat, and afterward spend his afternoon tangled up in the covers with a willing woman.

His plan made, Jason set off down the street.

The list of things he needed was a long one. The cook needed flour, sugar, salt and about two dozen other things. Jason left that portion of the list with the owner of the general store and crossed the street. He didn't find what he was looking for in that shop. Two stores later he did.

Construction on the brides' dormitory would get underway immediately, so materials had to be purchased. Everything not built with wood had to be bought. Jason had everything taken care of with a few more stops along Beaumont's main street.

As he went in and out of each store, Jason kept an eye out for Amanda and Meg. He hadn't seen them. Beaumont wasn't that big a town, and after a couple of hours it concerned him that he hadn't seen the women once. He hadn't even glimpsed them down the street somewhere, coming or going from one of the stores.

At first, he'd consoled himself that the two of them were holed up in one of those ladies' dress shops looking at fabric and patterns, or whatever it was that went on in those places. Now, he was beginning to worry.

Jason left the dry goods store and had started to consider looking for Amanda and Meg when he saw them in the distance, stepping out of a millinery shop on the other side of Main Street. For a second he wasn't sure it was them because the shop was so far away and there were a lot of people in town today blurring his line of vision. But he couldn't miss Amanda and that blue dress she wore.

He watched them for a minute and was about satisfied that the two women were all right, when he saw three men step in front of Amanda and Meg, blocking their path.

Jason's blood ran cold as the women moved around them, but the men blocked them again. They were miners, from the look of their dusty clothes, battered hats and beards. Likely as not they'd been up in the hills for weeks without a woman in sight.

Jason headed down the boardwalk.

He'd been afraid something like this would happen. His heart started to pump faster. Jason touched his thigh. He hadn't brought his pistol with him. There was a rifle in the back of the freight wagon, but it wasn't doing him a hell of a lot of good right now.

As he watched, Meg ducked her head and skirted around the men again. Amanda stood her ground. Meg touched her arm, trying to pull her away. Amanda didn't move. She looked square into the face of the man towering over her, jerked her chin, and started giving him a piece of her mind.

Jason cursed. He started to run.

Damn fool woman. She didn't know how to act in a place like this. She didn't know how to take care of herself. She didn't belong here. He'd thought it—and said it—more than once.

Dodging the stagecoach and a buggy, Jason dashed across the street and leapt onto the boardwalk. Desperately, he threaded his way through the crowd of people, never taking his eyes off Amanda. He had to get to her. He couldn't let anything happen to her. She couldn't take care of herself. Maybe in San Francisco she could. But not here. Not among these kinds of people.

Just then the man leaned down, bringing his face closer to Amanda's. Jason saw her spine stiffen, indignance bloom on her face. He saw her bring her satchel up with both hands and straight-arm the man's chest with it, throwing her weight behind it.

He stumbled backward, turned his heel on the edge of the boardwalk, and splashed into the water trough.

Jason skidded to a stop a few feet away. Everyone froze. The miner flailed in the trough, then struggled to his feet, soaked and dripping.

Amanda must have sensed Jason nearby because she turned to him, clutching her satchel against her stomach. Her cheeks glowed pink. Her eyes were wide, her breasts heaving. Her mouth puckered in a tiny *O*.

Jason's knees nearly buckled. God help him, he wanted to kiss her. Right there on the street, with everyone watching, and that mountain of a miner who'd likely pound the tar out of him if Jason turned his back on him. But Jason couldn't help himself. He wanted to take her in his arms and smother her against him. He wanted to be inside her. He wanted to own her.

A round of laughter erupted from the two miners standing beside the trough as they pointed at their friend dragging himself from the water. Jason hurried to Amanda and stepped in front of her.

"You swing a mean satchel, little lady," one of the miners called between howls of laughter.

"Yeah," the other one said, holding his belly. "Give a warning before you come to town next time. We'll know not to mess with you."

They caught their wet friend by the elbows and headed off down the street, all of them laughing.

"Amanda!" Meg gasped. "I can't believe you did that!"

She touched her hand to her throat. "I can't believe I did it either."

Jason spun around. All the desire he'd had a few seconds ago to kiss her, hold her, bury himself inside her turned to anger.

"What the hell were you thinking?" he demanded.

Amanda drew herself up a little straighter. "I was thinking that those three men had absolutely no manners at all, and had no business talking to us that way."

The fight went out of him. Only Miss Amanda Pierce of San Francisco would be outraged by the lack of proper decorum on the streets of Beaumont.

He shook his head wearily, and again, he wanted to kiss her.

"You're lucky you weren't the one thrown in the water trough," Jason said. "Or worse."

Her eyes grew wider still, realizing what she'd done, and she gasped, her quick intake of breath causing her breasts to heave.

Amanda looked up at him, slightly alarmed. "Goodness, you're probably right."

"Damn right I am," Jason told her, annoyed with her—and himself for looking at her breasts again. "You see what I'm talking about? You've got to learn how to take care of yourself in a place like this."

Amanda angled her face up at him and straightened her shoulders. "Excuse me, Mr. Kruger, but I think my actions here have demonstrated that I know exactly how to take care of myself."

A protest pushed its way to Jason's lips but didn't get any farther. Really, what could he say? Amanda had, in fact, handled the situation, though he didn't like it one bit.

Amanda waved her hand dismissing the entire incident. "Why don't we eat now?"

"Let's finish our shopping first," Meg said. "We only have a few more stops."

"We'll meet you at the restaurant," Amanda said to Jason and started down the street.

"Hold on," Jason said, going after them. "I don't want the two of you on the streets alone. That fella might dry off and decide getting dunked in the horse trough by a woman wasn't so funny after all."

Amanda shrugged away his concern. "We'll be fine."

"No, now wait—"

She huffed impatiently. "Mr. Kruger, we are not on your mountain now. We can do as we please."

"Maybe Jason is right," Meg said. "Just tell us where you'll be. If we have a problem, we'll come find you."

He pointed at the shop just down the street. "I'll be there, then I'll meet you at the restaurant."

"We'll be there," Amanda called, as she headed away from him down the boardwalk.

"Look," Jason called, "just be careful, will you?"

Meg turned back quickly. "Maybe you should warn Beaumont to be careful of Amanda!"

The two women burst into laughter, holding on to each other as they walked away.

Jason watched Amanda, his body still humming, his mouth dry. He wanted her. He wanted that woman like he'd never wanted another thing in his life.

How the hell was he ever going to find a whore to satisfy him now?

Chapter Fifteen

When Amanda approached the Red Apple restaurant beside the hotel she found Jason already there, as he'd promised. She smiled, a little surprised at how easily her lips curled up at seeing him.

It surprised her more that he smiled back.

She stopped in front of him. "Hungry?"

He regarded her from under the brim of his black hat. "I'm starving."

She thought he must be very hungry indeed because he had a desperate look on his face she'd never seen before.

Jason cupped her elbow and guided her inside.

The Red Apple had tables arranged neatly in its big dining room, all covered with clean checkered cloths. Other diners had already crowded inside, but Jason spotted a table in front of the window. He held her elbow all the way, then pulled out her chair and made sure she was seated comfortably before dropping into the chair across from her.

"Where's Meg?" he asked, realizing for the first time that Amanda was alone.

"She had something else to take care of," Amanda said, arranging her skirt. "She'll be along in a bit."

"She's not pushing anybody into a water trough somewhere, is she?" Jason asked, and laid his hat on the chair beside him.

Amanda saw that he was grinning and she did the same. "Meg is at the church talking to the minister," she said.

"What's that all about?"

Amanda sighed. "I think we both know."

"You were right about her and Ethan. I talked to him about it." Jason shook his head. "But I don't know that anything can ever come of it."

"Maybe the Lord will provide guidance today," Amanda suggested.

Jason grunted. "I think you've got an angel on your shoulder."

"Are you talking about that incident on the street again?"

He grinned. "Better get used to it. The whole mountain will be talking about it for days."

"I don't mean to cause such controversy," Amanda said.

"I guess the rest of us may as well get used to that."

Amanda smiled at his gentle teasing. She couldn't help it. He looked handsome, even more so than usual. He'd been an especially welcome sight when she'd accidentally pushed that miner into the horse trough. She hadn't meant for that to happen. And afterward, she'd been terrified by what the man might do to her. Amanda had never been so relieved to see anyone as she was when she'd turned and seen Jason standing behind her.

He had a way about him. She'd recognized it from the start, from the first time she'd laid eyes on him. Everyone else saw it in him, too. That's how he led his men. That's why they followed him. There was a command about Jason that few people could ignore.

But still, today there was something different about Jason. At times, he seemed more tense than usual. Yet now, sitting across the table from him, Amanda saw a side of him she'd never experienced before. He was more relaxed now. He smiled more easily. He'd even teased her a little.

The burden of responsibility on his mountain surely weighed heavily at times. It pleased Amanda that even Jason Kruger needed—and enjoyed—time off.

The serving girl stopped at their table, poured coffee and told them the cook's special. They asked her to come back when Meg arrived.

Amanda rested her arm on the table and gazed out the window.

"I never realized how big Beaumont was until today," she said, watching the people pass by on the boardwalk. "When I was here before it seemed smaller somehow."

Jason glanced out the window, then back at her. "It's not a bad place. It serves a good number of people, with the ranches and mines around here, not to mention the settlements and the lumber camp. There's talk about building an opera house here.''

She looked up at him. ''It's growing that fast?''

''I guess it doesn't look like much, though, after San Francisco,'' Jason said. ''You must be anxious to get back there.''

''As anxious as you are to stay on your mountain, I'd imagine.'' Her response didn't please him, she sensed, because he changed the subject.

''So,'' he said, ''what did you buy this morning?''

''More than I should have,'' Amanda admitted, smiling.

She told him about the things she'd bought to fix up her little cabin and make it seem more like home, and about the fabric she'd purchased for the brides' dormitory.

He frowned. ''Fabric? What for?''

''Curtains,'' she said. ''For the windows.''

''Oh.'' Jason grinned. ''Guess you've got to have those.''

''Most definitely,'' she said and smiled. ''And by the way, don't worry that you'll be spending time overseeing the construction of the dormitory. I'll take care of it.''

His brows rose. ''You?''

''Of course,'' Amanda said. ''No one knows better what the brides want than I do.''

Jason looked at her for a moment. ''Doesn't it bother you to do all this work, build the dormitory, make it livable, then just walk away?''

She considered it only briefly, then said, "No. I actually enjoy the work."

"And it doesn't bother you to see other women getting married when you're not?"

She glanced away. "No."

A few minutes passed while Amanda gazed out the window and Jason watched her. She felt him looking at her and finally he spoke.

"I asked you before why you never got married," Jason said, "but you didn't give me an answer."

"Didn't I?"

"You know you didn't."

Amanda shifted on the chair. "Well…"

"Well?"

"Well—Oh, Meg, you're here."

Meg appeared beside their table. "Sorry, to keep you waiting."

Jason got to his feet and assisted her into the chair beside Amanda, then sat down again.

"How did it go with Reverend Daley?" Amanda asked.

Meg smoothed back a stray lock of her hair and drew in a deep breath. "He wasn't without an opinion, I'll say that."

Amanda touched her arm. "I'm sorry."

"Oh, no. Don't be," Meg said. "The reverend didn't tell me anything I didn't already know."

"We all know that wedding vows are meant to last a lifetime," Amanda said, "but in your case—"

"The reverend means well," Meg said. "I'll have to make my own decision."

Meg put on a smile. "What's the special of the day?"

Jason waved the serving girl over and they ordered their meal. Talk of their morning shopping carried the conversation while they ate.

"That was delicious," Meg said to the serving girl as she took their plates away. "Even better, I didn't have to cook it myself."

"How about dessert?" Jason asked. Despite the groaned responses he ordered slices of apple pie for all of them.

When they finished, the three of them sat at the table awhile longer, none of them anxious to leave. When they rose, Amanda reached for the check the serving girl left on the table. Jason scowled and pulled it from her hand.

"I told you this was a thank-you for allowing my brides on your mountain," Amanda said.

"You're not buying this meal." Male pride swelled his chest, then he grinned. "You'll just have to find some other way to thank me."

A little jolt sliced through Amanda. She should have been offended, but instead it was all she could do to hold in a smile.

The afternoon sun had disappeared behind a bank of dark clouds, cooling the air and stirring up a little breeze as the three of them stepped outside the restaurant.

"We have a few more errands to run," Amanda said, standing on the boardwalk outside the restaurant.

Jason pulled on his hat. "I'll just walk with you."

Amanda frowned. "I thought you had more errands."

"Oh. Yeah." Stunned, Jason just stood there. He was supposed to go to the whorehouse this afternoon. It was the reason he'd come to Beaumont in the first place. How could he have forgotten?

Because he'd sat across from Amanda for the last hour. Looking at her. Smelling her. Admiring the way she held her fork, the way she turned her head. Enjoying her little laugh.

And now, rolling around in bed with a whore didn't seem so enticing. In fact, it hardly seemed appealing at all.

"You don't need to run your errand after all?" Amanda asked.

Jason considered it for a moment. Oh, yes. He still *needed* this errand. Needed it in the worst way. In fact, he might not be fit to live with if he didn't do something about this ache that wouldn't stop.

"I'm going," Jason said, with a firm nod, though his conscience pulled him in the other direction.

Amanda smiled. "All right. We'll meet you at the livery stable in a while."

"Sure thing," Jason said, and grinned. In fact, now that the moment was here, he couldn't stop grinning.

Amanda and Meg headed off down the boardwalk. Jason went the other way, then stopped. He turned back.

"You two watch out for yourself," he called. "Keep an eye out for those miners."

Amanda and Meg both stopped, looked at each other, then walked back to Jason.

"Do you think they'll bother us?" Meg asked.

"Just keep away from them," Jason said. "If you see them, walk the other way. I doubt they'll bother you again."

"You're probably right," Meg said, then turned to Amanda. "Come on. We'll be fine."

She nodded. "Yes, I'm sure we will be."

"And if anything should happen, Jason will be right here," Meg said.

A smile brightened Amanda's face as she gazed up at him. "That's good to know."

"Um, well…" Jason began.

"With a town this size how could he miss what was happening?" Meg said.

"Maybe you should tell us where you'll be," Amanda said.

Jason's stomach bottomed out. "Where I'll be?" he asked, his voice cracking.

"Yes," Amanda said. "Just in case."

Jason stared down at the two women. How in the hell could he tell them where he'd be? He was going to a whorehouse, for crying out loud. He intended to spend the next several hours mindlessly working off all the tension that had him nearly boiling in his own skin. How could he explain that to these two women?

Maybe he'd just tell them the truth. Jason almost smiled at the notion. He could just imagine the look on Amanda's face if he blurted it out. Hell, she'd caused it. She may as well know about it.

Maybe he'd tell her that it was her breasts that had created the problem in the first place. The left one. The one he hadn't gotten to touch yet. Maybe she'd let him, then. Just to even things up.

But as that delightful little fantasy played out in Jason's mind, he knew it would never happen.

And he knew he wouldn't make it to the parlor house. Not today, anyway.

He couldn't risk leaving Amanda and Meg alone in town. What if those miners did come back? They'd laughed off what had happened, but after they'd stewed about it awhile things might be different. How could he live with himself if something happened to Amanda or Meg while he was under the covers with a whore?

"I'll go with you two," Jason said.

"You're sure?" Amanda asked.

He hadn't made the statement with much enthusiasm, so he tried again.

"I'm sure," Jason told her. He managed to stretch his lips into a faint smile. "Where are we going?"

Amanda pointed across the street. "We haven't been in there, yet."

Jason looked at the store, a store in the opposite direction of the parlor house, the parlor house that was so far away it may as well be on the other side of the country.

He walked between the two women, holding their elbows as they crossed the street, then followed along behind as they wound through the store looking at every piece of merchandise on every shelf, talking about it, deciding on what to buy as if it were the biggest purchase either of them had ever made.

Women.

After so many months on his mountain surrounded by nothing but lumberjacks, he'd forgotten what it was like to keep company with women. The few females who lived on the mountain kept their distance, and that suited him fine.

But now, after having Amanda underfoot these past days, and after spending time in town with her, eating with her, watching her sashay down the street, giggle and talk about the things women talked about, Jason couldn't seem to recall just why he'd been so opposed to having women around in the first place.

Jason watched Amanda maneuver through the aisles. So delicate. So graceful.

One thing he did know for sure is that no whore would ever do now.

He wanted a fine woman.

Like Amanda.

Chapter Sixteen

A soft, steady rain tapped against the windows of the cookhouse, sounding louder than usual this morning because the loggers were so quiet.

Jason sat in his customary spot at the rear of the room where he could keep an eye on the door, the kitchen, the men. Only this morning there wasn't much to look at.

Amanda hadn't shown up for breakfast.

Her absence seemed to take the life out of the room. The lumberjacks barely spoke. No one seemed very hungry. Ethan had left the cookhouse already, his meal nearly untouched. Jason pushed his plate away, half-finished.

Maybe it was the rain, Jason thought as he rose from the table. Work on the mountain didn't stop just because of bad weather. None of the men—himself included—relished the thought of working in the cold rain today. Maybe that's what was wrong this morning.

Hell, it could have been one of a hundred things,

Jason decided as he strode toward the door. None of which had anything to do with Amanda.

Buck Johansen rose from the bench as Jason walked past. "Some of the men were wondering," Buck said, "if Miss Pierce was feeling poorly this morning."

Jason caught sight of the men seated at the tables, staring up at him expectantly.

"She was gone all day yesterday," Buck continued. "The men figured she'd be here this morning. She's not sick, or anything, is she?"

A knot of worry jerked inside Jason. He hadn't considered something might be wrong with Amanda.

"Far as I know she's all right," Jason said.

The men seated at the tables seemed none too relieved.

"Could be the weather," Jason said, and waved toward the door.

"Miss Pierce is a delicate little thing," Buck agreed. Behind him, the lumberjacks nodded and looked satisfied with that explanation.

"Make sure the crew works safe today," Jason said, and left the cookhouse.

The cold wind swirled around him as he stepped outside. Jason turned up his collar and fastened the buttons on his coat. Steady, misting rain fell as he hiked toward his office.

As had happened so many times before, Jason's gaze honed in on the littlest cabin, farthest up the mountain. Amanda's cabin. He didn't see any signs of life. No lanterns burned in her window in the morning gloom. Maybe she was still in bed.

Amanda in bed… Snuggled under the soft coverlet, deep in the feather mattress. An ache tightened Jason's chest.

Amanda in bed. Amanda in bed and him with her. Rain beating on the tin roof. The two of them together, alone, warm and cozy.

The ache in his chest sharpened, grew, and shot downward.

A rainy day was meant for rolling around in bed. Jason's imagination took over, playing out one little fantasy after another.

Amanda with her hair down.

Amanda naked.

Amanda's breasts.

Both of them.

Jason popped open the buttons of his coat, letting the wind and rain cool his body. Damn. He should have gone to that whorehouse yesterday.

The ache in him, the constant reminder of his desire for Amanda, was so familiar now it was almost bearable. Almost. He could have taken care of the problem in Beaumont yesterday, but had chosen not to. He could still go back anytime he wanted.

But somehow, the need in him was different now. The need wasn't for just any woman—only one woman—Amanda.

Where yesterday's ride down the mountain to Beaumont had been tense, the return trip had been a pleasure. Conversation flowed easily. Meg seemed to have a lot on her mind, understandably so, but Amanda hadn't missed a word he'd said.

They talked about how Beaumont was growing, the people they'd seen there, the things they'd bought. Jason was surprised that Amanda had listened to him talk about the economy of the state and the country, and how it affected his business. Not only had she listened, she'd understood.

And he hadn't minded hearing about the fabric she'd bought, the dress patterns she'd liked, the buttons, lace and colors of ribbon she'd told him about. For some reason, it was the most fascinating thing he'd ever heard.

When they'd pulled into camp just before dark, just ahead of the storm, Jason had been sorry to see her go. He'd offered to carry her packages to her cabin, but Shady had shown up with a couple of men and Jason had felt obligated to help them unload the wagon.

A gust of cold, wet wind hit Jason in the face as he glanced at Amanda's cabin once more. He knew better than to go there. He knew it last night. He knew it now.

Stepping under the shelter of the porch outside his office, Jason scraped his boots and pulled off his jacket and hat, shaking the rain off both. Ethan was seated at his desk when Jason walked in. The room was chilly and smelled of the coffee bubbling on the stove.

"About noon yesterday it hit me why you wanted me to go to Beaumont with you," Ethan said, "and why you *didn't* want the women to go."

Jason headed for the coffee on the stove, threw his brother a look and grunted.

Ethan sat back in his chair. "I never pretended to be the smartest brother in the family."

"I never pretended you were either," Jason said, and couldn't hold back a little chuckle as he poured himself coffee in a tin cup.

"So, how was it?" Ethan asked.

"Like I had any time to myself, saddled with two women to look after all day long?"

Ethan grinned. "The way I hear it, Amanda didn't need anyone looking after her."

Jason dropped into his chair. "I figured that story would get around sooner or later."

"She really knocked that miner into the water trough?" Ethan laughed. "Amanda is one hell of a woman."

Jason shuffled through the papers on his desk and didn't answer.

"I was going over some figures," Ethan said, holding up the tablet he'd been working on. "That idea she had about renting out the rooms in the dormitory after the brides get married is a good one. You'll earn back your investment pretty quick."

Jason sipped his coffee and dug through his desk drawers.

"She's a smart woman," Ethan said. "You ought to latch on to her before she marries somebody else."

Jason's gaze came up quickly and landed on his brother. "What makes you say something like that?"

Ethan shrugged as he rose from his chair. "Bound to happen sooner or later. A woman like her isn't likely to end up a spinster."

Ethan pulled on his coat and settled his hat on his head. "I'm heading up to the mill."

"How'd it go with Meg's boy yesterday?" Jason asked.

Ethan opened the door. "The kid needs a father. Meg's turning him into a mama's boy, fussing over him all the time."

"She's still married, Ethan."

"For now," Ethan said, then disappeared out the door.

"Hell...." Jason sat back in his chair and tossed aside the pencil he'd just picked up. Ethan was playing with fire. And nobody played with fire without getting burned.

Still, he couldn't blame him.

Jason turned his attention to the plans in front of him, trying to get started on his work, when something Ethan said popped into his head. It was about Amanda, and how she wouldn't remain unmarried forever.

He'd asked her before why she hadn't found herself a husband, especially when she had so many to choose from. She'd never answered him.

The more he thought about it the more he considered that Amanda was being deliberately evasive on the subject. Jason couldn't help but wonder why.

But every logical thought went right out of his head when the door to his office opened and Amanda hurried inside with a gust of wind. She closed it quickly behind her. Breathlessly, she looked around, spotted Jason behind his desk, and smiled.

"Good morning," she said.

It wasn't a good morning. It was one of the worst days possible to be on a mountain at a lumber camp. But Jason smiled back anyway and rose from his chair.

A light mist of rain moistened her face. Her cheeks flushed pink and her breath came a little quicker than usual. She wore a green dress and looked bright and cheerful on this dreary morning. He'd never seen her so delightfully disheveled.

He helped her take off her cloak and hung it on the peg by the door alongside his jacket. Amanda pulled off her scarf and turned away quickly.

"Gracious, that wind," she said, heading for the washstand in the back corner.

Jason draped her scarf over her cloak, then stopped still in the middle of the floor.

Standing before the little mirror over the washstand Amanda tucked an errant strand of hair back in place, then pinned it. She studied her reflection, turning her head left, then right. Then, dissatisfied, she pulled the pins from her hair.

All of them. One after another, Amanda plucked out pins, sending waves of her hair curling over her shoulders and down her back.

Thick hair. Dark hair, with a hint of red he hadn't noticed before. Couldn't notice with it all pinned so carefully, so neatly, atop her head.

Jason stayed where he was, silent, unmoving, not

wanting to shatter this private moment with Amanda. A decent woman never wore her hair down in public. A man never saw a woman's hair on her shoulders unless they were married...or as good as married.

Just why Amanda showed this trust in him he didn't know. He didn't deserve it. Now, when all he could think of was how he wanted to thread her hair through his fingers. How he wanted to bury his nose in it and smell it. How he wanted to see it fanned out across a white linen pillow.

While he watched, she produced a comb from her pocket and twisted her hair into place again. Efficiently, she pinned it, tucking every last strand where it belonged.

Jason pressed his lips together to keep from groaning. What he'd give to pull those pins from her hair himself. To watch that beautiful, shiny hair of hers fall—

"Did I miss something?" she asked.

"Huh?" Jason asked dumbly, then realized that she'd turned away from the mirror and was staring at him as he stared at her.

"Did I miss a strand?" she asked, turning and touching her hand to the back of her head.

Jason savored the moment as she stood still just for him. His gaze traveled down the long line of her back, to her waist, her hips, her bustle, to the hem of her skirt and the little glimpse of her ankles he got as her dress swirled around her. He held in another moan and lifted his gaze to her head.

Two little locks of hair curled at her nape, but

Jason didn't tell her. He liked seeing them there. Soft strands of hair, begging him to coil his fingers around them.

Amanda looked back over her shoulders, her brows raised, waiting for his answer.

"Fine," he murmured. "It's fine."

Jason cleared his throat and forced himself to head for his desk.

"Are those the plans for the dormitory?" she asked.

He sat down, only to find her leaning over his shoulder, studying the plans laid out on his desk. He picked them up to keep his hands busy, and off of her.

"I'm just about finished with them," he said.

"Can I see?"

He glanced up at her again and knew he was making a mistake. "Sure."

Amanda circled the desk and pulled a chair up to the opposite side. Jason pushed everything off to the right and spread out the plans between them.

When he'd drawn them up using the simple diagram Amanda had presented him with, he'd put no more thought into them than to include the things she'd asked for. Now, somehow, having her approve of his work meant the world to him.

They discussed the plans, each holding a pencil, pointing, asking questions, tossing out ideas. Amanda had a few more suggestions, but generally, she was pleased with what he'd done. And he was pleased at having her so close.

Finally, when they'd both agreed on every aspect

of the dormitory, Jason sat back and rubbed his forehead.

"I can't wait until this rain stops so we can get started," Amanda said, rising from her chair. "Do you think it will rain long?"

Jason squeezed his eyes shut for a minute. "Probably a day, the way the wind is blowing."

"Are you all right?" Amanda asked.

He glanced up and grimaced. "Got a little ache in my head, that's all."

"Women on your mountain," Amanda said softly. "We really are a pain for you, aren't we?"

Jason shrugged. "I've gotten used to the idea. And…it's all right."

She smiled. "Really? Do you really mean that?"

"Yep," Jason said. "I really do."

Amanda headed for the washstand. "Let me do something about your head."

"No, it's all right," Jason said, waving away her attention.

"Having women on your mountain may not be a pain, but it's my fault that your head is hurting," Amanda insisted, moving around the office. "My fault for keeping you hard at work over those plans."

He'd gotten a headache from the tension and pressure building up in his body. It had to go somewhere. But he couldn't tell her that.

"Sit back," Amanda said.

"No, look—"

"Oh, you men," she said, gazing down at him.

"You're so stubborn about this sort of thing. Now, sit back and close your eyes."

Well, why not? He'd wanted her to be closer. Now was his chance.

Jason closed his eyes and laid his head back. He felt her wedge her folded scarf under his neck so he rested comfortably on the back of his chair. A cool cloth covered his forehead. Her fingertips touched his temples.

Jason nearly came up out of the chair.

"Relax," she whispered at his ear.

Relax? How the hell was he supposed to relax with her so close he could smell her? When her soft fingers were twirling little circles at his temples? When every nerve ending in his whole body was standing on end? When he wanted her so badly he ached for her?

Gulping, Jason tried to relax. He tried to tune out the needs of his body. He tried to ignore every instinct he'd ever had.

Impossible.

Jason bolted from the chair.

"Didn't that help?" Amanda asked, holding the damp cloth she'd caught as it fell from his forehead.

He pulled it from her fingers and tossed it across the office. "Amanda...."

The look in his eyes warned her. The heat he gave off told her. His stance, drawing closer and closer, confirmed it.

But Amanda didn't back away.

She'd been aware of the force that pulled them

together—whatever it was—for days. She was helpless against it. Against him. Against herself.

Jason slid both arms around her and brought his mouth down over hers. Amanda's knees wobbled. A little mewl hummed in her throat. She threw her arms around his neck and angled her head back. Jason devoured her mouth with his.

A strange inner fire drove her. Amanda curled her fist into the hair at the back of his head. He kissed her harder. She leaned into him until their bodies touched. Her breasts brushed his chest. Her thighs rubbed his. She leaned closer until she felt his—

Amanda gasped. Jason groaned. He kissed a hot trail down her jaw, fumbled with the bow and fasteners at her throat, opened them, and laid his lips against her flesh.

Awkwardly, she pulled open the buttons on his shirt and long johns and laid her palms on his chest. A new, different sort of desire rushed through her. She raked her fingers through the dark swirls of hair on his chest. It was short, coarse…magnificent. Hard muscles lay beneath it. Amanda pushed her fingers deeper inside his shirt and touched his nipple. Jason groaned.

One by one she felt the buttons on her dress open—and she didn't care. She wanted this. She wanted this with Jason.

His long, hot fingers closed over her breast. His thumb caressed her nipple. Amanda moaned his name. His mouth covered hers again.

Heat sealed them together, their mouths, their bodies. Frantic, their hands explored. Amanda felt dizzy in his arms, yet driven to keep going. Clinging to Jason, she coiled her leg around his and pressed herself against him.

A harsh, ragged moan tore from Jason's throat. He lifted his head from the sweet valley of her breasts, breathing heavily.

"We shouldn't be doing this," he rasped.

"I know."

"We have to stop."

"I know."

They gazed at each other, their faces inches apart, their bodies full against each other.

"We have to stop," Jason said again.

"I know." Amanda caught a fistful of his hair. "Just...just once more."

He kissed her. Hard and wet and wild. He pressed against her until she bumped his desk, then leaned her backward, sealing her against him with his powerful arms.

Then he let go. Amanda plopped down on the desktop, crushing the dormitory plans beneath her, gazing up at him with passion-blurred eyes. He gazed back, looking just as dazed. Both their chests heaved. Their breathing was quick and their cheeks flushed.

Slowly, Jason straightened, putting distance between them but never taking his eyes off her.

"Somebody might walk in," he said, his voice a hoarse whisper.

A few seconds passed before the haze of passion lifted and Amanda realized what Jason was saying.

She glanced back at the door recognizing how vulnerable—and how foolish—she'd been.

Still, she wasn't embarrassed. Or sorry.

"You'd better go," Jason told her, and took a step back.

Amanda got off the desk and saw his gaze follow her. She glanced down. Her blouse was unbuttoned, exposing the swell of her breasts. But instead of pulling the fabric closed, her gaze went to his chest, visible through his open shirt.

Desire arced between them again. Their gazes met. But Jason backed away.

He couldn't stop watching her though as she buttoned her blouse and straightened her clothes, and his body burned for her. She grabbed her cloak and scarf and opened the door. She looked back, then left.

The only thing that kept him from going after her was knowing what would happen if he did. And fearing what that meant.

If word got out—and it would—she'd be ruined.

And he'd have ruined her.

Amanda crawled into bed that night and pulled the coverlet over her, exhausted. She didn't even think about the strange sounds in the forest around her that made her nervous, made her imagine all sorts of things were lurking in the trees surrounding her cabin. All she could think of was Jason.

He'd occupied her thoughts all day. He'd warmed her stomach, made her heart beat faster, caused her to quiver and feel dizzy. She'd worked herself silly today cleaning her cabin, cooking, making lists, planning, but Jason hadn't been far from her thoughts.

She didn't know why she'd done the things she'd done with him in his office this morning. Scandalous things. Things she'd never imagined doing before.

Things that would have devastated her reputation if Jason hadn't come to his senses.

Good thing that he had, Amanda decided, staring into the darkness of her little cabin, because this morning in his office, in his arms, she'd had not one bit of sense. Something had driven her to do those things. Something Jason had awakened in her.

Amanda rolled over and fluffed her pillow. She'd awakened something in Jason, too. Something beyond the passionate fever pitch they'd experienced this morning.

He'd come to accept women on his mountain. He wasn't just tolerating them, or putting up with them, he was actually accepting them. Acknowledging that the women had a place there, and it was all right with him. That pleased her.

Amanda never blamed Jason for the way he felt about women. He'd told her about his mother, her domineering ways, how she ran the family, how his father had done nothing to stop her, and the hardships she'd placed on Jason and his brothers and sisters.

Somehow, he'd come to terms with that now. He'd forgiven and forgotten. Accepting her brides on his mountain proved it.

Amanda smiled into the darkness. Had she been

responsible for his change? Jason was a stubborn, determined man. A man didn't own a mountain and run a lumber camp without those qualities. She wouldn't kid herself into believing she was solely responsible for his change of heart. But maybe, just maybe, she'd had a little something to do with it.

But whatever the cause, it pleased Amanda. He trusted her. He'd accepted her into his life. He'd told her his secrets, he'd given her a chance, and he'd come around. Things had gotten better between them. So much better, in fact, that they'd nearly torn each other's clothes off this morning.

Amanda pressed her lips together. Jason trusted her. With his past, with his future.

Where would that lead?

Chapter Seventeen

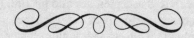

At breakfast the next morning, an argument broke out between three loggers who wanted to assist Amanda into her chair. This surprised her, given that Jason wasn't at the table, glaring at the men, barking out orders on their conduct.

"Gentlemen, thank you," Amanda said, raising her voice over that of the three men. "I'm so pleased that you've all remembered your manners."

The three men stared at each other, and two of them backed off. The third man helped Amanda into her chair, then they all sat down on the benches that surrounded their large table.

"We heard about what happened down in Beaumont, Miss Pierce," Henry Jasper said after they'd filled their plates. "Did you really dunk that miner in the horse trough?"

Amanda almost blushed. She'd feared this story would get around the lumber camp and would have preferred to keep it quiet. It wasn't the kind of story that would do her image as a genteel lady any good.

How could she ask the loggers to act like gentlemen if she couldn't conduct herself as a lady?

"Yes, Henry," Amanda said. "It's true."

"Well, hot damn!" Bill Braddock pounded his fist on the table and a round of hoots and yells rose from the men.

"Good for you, Miss Pierce," Henry said, grinning.

"Don't take nothing off them miners," another man called out. "Show 'em what it means to work the high timber."

The men cheered and clattered their silverware on the tabletop.

Amanda stared, forcing her lips together to keep her mouth from sagging open in amazement. The loggers were actually pleased by what she'd done.

"'Course now, Miss Pierce," Henry said, "we're sure you dunked that fella in the most ladylike way possible."

Another chorus of agreement circulated around the table.

Amanda couldn't help grinning. "Thank you, Henry."

"You want to tell us more about them manners we're supposed to be learning?" Bill asked. He waved his fork around the table. "Some of these jackasses—excuse me, ma'am—some of these gentlemen don't seem to remember."

A big smile spread over Amanda's face. "Of course."

"Then we want to hear all about what happened

in Beaumont,'' Henry said. ''Straight from you, ma'am.''

''Well, certainly,'' Amanda said, and proceeded with their manners lesson for the morning.

Afterward, the prospective husbands crowded close as she told them what had happened in Beaumont. The men at the adjoining tables fell silent, as well, listening. She tried to downplay the incident, but the men wouldn't hear of it. Some of the details they made her tell twice. By the time the loggers left the cookhouse Amanda felt a closeness with the men, as if a new respect and camaraderie now bound them all together.

''You're going to have every man on the mountain after you, if you keep telling that story.''

Amanda turned and found Jason standing behind her. She hadn't realized he'd been there, listening.

When he hadn't been present at the table of prospective husbands this morning, Amanda thought he wasn't in the cookhouse at all. She wondered why he hadn't eaten with them. Now, seeing him, she knew why.

The passion they'd shared in his office yesterday morning showed on his face. She knew it was displayed on hers as well, evidenced by the way her heart quickened and her knees trembled. Anyone seeing them together would have seen it immediately. Jason wouldn't want his men knowing his feelings for her. And really, Amanda didn't want that either.

He'd been wise to stay away from her. Still, she'd missed him. And she was glad to see him now.

"I'd think they'd be put off that I'd acted so brazenly," Amanda said, watching the last man disappear out the door.

Jason came forward, shaking his head. "It's a rough life up here on the mountain. A man prizes a woman who can take care of herself."

She wanted to ask Jason if he included himself among that type of man, but didn't. She thought it better to get on with business.

"Would it be all right if I used the cookhouse for a while this afternoon?" Amanda asked. "I thought it would be a good idea to have a meeting with all the women on the mountain, try and get them involved with the brides' arrival."

The idea had come to her last night during one of the hours she'd lain awake. She didn't want the women already living here to feel threatened by the newly arrived brides. The last thing she needed was discontent on the mountain among the women.

Jason nodded toward the kitchen. "I'll tell the cook. You won't have much time."

She understood. The cookhouse was the busiest place in the camp, busier than the sawmill or logging operation. As fast as one meal was served and cleared, another got under way.

"We're breaking ground on the dormitory this morning," Jason said. "Looks like we'll have sunshine all day."

Amanda glanced out the door at the gray dawn receding into the trees. The rain had stopped during the night. The ground was soft, but wouldn't be that way for long.

Amanda smiled. "Looks like things are moving right along."

"Looks that way," Jason said.

They stared at each other for a long minute, neither anxious to move on or say anything. Looking was enough. For now.

Finally, Jason broke eye contact. "I'd better get to work."

"So had I," she said and gave herself a little shake.

He smiled, and she smiled back at him.

"Well, I'm going now," he said.

"Yes, me too."

"Let me know if you need anything," Jason said.

"I will."

He headed toward the door.

"Jason?"

Stopping quickly, he turned back. "Yes?"

Amanda walked nearer but stopped before she got too close. "A couple of times you've asked me a question. I've been deliberately evasive. I wondered—if you're still interested—if you'd have some time to talk later this evening?"

He nodded thoughtfully. "Sure."

"Good. After supper?"

He smiled. "Sounds fine."

As he left the cookhouse, Amanda couldn't help but follow him with her eyes. He stopped at the door and looked back. She saw the tiniest smile on his lips before he disappeared outside. A little piece of her went with him. A little piece of him stayed with her.

* * *

"Ladies? Could I have your attention, please?"

Amanda lowered herself onto one of the three benches surrounding the two tables in the cookhouse that had been pushed together for her manners classes. Seated around her was the total population of women on the mountain, all six of them.

Meg McGee was there, of course, and Amanda was glad to have her. Of all the women on the mountain, Meg was the one she could count on the most. Amanda had explained the reason for this meeting to Meg, who'd agreed that it was necessary.

Becky sat at the table beside her aunt, Polly Minton, who ran the laundry on the mountain. Gladys Duncan sat next to Polly, the two of them good friends since their recipe dispute had been settled by Amanda the night she'd arrived in the lumber camp.

The other two ladies Amanda hadn't met before. Idelle Turner's husband worked in the sawmill. She served as schoolteacher for the few children who lived there. Frances Conroy's husband ran the barber shop in town.

"Would anyone care for more coffee?" Amanda asked, holding up the tin pot.

The blue, speckled table service wasn't exactly what Amanda had wanted for her meeting today, but since there wasn't a single teapot to be found on the entire mountain she'd had to make do. The cake Meg had baked had gone over well, as had the selection of candies she'd bought in Beaumont.

"So, what's the point of this here get-together?"

Frances Conroy asked, holding out her cup for more coffee.

Amanda poured and set the pot aside. "All you women here have a very important role in the arrival of the brides. I wanted to consult with you before things proceed any further."

"Yeah?" Polly Minton asked. "Like what?"

"A number of things," Amanda said. "First, there will be a number of financial opportunities coming available. I want you ladies to have first chance at them."

Gladys Duncan angled her wide shoulders closer to the table. "What did you have in mind?"

"Polly's general store, for example," Amanda said.

"Shoot, it's not much of a store," Polly said.

Amanda couldn't disagree. Polly ran the laundry out of half her building and used the other half for a small general store that offered a few essentials the lumberjacks needed.

"I expect that to change when the brides arrive," Amanda said. "The women will need things, for themselves, for the homes they'll be making. The trip down the mountain to Beaumont is long and hard. I think a fully-stocked store right here beside the lumber camp would do well."

Becky perked up. "Heck, yeah. That's a great idea."

"Naw, I don't know," Polly said. "Truth is, I don't make much of nothing off those dry goods I sell."

"But all of that would change when the brides arrive," Amanda said.

"Can you guarantee that?" Polly asked.

"Well, no," Amanda admitted. "I can't guarantee anything. But I see it as a strong possibility."

"Sure," Becky said. "Those new brides will be shopping to beat the band."

"To tell you the truth, I don't much like selling stuff, putting out my hard-earned money, then watching it sit around on a shelf hoping somebody will take a notion to buy it," Polly said. She shook her head. "Besides, I haven't got the kind of money it takes to buy that much stock."

Amanda looked around the table. "What about you other ladies? Would any of you care to take on that business?"

They glanced at each other, then shook their heads.

"I'm just like Polly," Idelle said. "I haven't got enough money to start up a store."

A murmur went around the table and Amanda realized that was the general consensus of the women.

"All right," Amanda said. "That's understandable. I just hope each of you will keep your mind open for the business opportunities that come along."

The women nodded and Amanda moved on.

"I'm planning a get-acquainted social when the brides arrive," Amanda said.

"You mean like a dance?" Becky asked.

"Yes," Amanda said. "I'd like to get your suggestions on what we should do."

While the women hadn't shown much interest in expanding or starting businesses on the mountain, they had lots of ideas for the social. Amanda made notes, committees were formed, food and decorations decided on.

"My husband picks banjo, a little," Idelle said. "He and some of the other boys get together every once in a while. They got a guitar, fiddle and harmonica. I bet they'd play, seeing as how it's a special occasion."

"Sounds wonderful," Amanda said, making a note on the tablet in front of her. "If you ladies think of anything else we should do, please let me know."

Frances sipped the last of her coffee. "Did you ever figure out who it was that sent you that letter in the first place? The one claiming to be Mr. Kruger looking for a wife?"

Amanda had been so busy she hadn't thought any more about the forged letter that had brought her to the mountain.

"Whoever sent it," Meg said, "I'm glad they did. Otherwise, we wouldn't be getting any more women up here."

"Amen to that," Gladys said.

The ladies got up from the table and headed for the door. Amanda gathered up the dishes. Meg stayed behind to help.

"I think you could run a store," Amanda said. "In fact, I think you should do it."

Meg looked up. "Me?"

"Yes, you," Amanda said. "You told me you

and your husband ran several businesses. You certainly have the experience.''

''But I don't have the money to get started.''

Amanda thought for a moment. ''What you need is a partner. Someone who could put up the money for the inventory. You could run the store. Then, you two could split the profits.''

Meg shook her head. ''I don't know where I'd find someone willing to do that.''

''But you'd do it if you had a partner?'' Amanda asked.

''Of course,'' Meg said. ''I have Todd to provide for. I barely scrape by now. Having a business with a steady income would be the answer to my prayers.''

''I might have a partner in mind for you,'' Amanda said.

''You?'' Meg asked hopefully.

Amanda shrugged. ''You never know what could happen.''

Meg lifted the tray of dirty cups and plates and headed for the kitchen. ''I'll get started on the curtains this afternoon.''

Amanda had hired Meg to sew the curtains for the brides' dormitory. She could have done the work herself, but knew Meg needed the money. It was a good way to help out her friend.

''Good,'' Amanda called, just before Meg disappeared into the kitchen. ''Jason says the dormitory will be ready pretty quickly.''

Standing alone in the cookhouse, Amanda felt a warmth creep through her. She turned and saw Jason

striding through the door. He smiled and she realized how glad she was to see him.

"How did your meeting go?" he asked, stopping
in front of her.

"Very well. The ladies are all excited about the
arrival of the brides. The social should be quite an
affair."

"The biggest this mountain has ever seen," Jason
said and grinned.

Amanda smiled back because they both knew
there'd never been a social on Jason's mountain before.

"I got a crew started on the dormitory," Jason
said.

"I guess you really are agreeable with having
women on your mountain."

His gaze deepened. "Some more than others."

Amanda blushed.

"Want to come take a look?" Jason asked, and
nodded toward the door.

Shady ambled into the cookhouse and stopped
just inside the doorway. His eyes narrowed.

"You'd best get down to your office," he said.

A feeling of dread tingled down Amanda's spine.
She glanced up at Jason and saw him tense.

"What's wrong?" he asked.

"Somebody just rode up from Beaumont looking
for you. You and Ethan both."

"Who is it?" Jason asked.

"Didn't get the name." Shady hitched up his
trousers. "But he claims he's your brother."

Chapter Eighteen

Amanda would have known the boy standing on the porch of Jason's office was his brother, even if no one had told her.

She couldn't have guessed it, however, by Jason's reaction to him.

The young man was around thirteen, Amanda guessed, with the same dark hair and green eyes that Jason and Ethan both had. He was small and skinny. His facial features were soft but would grow into the same hard lines as his brothers.

And like Jason, he didn't look all that pleased to see his brother.

Amanda shared an uncomfortable glance with Shady, who'd come down from the cookhouse with them. Shady flipped a coin to the driver who'd brought the boy up from Beaumont and sent him on his way.

The brothers hadn't rushed together for an embrace, not even a handshake. The boy stood at one end of the porch surrounded by a valise and several boxes held together with twine. Jason stood at the other. They eyed each other warily.

Jason glared at him. "Which one are you?"

"Brandon," he replied. "Which one are you?"

"Jason."

"The oldest. Right?"

"And you're the baby."

"The youngest," Brandon corrected him, and bristled slightly. He pulled an envelope from his coat pocket. "This is for you. From Mama."

Brandon crossed to the center of the porch, exactly halfway to Jason, and stopped. He held out the envelope. Jason strode forward with one big step, snatched it from his hand and ripped it open.

"Hey there, little brother."

Ethan's voice carried to them as he hiked down from the sawmill. He leapt up the porch steps and threw his arms around the boy, then stepped back and held him at arm's length.

"You're not Brandon, are you?" Ethan asked, smiling.

"Yeah," he replied, and looked uncomfortable with the brotherly embrace.

"Damn, boy, when did you do all that growing?" Ethan hugged him again. "When did I last see you?"

Brandon shrugged as if he didn't know and didn't care. Ethan patted his shoulder. "What brings you here?"

"*She* sent him." Jason slapped the letter against his palm and spoke the worse curse words Amanda had ever heard. Even Shady cringed.

"Ma sent him?" Ethan asked.

"She's gone to England with Pa." Jason cursed again and looked at Brandon. "How come she dumped you here? Has she already sent you to every other relative we have?"

"Look," Brandon said, "all I want to know is if I'm staying or going."

"Staying, of course," Ethan said before Jason had a chance to speak. He picked up the valise. "Come on. Let's get you settled."

"You handle it," Jason barked. "I've got work to do."

He spun around and stalked away.

Stunned, Amanda stood there for a moment watching him go, his anger showing in his strides. She turned back to Brandon. If he was hurt, he didn't show it. But neither was he happy to be here, even though Ethan was going to great lengths to balance out Jason's reaction to him, to make him feel welcome.

Amanda went after Jason. She called his name twice and was sure he heard her, but he didn't stop. She hiked up her skirt and ran, and finally at the bottom of the skid road that led up the mountain he whirled around.

"What?" he barked.

Amanda fell back a step, unprepared for the venom in his tone or the raw anger on his face. She didn't know what to say, what she expected to do when she went after him. Except that he was hurting and she wanted to help him.

"I know you're upset—"

"*Upset?* You're damn right I'm upset!" Jason pointed down the hill to the office. "Is this what I have to look forward to having women on my mountain? Kids showing up? Kids getting dumped off? Families falling apart? Mothers who care more about the almighty dollar than their own children?"

Amanda faced his anger calmly. "I know you resent your mother for the way she raised you, but that's no reason to think that sort of thing will happen when the brides arrive."

"And why the hell not?" Jason cursed bitterly. "I'm supposed to look forward to seeing my men turn into sniveling cowards who knuckle under to their wives' wishes? Watch them become sissies afraid to speak their minds?"

"I know you blame your father for not standing up to your mother," Amanda said, "but there's no need to take it out on your brother."

"What the hell am I supposed to do with him? He ought to be in school. He ought to have his parents looking after him. How the hell am I supposed to know how to take care of him?"

"If you'll just give it a little time—"

"Time?" Jason demanded. "That's just what I want. Time. Time to look at that kid every day and be reminded of how I got passed around from one relative to the next. How nobody wanted me. How they couldn't wait until I left."

"Then perhaps a little compassion would smooth things between you two," Amanda said softly.

"I run a lumber camp—not an orphanage. I've

got a business to build, a railroad contract to fill, and—thanks to you—brides to get ready for.''

The words hit Amanda as if she'd been slapped. ''Are you sorry now that you agreed to having the brides here?''

''Damn right I am!''

''Then you're sorry that I'm here, too?''

''Why the hell shouldn't I be?''

She'd come after Jason to help him, soothe things for him because she could see how hurt he was. She'd been prepared for his anger. But she hadn't expected this.

''You're sorry I'm here?'' she asked again softly.

''Everything was going just fine before you got here!'' Jason swung his arm encompassing the entire camp. ''And now look at what's happening!''

Amanda braced herself, warding off the hurt she felt. ''You don't mean that,'' she said softly.

''Hell if I don't.''

Jason stalked up the mountain and didn't look back.

The house shared by the Kruger brothers was the largest on the mountain, built with slightly more care than some of the other buildings there. Amanda climbed the steps to the porch wondering what she'd find inside, wondering why she didn't have better sense than to go there.

The front door stood open so she knocked on the frame and glanced inside. She could see that the house wasn't one big room, as the others on the mountain. It had a parlor and kitchen, and a hallway that led to bedrooms.

"Ethan?" Amanda called.

She heard muffled voices from down the hallway but got no response. Amanda knocked and called his name once more.

She'd left Jason hiking up the skid road a short time ago. A few minutes had passed while she watched him, while she tried to rein in her own feelings. Understandably, he was angry. She accepted that and couldn't blame him. But still, she was torn between understanding and dealing with the hurt he'd inflicted on her.

He'd said he was sorry she'd come to his mountain. He'd said it and meant it. Amanda had no doubt about that. Her throat tightened. She gulped to keep tears from springing to her eyes.

At that moment she'd never felt more alone in her life—and she'd felt alone more than once—standing at the foot of the skid road watching Jason walk away, and knowing how he felt about her. He'd spoken the words in anger, but he'd meant them.

Amanda gave herself a little shake and rapped harder on the door frame. "Ethan?"

His head poked out of one of the rooms down the hall. He smiled when he saw her and walked to meet her.

"I'm getting Brandon settled," Ethan said, and nodded back down the hallway.

Amanda glanced out the door, up the mountain. "I'm worried about Jason. I think you should talk to him."

Ethan peered out the door, then turned back to Amanda. "Nope. No sense trying to talk to him when he gets like this."

"He's very upset about your parents leaving Brandon here."

"I know," Ethan said. "But it's best to leave him alone."

Maybe she should have done just that, Amanda thought. Maybe she shouldn't have gone after him. Maybe she'd made a mistake.

But she'd thought she meant something to him. She'd thought he'd want her with him when things went wrong, when he was upset. He'd acted as if he cared about her, needed her.

Had all that been just that—an act? Had Jason held her and kissed her, and all along she meant nothing to him?

So it seemed. Amanda's chest ached at the realization.

Jason Kruger was a hard man. He didn't need anyone. Not even her.

"Come meet Brandon," Ethan said. "He could stand seeing a friendly face besides mine."

That was certainly true. Amanda gulped down her feelings and followed Ethan down the hallway.

The parlor she passed was sparsely decorated: a settee, one chair, a table and lamp. The curtains hung crooked at the windows. A table and chairs sat in the kitchen, along with a cookstove and cupboards, none of which looked as if they'd been used in a while since the Kruger brothers ate their meals at the cookhouse. A fine mist of dust covered everything and dirt was scattered across the floor. The house wasn't filthy; it just looked as if two men lived there.

Two men, and now a boy.

Brandon sat on the edge of a big brass bed rubbing his eyes when Amanda and Ethan walked into the room. She hadn't noticed how tired he looked when she'd seen him outside Jason's office, nor had she noticed how rumpled his clothes were, as if he'd slept in them a number of times.

Ethan introduced them. Brandon rose from the bed and nodded politely. "Nice to meet you, Miss Pierce."

Someone had taught the boy manners, whether it was his mother or the relatives he'd been living with, Amanda didn't know.

"Welcome, Brandon," she said, and glanced around the room at his belongings stacked up in the corner. "Can I assist getting you settled?"

"That would be a big help," Ethan said. "I've got two new men who started at the mill this morning. I need to be there and make sure they don't do anything stupid—and lose a hand or something in the process."

"Certainly," Amanda said. "Run along. I'll see to Brandon."

Ethan gave his brother an affectionate half hug. "I'll see you at supper time. Come up to the cookhouse."

Brandon watched him leave but didn't say anything.

"Well," Amanda said after Ethan had left the room, "how was your trip?"

"Long," Brandon said and yawned, remembering at the last second to cover his mouth. "Five or six days. I'm not sure now."

"You traveled nearly a week by yourself?"

Brandon nodded, rubbing his eyes.

"Gracious...." That certainly made her trip from San Francisco seem small.

"Missed the train, once. Stagecoach broke down and left us stranded."

For having endured such a harrowing trip the boy looked none the worse for wear, except that he was tired. Still, it didn't sit well with Amanda that Brandon's parents had sent him on this odyssey alone.

So this was how Jason had lived his youth. Left to fend for himself. It had made him strong, built him into the man who commanded a lumber camp, secured a prized railroad contract and owned a mountain.

But it didn't make for pleasant childhood memories.

"Let's get you unpacked," Amanda said.

"Not much to unpack," Brandon said, and sat on the edge of the bed again. "Our stuff got mixed up. Most of my things are halfway to England by now. Those boxes were supposed to go with Mama."

"Oh, dear. That's a shame." Amanda lifted one of the boxes by the twine. "It's not very heavy. What's in here?"

"Old junk." Brandon set the box on the bureau

and unknotted the twine. He pried off the lid. "See? Just papers and letters and things like that."

Amanda peered into the box at the assortment of folded documents. A packet of letters was held together by a pink ribbon. Several other small boxes were inside as well.

"Do you suppose your parents need these things in England?" Amanda asked.

Brandon shrugged indifferently, then opened the other box. "I don't know. Mama carries these things around with her all the time."

"Perhaps we should ship it to them."

"I don't think it's important," Brandon said, "but you can look through it if you want, see what you think."

Amanda glanced inside the two boxes sitting on the bureau, a little uncomfortable at being invited to look through the private papers of a man and woman she didn't know. Although she felt as if she knew them simply by knowing Jason and Ethan, and now Brandon.

"I don't know if I should," Amanda said. "Maybe one of your brothers should do it."

A few seconds passed with no response. Amanda turned and found Brandon stretched out on the bed, lying on his belly, arms spread, sound asleep. He hadn't taken off his jacket or shoes. Amanda smiled. He looked peaceful, dead asleep.

Was this what Jason looked like when he slept? Sprawled across the bed, not a crease or worry line on his face, muscles relaxed. She couldn't imagine seeing him so calm and unguarded.

Now she never would.

Wanting to stay busy, Amanda turned back to the boxes and valise and decided to unpack for Brandon. She emptied his few meager possessions from the valise, then her gaze settled on the two open boxes still sitting on the bureau.

Maybe she should look through them. No one else was likely to do it. Ethan and Jason were too busy. And Jason certainly wasn't inclined to rehash old memories, not to mention do his parents any favors.

Amanda settled into the cane-bottom chair in the corner and put the boxes on the floor at her feet. As she dug through the documents she began thinking Brandon's assessment was correct. They were just old papers of no value.

She changed her mind when she reached the bottom of the first box and found the Kruger family bible.

It was a large leather volume with a hinged clasp and gold foil on the edges of the pages. Amanda opened it on her lap and carefully turned the tissue-thin leaves. In the center were several thicker pages with ornate drawings depicting images of Jesus, haloed angels and divine lights beaming from the heavens. On these pages the history of the Kruger family was recorded.

Amanda read the names of Jason's ancestors going back nearly a hundred years. His grandparents, his parents, his brothers and sisters, aunts, uncles, nieces, nephews, their births, deaths and marriages.

As Jason had said, he and his siblings had all been

born in different parts of the country, as indicated by the places of birth recorded on the pages.

Tracing her finger to the last entry, Amanda read Brandon's name and glanced up at the boy sleeping on the bed. Jason, the first born, was nearly nineteen years older than Brandon, the last born. Small wonder there was no brotherly bond between them.

Sadness settled over Amanda. She had neither brother nor sister. Both parents were dead. Her family consisted of a few cousins she corresponded with occasionally.

She touched her finger to the bold script of the Kruger family tree. Such a large family. Scattered. Rarely seeing each other. Near strangers, really. Perhaps that loss was greater than what she felt at having no one.

Amanda closed the bible carefully and picked up the stack of letters bundled together with a ribbon. She sorted through them, quickly skimming the contents, not wanting to delve too deeply into the Kruger family business.

She expected to find correspondence among family members, talk of the weather, births, marriages, stories of growing children and growing old. News that was the common bond that held families together.

Instead, Amanda's brows pulled together in a frown. She went back and read each letter again, slowly and carefully.

When she'd finished the last, Amanda sat back in the chair, her chest heavy. This wasn't what she'd expected to find. Not at all.

Briefly she considered what she should do with these letters, with this newfound knowledge. Tell someone, or let it go?

Jason was already angry at her and wouldn't appreciate another attempt by her to butt into his life. Still, he needed to know.

Because it was quite obvious to Amanda that Jason didn't know the truth about his parents.

Chapter Nineteen

"Morning, Miss Pierce."

A welcoming chorus greeted Amanda as she entered the cookhouse for breakfast. The prospective husbands, already seated at their table, rose to their feet as naturally as if they'd been doing it all their lives, rather than just a few weeks.

"Good morning, gentlemen," Amanda said, as one of them assisted her into her chair. "Lovely day, isn't it?"

The loggers all agreed that it was in fact a lovely day as they put their napkins in their laps, passed the food platters around the table, and began eating.

For over a week now, Amanda had sat alone with the soon-to-be husbands. Jason had returned to his usual spot at the rear of the cookhouse.

Over a week had gone by since Brandon arrived and not once had Jason spoken to her. He'd not even glanced in her direction. This morning was no exception.

Amanda tried to eat breakfast, tried to focus on

the conversation at the table, but it was nearly impossible. Through the shifting crowd of men in the cookhouse she could see Jason seated at his table, eating. She could see him, but that was all.

And it wasn't enough. Her arms ached to hold him, touch him. She wanted to see him smile, hear him tell her how work on the mountain was going.

Her heart ached. Jason, so close. Jason, so distant.

The pain was almost unbearable. Over the last week she'd seen him going about his business, talking to his men, hiking up the skid road, conversing with Ethan at the sawmill. Her gaze seemed to find him wherever he went, drawn to him so naturally.

She'd considered trying to talk to him, smooth things over, but rejected that notion each time. Ethan had said to leave him alone because there was no use trying to talk to him when he was angry.

It went against Amanda's instincts to simply let things lie. She preferred talking, getting things out in the open. But his brother knew him better than anyone so she bowed to his advice.

Jason knew where she was. If he wanted to talk to her, he could. When he was ready he'd do just that.

Hopefully.

"Miss Pierce?"

Amanda's attention snapped back to the husbands at the breakfast table and saw that they were all gazing at her.

"Miss Pierce?" Henry Jasper said softly. "Just so you know, none of us are sorry you came to the mountain."

The men all nodded solemnly.

Tears sprang to Amanda's eyes, touched that the men would say that to her. Word had spread across the mountain that Jason was angry and sorry he'd allowed her to bring her brides here…sorry that she was here.

"Thank you," Amanda said, sniffing. "Thank you all very much."

"We appreciate everything you've done for us," Tom Redford said.

"Yes, ma'am, that's the truth," Henry said above the murmur of agreement around the table.

"Thank you," Amanda said again. She laid her napkin aside. "If you gentlemen will excuse me?"

She got to her feet and the loggers clambered to theirs. They nodded respectfully as she left the cookhouse. It took all her strength not to glance at the rear of the room where Jason sat.

Amanda stepped outside into the cool air. Gray clouds hung over the mountain, the morning sun only a hazy glow at the treetops. In the distance she saw the dormitory taking shape. Work was proceeding quickly. The crew Jason assigned to the job worked diligently. The prospective husbands joined the effort after their shift was over for the day. Some of them were also building cabins on the mountain for their brides.

Tears stung Amanda's eyes again and this time threatened to fall. In a short time the brides would arrive. Marriages would take place. Lonely people would find partners. Families would grow.

And Amanda would leave.

She sniffed. There would be no marriage for her. Not now. Not ever. How could she marry anyone when her heart belonged to Jason Kruger? And he didn't want it.

Angrily, Amanda swiped away her tears. It was her own fault. No one else's. She should have known better than to lose her heart to a man. Hadn't she learned that the hard way once already in her life?

The rustle of footsteps sounded behind Amanda and she realized the loggers were leaving the cookhouse, heading to work. Well, she had work to do, too.

Ethan, calling her name, stopped her. She waited until he caught up.

"Have you seen Brandon this morning?" he asked.

Amanda glanced at the men filing past, then thought back to breakfast. Though most of her attention had been fixed on Jason she had noticed that Brandon wasn't present in the cookhouse again this morning.

"No, I haven't see him," she said.

"That boy." Ethan shook his head. "I don't know where he's been going or what he's doing, but I don't like it. Having a boy his age at loose ends is just asking for trouble."

"Yes, I agree," Amanda said. "He told me he wants to work but Jason won't let him."

Even though the oldest Kruger brother had little use for her, the youngest had spent quite a bit of time with her over the last week. Unlike Jason,

Brandon wasn't shy about saying what was on his mind.

"I told Jason we need to give the boy a job," Ethan said, "but he won't hear of it. Says he's too young to have to work for a living. Says all he has to worry about is getting an education."

"Brandon goes to Idelle Turner's school every day," Amanda said. "I see him walking back and forth."

"That's not enough to keep him busy."

Amanda agreed. Because there were so few students, their lessons were completed quickly and class dismissed before noon. That left hours and hours of empty time to fill somehow.

"Maybe you could train him at the sawmill?" Amanda suggested.

"If I had time I would," Ethan said. "But with that railroad contract to fill I can't spare the time or manpower to train somebody. Especially a kid with no experience."

"Isn't there something you can give Brandon to do?"

Ethan shook his head. "The sawmill is too dangerous to work without proper training. One wrong move and—well, let's just say it could be your last wrong move."

Amanda cringed at the mental picture Ethan's words conjured up. She'd been to the sawmill, seen the huge blades spinning. They sliced through the thick trees like butter. She'd heard the stories of the men who'd lost limbs—and lives—to those blades.

"Jason hasn't warmed up to his brother yet, has he?" Amanda asked.

"No," Ethan said. "But he'll come around."

"I hope so," Amanda said softly. She felt tears burning at her eyes again, so she straightened her shoulders and changed the subject.

"Ethan, there's a business opportunity I'd like to discuss with you. A partnership, actually."

He grinned. "A partnership with you? I wouldn't think twice about saying yes to that, Amanda."

She couldn't help smiling. Ethan had that effect on her. Why couldn't she have fallen in love with *this* Kruger brother?

"No, not me. I'll be leaving soon."

Ethan scowled. "I can't imagine this mountain without you on it, Amanda."

She gulped hard, holding back a fresh flood of tears. "Let me explain what I have in mind."

"Yes? He said yes?" Meg dropped the curtain she was hemming and came out of her chair in the little parlor of her cabin. "Ethan said yes?"

"He said yes," Amanda told her.

Meg squealed with delight and threw her arms around Amanda. They hugged, then Meg spun away.

"I should be mad at you," she said.

Amanda nodded. "You should."

"Going behind my back, asking Ethan to be my partner in the new general store."

"I knew you'd never ask him yourself," Amanda said. "And he jumped at the chance."

"He did?"

"Of course he did," Amanda said. "It's an excellent business opportunity."

Meg glanced down at her hands. "Was that the only reason he agreed?"

"You know it wasn't," Amanda told her.

"No, I don't know that," Meg said, twisting her fingers together.

"Ethan is wild about you. He'd do anything to make you happy." Amanda walked closer. "Have you decided what you're going to do about your husband?"

Meg pressed her lips together. "My head tells me one thing, but my heart says another."

"There's no rush," Amanda said. "The only thing you need to concentrate on is getting your store ready to open. You're meeting Ethan tonight after supper to discuss your arrangement."

"I am?"

"You are." Amanda plucked a curtain from the stack beside Meg's chair. "Now, let's get these things finished. We have a lot to do."

Darkness had fallen over the lumber camp, and while this was normally Jason's favorite time of day, he found little comfort tonight as he walked toward his office. That puzzled him because things were going well. Better than usual, really. The railroad contract was ahead of schedule. The dormitory was coming along. His crew was working hard. No one had gotten hurt in weeks. The men had even stopped fighting among themselves over the arrival of the brides, especially since it had been decided that bride number nine was more compatible with Tom Redford.

There was no reason for the foul mood he'd been in, Jason decided. Not on the face of things. Not concerning the important matters in his life.

Or at least in the matters he used to consider important.

Jason stepped up onto the porch of his office. Lantern light glowed in the window, indicating Ethan was inside.

At once, Jason wanted to talk to his brother. For over a week now he hadn't wanted to talk to anybody. Hadn't wanted anybody to talk to him. And his grumpiness had ensured that nobody had.

Laughter drifted out of the office, freezing Jason on the porch. He backed up a step and peered through the window.

Ethan sat at his desk writing on a tablet. Across from him sat Meg. Jason was more than a little surprised to see them together in the office.

Both leaned forward until their heads nearly touched, discussing whatever Ethan had written on the tablet. They looked good together, the two of them. Jason couldn't deny that.

He shifted on the porch ready to walk inside when another person stepped up to the desk. His stomach bottomed out.

Amanda.

She positioned herself at the end of the desk, facing the window where Jason could see her clearly. With her attention on the tablet, she didn't see him at the window. Amanda spoke and both Ethan and Meg looked up at her. She pointed. They nodded. She said something and all three of them laughed.

Jason's heart ached. He curled his hands into fists to ward off the pain. It didn't help.

Over a week had passed and they hadn't spoken. It was his doing, his fault. He knew that.

He'd taken his anger out on Amanda. After he'd cooled off he'd realized what he'd done. Yelled at her. Said things he didn't mean. Things that couldn't be unsaid.

Now she stayed out of his way. She went about her business, though, seeing that the things on the mountain that needed doing got done.

Each morning she gave her manners classes in the cookhouse. When he'd first met her Jason had thought her an uppity city woman capable of nothing more than knowing proper etiquette. But she'd shown him she was much more than that. In fact, Amanda was a lot of things.

Just as she'd promised, she had overseen the work on the dormitory. She was there throughout the day, talking to the men, complimenting them, discussing things with Tom Redford, whom Jason had put in charge of the project.

Jason kept an eye on the construction, too. It wasn't easy. Every time he looked at the plans, the big wrinkle across the middle reminded him of the morning in his office when he'd kissed Amanda so hard she'd sat down on the plans.

He'd wanted her so badly that day. He'd lusted

after her, hardly able to find the strength to stop what they were doing.

Now, he missed her. He just plain old missed her. The ache in Jason's chest deepened.

He knew he could change that. He could change it this minute, if he wanted, simply by walking into his office and talking to her.

But doing that meant carving off a big chunk of his pride and gulping it straight down. It meant acting just the way his father had, always bending to the will of his wife, consequences be damned.

Jason had seen it happen over and over growing up. He'd had to live with the results. And he'd sworn, over and over, that he'd never let any woman run his life.

He looked at Amanda through the window. Lovely, lovely Amanda....

Jason turned and walked away.

Chapter Twenty

"Step, two, three. Step, two, three. That's it. Keep going."

Amanda clapped her hands to the beat of Jim Hubbard playing "My Darling Clementine" on his harmonica, pacing off the steps, smiling, and trying to encourage her dance class. The men were first-rate lumberjacks, but on the dance floor they had a long way to go.

The afternoon breeze blew gently through the first floor of the brides' dormitory bringing the sweet smell of sawdust with it. The building was ready, all but a few finishing touches. Freight wagons came from Beaumont daily, and more were expected with the brides' arrival, which was now only days away.

The loggers on the dance floor had finished their noon meal; Jason had given them extra time off for their lesson. This was their third lesson and things hadn't improved much.

They'd drawn a good crowd, however. Even men who weren't expecting brides had shown up, lining the perimeter of the room, watching. Shady was there, standing by the door, keeping a watchful eye on things.

About a dozen of the bravest men were assembled in the middle of the room, stumbling along, stomping their boots against the wooden plank floor, mimicking Amanda's dance steps, trying to follow the beat of the music. The other men looked on, wary and not quite ready to make fools of themselves yet.

Amanda sighed inwardly. At this rate, her get-acquainted social would be a total failure.

"All right, let's take a little break," she called. The men wiped their sweaty brows looking grateful.

"Brandon?" she called.

The boy hopped from his perch on the windowsill and hurried over. He seemed to be everywhere in the lumber camp, and nowhere. Brandon, apparently accustomed to keeping himself entertained, had an easy way about him, more like Ethan than Jason. He'd made friends with Todd McGee, despite their age difference. Ethan had taken them both fishing. Amanda had heard that Brandon helped out in the cookhouse and at the millpond, but Jason had put a stop to it when he found out.

Amanda gazed at her dance class trying not to look discouraged. While the lumberjacks on the floor were trying, most were simply going through the motions. The others hadn't even joined in. Dancing was not a priority to them, obviously. Something was needed to spur their interest. Amanda jotted a note on the tiny tablet she kept in her skirt pocket and presented it to Brandon.

"Would you take this to Meg, please?" she asked.

"Yes, ma'am," he said.

She leaned a little closer and smiled conspiratorially. "It's an emergency, of sorts. Please hurry."

He glanced at the note and smiled back, understanding her meaning right away.

"Sure thing, Miss Amanda," Brandon said, and took off.

Amanda spoke quietly with Shady for a few minutes. By the time the men had caught their breath and gotten water, Amanda heard the chatter of women's voices and knew her dance lesson—and social—had been saved.

"Gentlemen," she called. "Since you're all doing so well, I've decided to move things along a bit. This afternoon, you'll be dancing with partners."

A rumble went through the men, heads snapped around, and they came a little closer as Meg, Becky, Idelle Turner and Frances Conroy came up the stairs into the dormitory.

"These ladies have graciously donated their time to help with your lessons," Amanda said, gesturing to the women grouped together by the door. "Now, if you'll come onto the dance floor, we'll get started."

All the men—even those who hadn't participated before—rushed to the center of the room. There was some pushing and elbowing as they lined up.

"First of all," Amanda said, "you must remember that when dancing with a lady you are to be respectful at all times. Any man who is not will be shot.''

Faint laughter rippled through the loggers until Shady stepped forward and pulled his pistol from his holster, and waved it in the air.

''That's for dang sure!'' he shouted, quieting the men.

''Now, let's proceed,'' Amanda said. She almost asked for volunteers but, fearing a stampede, selected men to partner with the women.

At Amanda's signal Jim Hubbard blew into his harmonica and the dancing began. Such as it was.

Amanda circulated through the dancing couples offering encouragement and making suggestions. The men took her instructions to heart, trying harder.

After a few minutes, Amanda ordered partners to change, giving other men a chance to dance. None of them were shy about being on the dance floor now.

Ethan appeared in the doorway. When Amanda called for the next partner change, he approached Meg and they danced around the room. At the next break, he still didn't give her up. Nobody protested.

Watching from the sideline, Amanda couldn't help but feel happy for Meg. Ethan gazed down at her with affection, not bothering to hide it. Amanda had worked with the two of them a couple of times as they'd made plans for opening the store on the mountain. Ethan and Meg were well-suited for one another. She didn't have to be the owner of The Becoming Brides Matrimonial Service to see that.

Her thoughts went to Jason then, as they often

did. Amanda had about run out of patience with him. They still hadn't spoken. She missed him.

She understood he needed time to come to terms with things. Having Brandon—the reminder of his own unhappy childhood—on the mountain wasn't easy for him. She didn't want to crowd him, or make the situation more difficult for him, but things couldn't go on like this much longer.

"Miss Amanda?"

She turned to find Brandon standing behind her.

"There's a man down at the office," Brandon said, nodding in that direction. "He's looking for Miss Meg."

"Who is it?"

Brandon shrugged. "Name's McGee. Gerald McGee. Claims he's her husband."

"I know this is asking a lot, but—"

"Don't give it a thought," Amanda insisted as she helped Meg carry her belongings into Amanda's cabin. Todd came through the door behind them, dragging blankets and scowling. Meg tried to hug him, but he pulled away.

"I don't want to live here," Todd grumbled and dropped the blankets on the floor.

"I know, Todd, but—"

"Will Pa take me fishing? Like Ethan did?" he asked.

"We'll see." Meg patted his shoulder. "Why don't you run along and play? I'll call you when supper's ready."

Todd ran outside and Meg collapsed onto the bundle of blankets on the floor. She covered her face with her hands and started to sob. Amanda sank down beside her. She felt like crying herself.

"I—I don't understand," Meg said, looking up at Amanda with tear-streaked cheeks. "Why did this have to happen? I waited nearly a year. A year without a word from him. And now he simply shows up?"

Amanda passed her the lace handkerchief from her pocket. "I don't understand either."

"No one knows how I struggled when Gerald left," Meg said, still sobbing. "I could barely feed my child. I was alone, and lost, and—and I didn't know what to do. And now, he just shows up again, saying he's sorry, and expects everything to be all right?"

Amanda had walked to the office with Meg to meet her long-lost husband, but the two of them had gone to the privacy of their cabin to talk. Amanda didn't know exactly what had been said, but Meg had left a short time later and asked Amanda if she and Todd could move in with her for a while.

"What does Gerald want?" Amanda asked. "Where has he been all this time?"

Meg sniffed. "Looking for work, he claims. Now he's found a job near Los Angeles."

"Los Angeles? That's so far away."

"And he expects me to go with him," Meg said. Fresh tears spilled over her cheeks. "Gerald says he wants his family back."

"No...."

"I told him I needed some time to think. He can't

come waltzing back onto this mountain as if nothing had happened and expect us to…well, you know. I won't stay in the same cabin with him. Not yet, anyway.''

"Stay here with me as long as you need," Amanda said.

Meg clutched the handkerchief in her fist, tears rolling down her face. "Just when things were turning around for me. Just when I had a chance to make something of myself, and for Todd. A chance to build a solid future."

A fresh wave of sobs shook Meg. "Oh, and Ethan…Ethan…."

Amanda put her arm around Meg and pulled her close. "What are you going to do?"

"What can I do?" Meg looked up at her. "He's my husband. The father of my child. I have to go with him."

"Dammit!"

Jason paced across the office, swearing and mumbling under his breath. He stopped and looked down at his brother. Ethan sat at his desk, elbows planted, his palms covering his face.

"That McGee bastard shows up," Jason said, "after nearly a year. Just shows up like nothing happened. What the hell kind of man would abandon his wife and son like that, then come back expecting to pick up where they left off?"

When Ethan didn't say anything, Jason started pacing and cursing again. After a few minutes, he stopped.

''What are you going to do?'' he asked.

Ethan dragged his palms down his face and sat back in the chair. ''What can I do?''

''You can't let McGee take Meg off this mountain,'' Jason insisted. ''Not if you love her.''

''Great advice,'' Ethan snapped. ''Especially coming from you.''

''What the hell is that supposed to mean?''

''You know what I mean!'' Ethan surged to his feet. ''You've been acting like a bigger horse's ass than usual these past few weeks!''

''I've got nothing to do with what happened between you and Meg!''

''But you sure as hell have something to do with what's happening between you and Amanda!''

Jason backed off, shaking his head. ''One's got nothing to do with the other.''

''At least I tried!'' Ethan told him. ''Meg knows I care about her. All you've done since Amanda got here is try to run her off this mountain. And all because of something that happened years ago that has nothing to do with the two of you!''

Jason looked at him for a long minute but didn't say anything. He fell back to pacing again. Ethan sank into his chair after a while.

Arguments between the two of them never lasted long. The fact that they disagreed on something gave Jason no cause for concern. He respected his brother for having a different opinion, they talked it out— sometimes fought it out—and moved on. It had always been that way between them. It suited them both.

But it didn't suit Jason that Ethan was hurting right now. He had half a mind to go up there and run Gerald McGee off his mountain, once and for all. It would feel good. He'd wanted to hit somebody for a while now. He'd do it, too, except that it wouldn't accomplish anything in the long run. Things had to be settled, one way or the other.

Jason dropped into the chair in front of Ethan's desk. "What are you going to do?"

"I know what I'd like to do."

Jason nodded. Knowing his brother, the same solution had crossed both their minds.

"But I can't." Ethan sighed heavily and slumped deeper into the chair. "I can't force Meg to choose. She's married to the man. She bore him a son."

"And he abandoned both."

"McGee is a son of a bitch, no doubt about it," Ethan said. "But what kind of man would I be if I asked her to choose between me and him? Asked her to break her marriage vows, vows she made in church, before God? How can I ask her to do that?"

"She loves you," Jason said. "She'll pick you over McGee in a heartbeat."

Ethan shook his head. "They're married. They have a son. That's a strong bond. Besides, if I asked her to choose, in the end she'd just resent me for forcing her to make the choice."

Jason shook his head. "Damn."

"And what about Todd? That man's his pa. What right have I got to come between the two of them?"

"You've got to do something," Jason insisted.

"You tell me what I should do and I'll do it."

Jason got up and started pacing again. A timid knock sounded on the door and he yanked it open.

Rory Connor stood in the doorway, his face white, his hat crumpled against his chest.

"You'd better come quick, Mr. Kruger," he said. "Your little brother's damn near cut his hand off at the sawmill."

Chapter Twenty-One

Meg had asked for some time alone to think and compose herself, and Amanda agreed it was for the best. She left Meg sitting at her table, staring at a cup of coffee, clutching her lace handkerchief and sniffling.

Amanda closed the door of her little cabin and walked down the front steps. Her thoughts were with Meg and the decision she faced, so at first Amanda didn't notice the eerie silence on the mountain.

She stopped, her senses alert. No voices carried on the breeze, the birds didn't sing in the treetops. And there was no sound from the sawmill.

The door to Jason's office burst open and Jason and Ethan both ran up the mountain. Rory Connor, the sawmill foreman, trotted behind them, as if uncertain whether he wanted to follow.

A sick knot jerked in Amanda's stomach. She picked up her skirt and ran.

She reached the sawmill only a moment after Jason and Ethan went inside, and just seconds ahead of Rory Connor. The crew had broken back against the walls, unmoving, staring. The saws and their spinning blades were silent. The air was thick with tension.

Jason stood in the center of the room, glaring at his men. Ethan huddled with three other men in the corner. Amanda pushed her way to Ethan's side.

She gasped aloud.

Brandon sat on a small keg, his head resting against the hard wooden wall, eyes closed against his colorless cheeks. His right hand and arm were wrapped in rags, and soaked in blood. Dark red stains streaked across his shirt, his neck, his cheek.

"Who's responsible for this?" Jason's voice boomed in the silence.

Ethan pulled back the rags and sucked in air between his teeth. Amanda looked at the bloody mess and her stomach heaved.

"Who's responsible?" Jason demanded again, turning in the center of the room, eyeing the crew. "Who was running that saw?"

A tall, thin man with a heavy beard stepped forward. "It was me, Mr. Kruger."

"You're fired!" Jason swung the other way. "Where's the foreman?"

Rory Connor reluctantly held up his hand. "Right here, Mr. Kruger."

"You're fired!" He swung the other way. "Who else was involved in this?"

Amanda left Brandon and stepped up to Jason. She touched his arm. "Jason—"

"I want to know who saw this and did nothing about it!" Jason shouted, glaring at the crew.

"Jason," Amanda said softly. "Your brother needs to go to the doctor."

Fierce anger contorted his face and he looked down, as if seeing her for the first time.

"Now, Jason," she said quietly. "Now."

His gaze darted to Brandon in the corner, the urgency of the situation dawning on him. He looked again at Amanda, but she'd already turned away.

She pointed at the three men standing closest to her. "You, get the wagon. You, fetch blankets and put them in the back. You, bring clean towels and water. Now!"

The men scattered.

Ethan and Amanda washed Brandon's wound and wrapped it tightly in the clean towels. Brandon groaned softly, fading in and out. Blood seeped through the towels.

Jason went outside and shouted at the driver of the freight wagon—and anyone else standing around—as it pulled up outside the sawmill. Then he scooped up Brandon and placed him on the pallet of blankets. When Jason tried to climb up onto the seat, Amanda stopped him by touching his arm.

"No," she told him.

Jason glared at her, somewhere between stunned and annoyed at her handing out orders.

"You're too upset. Brandon needs a smooth ride. Get in the back and help steady him. Ethan, you drive."

Amanda climbed into the back of the wagon with

Jason and they sat on either side of Brandon as they made the long trip down the mountain.

The boy looked frail and helpless wrapped in the woolen blankets, his eyes closed, mercifully unaware of most of the pain. He moaned occasionally, bringing a new pang of worry to Amanda. She glanced up at Jason, his face grim.

When they reached Beaumont the doctor was in his office. Jason carried Brandon inside and they all crowded into his surgery. The small, dim room smelled of chemicals and illness. When the doctor pulled away the blood-soaked towel, Jason reeled back, then went out the door.

Amanda watched him, torn between whether to follow or stay with Brandon. Ethan caught her eye and nodded toward the door. Amanda went outside.

She waited on the front porch of the doctor's office until Jason came from around back, dragging his fist across his mouth. He stopped when he saw her, hesitated for only a second, then stepped up onto the porch.

Amanda turned away and rested her hands on the porch railing. The evening breeze ruffled her hair and cooled her face. On the street in front of her a few horses and wagons plodded by. Stores were closing. Beaumont was settling in for the night.

She felt Jason's presence on the porch near her, sensed him at her side staring at the dusty street. A long moment passed before he spoke.

"Do you think he'll lose his hand?"

"I don't know," Amanda said.

From the corner of her eye she saw Jason scrub

his palms over his face. "I—I can't look at…that sort of thing without—"

"Throwing up?"

He glanced down at her, mildly surprised she'd use so unladylike a term. Saw, too, that she was unwilling to allow him at least a little dignity.

"Yeah," Jason said.

Another few minutes dragged by. Jason eased a little closer, and turned to face her.

"I know this is my fault," he said, and nodded toward the doctor's office.

"Yes, I'd agree with that."

Jason's cut his eyes away. "Thanks," he said sourly.

"What kind of friend would I be if I told you lies just to make you feel better?" Amanda asked. "What happened to Brandon is partially your fault."

"Everything that happens on that mountain is my responsibility."

"You should have given him something to do," Amanda said. "A boy his age can't be left to wander."

"Look, he had no business in that sawmill. This just proves I was right."

Amanda whirled to face him. "This only proves that you're stubborn and pigheaded, as I've said all along."

He glared at her. "I'm not getting into this with you."

"I don't care whether you want to talk about it or not!" Amanda told him. "You need to consider the possibility that you may not be right all the time!''

Amanda waited for him to say something, but he didn't. Jason just looked at her. She couldn't read his expression at the moment. Was he angry? Hurt? Did he really believe what had happened to Brandon was his fault? Or that she might be right?

Something was different about him. His stance was a little softer. The edges of his face weren't so hard. There was a vulnerability about him she hadn't seen before.

It tore at her heart. For all the anger she felt, Amanda wanted to hold him. She wanted to loop her arms around him and press against him. Give him the strength she had. Take the strength he offered.

But he hadn't offered any. He hadn't asked for any.

Amanda crossed the porch and went inside the doctor's office.

Darkness had fallen by the time the freight wagon pulled into the lumber camp. Ethan drove the team up to the Kruger house. Lanterns sat on the porch, along with Shady and Buck Johansen. They came to their feet as the wagon pulled to a stop.

''Well, what about it?'' Shady asked as he ambled to the rear of the wagon.

''Everybody's been asking,'' Buck said. ''The whole mountain's worried.''

Ethan jumped down from the driver's seat. ''The

kid got lucky. Didn't break the bone, just sliced everything open.''

Jason climbed out the back of the wagon and lowered the tailgate. He caught Amanda at the waist and lifted her to the ground.

"No permanent damage?'' Buck asked, peering over the side of the wagon.

Brandon lay bundled in the woolen blankets, sleeping, his right arm wrapped in bandages. Jason lifted him out, resting the boy's head on his chest.

Amanda touched her hand to Brandon's forehead. "The doctor can't be sure at this point. Only time will tell. But things look good.''

Shady chuckled. "Sounds like the boy's got Kruger luck.''

"He'll have to be very careful,'' Amanda said. "The arm needs special care until it's healed.''

"Ain't nothing to fool around about.'' Shady shook his head. "The boy needs a doctor up here to look after him.''

"He needs his mother,'' Jason said curtly and brushed past them.

Ethan followed him inside. Amanda waited on the porch talking to Shady and Buck, giving them details of what the doctor had said. They told her how everyone on the mountain was worried about Brandon.

"The two men Jason fired at the sawmill,'' Amanda said. "Do you think he was serious?''

"Yes, ma'am,'' Buck said. "Dead serious.''

"But mightn't he reconsider?''

Buck shook his head. "I'm sure not going to be the one to ask him, ma'am."

Amanda doubted any man on the mountain would question Jason on his decision. He ran the place. His word was law. And in this case, Amanda couldn't disagree with him, even though she hated to see the two men lose their jobs.

"Well, 'night, ma'am," Buck said. He tipped his hat and hiked up toward the bunkhouse.

Shady lingered, rocking back and forth from his toes to his heels. "I heard tell that Gerald McGee is back on the mountain wanting his wife and boy."

Fatigue swamped Amanda. Today had been one of emotional ups and downs. For herself, and for so many others. She was tired, worn out by everyone else's—and her own—problems.

"Yes, Shady," she said. "I'm afraid you're right."

He sucked his gums. "Just don't seem right."

"No, it doesn't."

"She a-gonna go with him?"

"I think so."

Shady grunted. "Guess she's got no choice, seeing as how she's married to him. Reckon that's why I never got hitched. Didn't like not being able to choose things for myself."

The sounds of the night closed in around them. The camp seemed peaceful. After a time, Shady ambled away.

Amanda pinched the bridge of her nose, tired and anxious to get to her little cabin. Somehow, in the past weeks, it had begun to feel like home. The sounds in the woods no longer frightened her. The simple furnishings seemed inviting. Tonight, the feather mattress waiting for her seemed more welcoming than the finest bed she'd ever lain on in San Francisco.

But she wanted to make sure Brandon was all right before she left. She expected Ethan to come outside and let her know he was settled in for the night. She waited for a while and was surprised to see Jason come through the front door.

"How is he?" she asked.

"Sleeping."

"Good. He'll need lots of rest."

In the dim light from inside the house Amanda watched Jason closely. For a second he looked as if he wanted to say something, or ask something, but in the end didn't. She stepped off the porch and headed for home.

"Thanks," Jason called.

She was surprised to hear him say that, but wouldn't allow herself to make too much of it. "You're welcome," she answered, and kept walking.

"You were right."

Amanda froze, her spine tingling. Slowly she turned. Jason stood on the porch. She never expected to hear those words from him, and for a moment wondered if it was her imagination. Then Jason spoke again.

"You were right," he said. "I should have paid more attention to him, given him something to keep him busy."

"You were right, too," Amanda said. "He does need his mother."

They stood like that for a few minutes, yards apart, staring, saying nothing. The yards separating them may as well have been miles. The ground between them a yawning abyss.

Amanda considered marching right up to Jason then and there and telling him she'd had enough of this emotional gulf that separated them. She almost did it, too. Definitely would have if he'd taken the tiniest step toward her.

But tonight she was tired. Simply too tired. She wanted to lie in his arms and collect herself, soothe him and make his problems go away. But Jason didn't want that. And Amanda was too tired to fight for it. She turned and hiked toward her cabin without another word.

Jason watched until she disappeared into the shadows and still didn't take his eyes from her. He caught glimpses of her as she crossed the camp, highlighted by shafts of light from windows and open doorways. When lanterns flickered inside her own cabin he still couldn't turn away.

If things had gone a little differently today, he could have lost his brother. The brother he hadn't even gotten to know yet.

He still might lose his other brother. If Meg left with her husband, no telling what Ethan would do. Expecting him to stay on the mountain, looking at Meg's vacant cabin, remembering and being reminded of what he almost had might be too much. Ethan might just take off.

And what would that leave him with? A mountain full of newlyweds. A railroad contract. A business to run.

Jason leaned his head against the roof post. What the hell good was any of it? Without Amanda?

Chapter Twenty-Two

"Brides! Brides on the mountain!"

Amanda had heard the shouts echo through the lumber camp since the first wagon pulled into sight at midday yesterday. First from the men at the sawmill, then from those at the millpond, the cookhouse, the barns and now from the loggers who trekked down the skid road for their noon meal.

Tablet and lists in hand, Amanda stood in the swirl of confusion inside the dormitory as the last six of her twenty-three brides arrived from Beaumont. All brought baggage, all needed their room. All asked a dozen questions. All were tired and hungry. Meg and Becky helped out as best they could.

"Yes," Amanda said, flipping through her lists, "you're in room eight. Upstairs. Yes, yes, and you're right next door. Supper is at four tonight. Baths will be available afterward. The social begins at seven."

"Y'all just follow me," Becky called out, leading the duck line of brides up the stairs.

"Gracious...." Meg blew out a big breath and sidled up to Amanda.

"Things will settle down now that they're all here." Amanda grinned. "Hopefully."

She glanced out the window at another freight wagon pulling up out front. Though the supplies for the brides had been ordered some weeks ago, not everything had come as quickly as needed. They continued to arrive daily with more expected over the next couple of days. Wagons from Beaumont were wearing dozens of new ruts in the mountain road.

"The men are getting anxious," Meg said, peering out the side window.

Amanda pressed her nose against the glass. The loggers, prospective husbands and others, were gathered just down the hill from the dormitory. They talked, occasionally pointed, stretched their necks and jockeyed for a better position.

One of the rules in the camp was that no men were allowed in the brides' dormitory without express permission from Amanda, although she didn't think any of the men would be brave enough to venture in at the moment.

Was Jason out there? Though she didn't want to, Amanda found herself searching the faces of the men assembled outside. She hadn't spoken to him since the night before last when they'd come back from Beaumont. She'd been tempted, though. Once she'd even marched halfway to his office before stopping. But in the end Amanda had turned back, not as eager for a confrontation as she'd thought since she feared the outcome might not be what she wanted. Besides, she was running out of time.

Among the men assembled outside, Amanda saw Gerald McGee, Meg's husband. At the other end of the gathering she spotted Ethan Kruger. Amanda glanced at Meg beside her and wondered which man her friend was looking at.

"Just as well we're having the social tonight," Meg said, turning away from the window.

"And the weddings tomorrow." Amanda checked her list, getting back to business. "Reverend Daley will arrive around noon. I have a crew of volunteers to set up the benches for the joint ceremony, Idelle Turner is in charge of decorations, Gladys Duncan and Polly Minton are handling the refreshments. Everything should go like clockwork."

Meg's eyes widened. "Do you think so?"

"Of course," Amanda said. "Everything will go just as planned."

"Let's hope things go smoothly tonight at the social."

Amanda waved away her concern. "I've done dozens of these. This is the easiest part. Just wait and see."

A disaster! Her get-acquainted social was a disaster.

Stunned, Amanda stood among the crowd at the edge of the dance floor. How could this be happening?

At Amanda's insistence, Jim Hubbard and the other four musicians pushed on, playing the dozen songs they knew. The dormitory was decorated with wildflowers and candles. At the far end of the room, tables covered with pink cloths held trays of food. The brides were turned out in their finest, the loggers were clean-scrubbed, with fresh haircuts and neatly trimmed beards.

But nobody moved. The men stood on one side of the room, the women on the other, lined up as if awaiting execution. And between them yawned the gaping expanse of empty dance floor.

"What's wrong with everybody?" Meg whispered from beside Amanda.

She surveyed the scene in front of her. At the start of the evening, she'd introduced each bride to her prospective husband. They knew who each other was, why weren't they dancing?

"We need one man brave enough to cross the floor and ask a woman to dance. Once that happens, everyone will join in," Amanda said.

"But they've been in this standoff for nearly a half hour," Meg said. "I don't think there's a brave enough man among them."

Amanda gulped. "If something is not done soon I may have to cross the floor and ask one of the men to dance."

"Oh, Amanda, you can't possibly do that," Meg insisted, shocked at the very idea.

"I can't simply stand by and—"

Meg gasped. "Oh, look. Here comes someone."

Amanda wheeled and in the soft light saw one man step away from the group knotted on the other side of the room. Her hopes soared, then stumbled.

"It's Jason," Meg said.

"Oh." Disappointment sank Amanda's shoulders. She'd hoped it was one of the prospective grooms, a brave one, who'd stepped out to ask his bride to dance. Instead, it was Jason Kruger crossing the floor, heading her way.

"It's all right," Amanda said, her spirits lifting. "I'll make Jason talk to the men, insist he send one of them over here to invite his bride to dance."

Meg shook her head, eyeing the large expanse of dance floor separating the sexes. "I don't know if even Jason can force the men to do that."

"Well, I've got to do something."

Amanda wrung her hands together, watching Jason. As he approached, his height increased, his chest grew wider, his shoulders broader. He'd been to the barber like the other men, she saw. His dark hair looked neat and freshly cut. He had on a white shirt with a string tie, and a vest she'd never seen before. He looked handsome. And he was going to save her social—whether he wanted to or not.

Every eye in the room followed Jason across the floor. The men edged slightly closer. The women shifted for a better look. A low murmur rumbled through the room.

Jason took his time, walking at an unhurried pace, like a man used to being at the center of things, a man who owned everything around him. A man who enjoyed every moment of it.

He stopped in front of Amanda and her heart skipped faster. Thank goodness, he'd come to her.

Somehow, he'd sensed her distress. He'd come to help her, to save her social.

Jason gazed down at her. "Would you like to dance?"

"Oh, thank goodness you're here." Amanda latched onto his forearm, glancing around. "You've got to make one of your men ask one of the brides to dance."

"I just asked you to dance."

She rose on her toes to see around him, to the men lined on the opposite wall. "He'll have to be a brave one. Offer him money if you have to. I'll pay. I can't let my social fall—"

"Amanda." Jason touched his finger to her chin and tilted her face up to look at him. "I just asked you if you'd like to dance."

"Me?" She gasped, suddenly aware that every eye in the room was on them. Amanda looked up at him and he smiled and raised his brows in a question.

Amanda's cheeks warmed and her heart did a little flip. Jason wanted to dance with her? Her? He'd crossed the dance floor under the scrutiny of everyone on the mountain, and asked *her* to dance?

"Well, certainly, Mr. Kruger. It's kind of you to ask."

Jason led her to the center of the room, settled her in his arms and off they went. She was glad she'd selected her pale yellow dress to wear tonight, especially now that every eye in the room was on the two of them. It was her favorite dress and she hadn't worn it on the mountain before.

Amanda smiled up at Jason as they waltzed around the floor. "I didn't know you could dance."

"I haven't done it in a while," Jason admitted. Then he grinned. "In fact, there's a few things I haven't done in a while that I'm anxious to get practiced up on."

"If you do them as well as you dance," Amanda said, "they should prove a delightful experience."

Jason's expression deepened and a flash of heat emanated from him. Amanda thought for a moment he would say something, but he didn't.

The song ended and they stopped at the far end of the dance floor. A little round of applause followed for the musicians. Immediately, they took up another song and Jason swung Amanda onto the floor again.

"Oh, look, Jason," Amanda said as they danced past the line of loggers, "the men are moving."

Jason looked back over his shoulder at the three men crossing the floor. Another group of two followed, then others trailed after them.

"It would suit me to have the place to ourselves," Jason said, smiling down at her.

Amanda basked in the warmth of the moment, of his smile, of the feel of his hands on her. She'd missed him. Being close to him now was like coming home. As if this was the one place in all the world she belonged.

The dance floor filled up quickly as other couples joined in. Some of the men who didn't dance ventured across the room to the brides and stood talking.

When the song ended, Jason took Amanda's hand

and led her out the open double doors onto the porch. The air was cool out here, away from the press of the other dancers. A full moon hung over the tops of the trees.

"It was thoughtful of you to do that," Amanda said, moving away from him. "You saved my social."

"Is that why you think I asked you to dance?" Jason asked. "Just to get the other men on the floor?"

"Well, yes." Amanda glanced back at him. "Why should I have thought otherwise?"

Jason walked closer and put his hands on her shoulders. He turned her to face him, and grinned. "Maybe I just wanted to dance with you?"

An energy sprang up between them. Amanda felt it now, as she'd done before. She put her palms against his chest, as comfortable in his embrace as she'd ever been. As if they hadn't exchanged harsh words, as if he hadn't said he was sorry she'd come to his mountain, as if she hadn't felt sorry to be there.

When they were together, just the two of them, everything seemed right with the world. And Amanda wanted to be no place but in Jason's arms.

He eased closer. He lowered his head. Her mouth quivered, awaiting the kiss she knew was coming. Amanda's heart thumped harder in her chest.

"Stop," she whispered.

Amanda pushed against his chest and leaned her head back, unable to escape his reach but far enough away to discourage him.

Jason didn't discourage easily. He pulled her closer. The heat of his body seeped into hers. It weakened her will. His lips brushed hers, and her knees nearly gave out.

But she turned her head away.

"I don't want you to kiss me," she said.

Jason stopped and gazed down at her, his brows drawn together. "Why not?"

"Because things aren't settled between us, and this will only complicate matters."

He backed off then, releasing her. "All right, then, let's get them settled."

She was surprised he'd said that so quickly, so easily. "I don't like it when we don't talk. It doesn't solve anything when you're upset but refuse to speak to me."

"Yeah?"

"It's childish."

"So is name-calling."

She looked up at him, realizing that she'd done just that. "You're right. I'm sorry. I shouldn't have said that. But you have to—"

"Change?" Jason demanded. He stepped a little closer. "Isn't that what this is all about? Me not doing things to suit you? You trying to change me?"

In the dim light she saw the anger in his expression, and the hurt. He'd told her before he wouldn't bend his life to suit the will of a woman, as his father had done for his mother. Amanda didn't see this as the same thing.

"No," she said quickly. "It's not that at all. It's

just that we can't solve our problems unless we're willing to work at them.''

"Unless I'm willing to do it your way, you mean.''

Amanda stopped, gazing into the tight lines of his face. "No, Jason, that's not what I mean.''

"Yes, it is,'' he insisted, drawing closer, crowding her. "That's what you want, isn't it? For me to change the way I do things? Do them like you want them done?''

"I don't think it's unreasonable to ask you to talk about things rather than—''

"I'm not going to change. Not for you. Not for any woman.''

"I'm not worth it? Is that what you're saying?'' she asked.

Jason drew back, as if surprised by what she'd said.

"Are you still sorry I came to your mountain?'' she asked.

He shook his head. "I shouldn't have said that.''

"But you meant it. Didn't you?''

"I liked things the way they were,'' he admitted. "They were simpler.''

Amanda searched his face in the pale moonlight hoping to find some softness there, but saw none.

"Well, then,'' she said quietly, "I guess we have nothing to discuss.''

Amanda gulped down the tears that sprang to her eyes and walked into the dormitory. She felt Jason's gaze on her but he didn't call her back.

The dance floor was crowded with couples now.

A few men and women lined the perimeter of the room. Amanda didn't want to talk to any of them. Her chest ached. Her heart hurt. And she was about to cry.

Quickly, she made her way to the opposite end of the building and into the kitchen. The room was warm from the big cookstove Gladys and Polly had used to prepare tonight's refreshments. She headed out the back door, but voices stopped her.

Meg and Ethan stood by the pantry on the other side of the room. Pausing in the doorway, Amanda had a clear view of them, but neither Meg nor Ethan saw her. Small wonder. Looking up at Ethan, Meg's face had gone white. He stood a few feet away from her as if afraid to get too close.

"I'm not asking you to choose, Meg," Ethan said, his voice soft but rich in sincerity. "McGee is your husband and I respect that. I'm just telling you how it is so you can make your choice."

Ethan took a step closer to her. "I love you, Meg. I've loved you since the minute I first laid eyes on you. I'll take care of you. You and your son both. I'll never abandon you. You'll never want for a thing as long as I've got a breath of life left in me."

Meg didn't say anything and Ethan looked as if he didn't expect her to.

"But regardless of what choice you make, Meg," Ethan said, "I'll always love you."

Tears splashed onto Amanda's cheeks. She tore the kitchen door open and rushed outside, up the hill toward her cabin.

Oh, to be loved like that....

She'd hoped she'd found it with Jason. But no, it was not to be. It just wasn't meant to be.

When his office door opened and slammed shut, Jason expected to look up from his desk and see Amanda standing over him. In fact, he wished it were Amanda. He hadn't seen her since she'd left him standing on the porch outside the dormitory at last night's social.

Instead it was Meg McGee walking through his office door. She was frowning just as Amanda would have done, looking none too pleased with him.

"This is for you," Meg said, and tossed an envelope on his desk.

"What's this all about?" he asked.

"It's from Amanda."

Jason frowned and picked up the envelope. "Amanda?"

"She's gone."

"Gone?" He came to his feet.

"Yes, gone. Gone back to San Francisco."

"But she can't leave. The weddings are taking place today."

"She never goes to weddings," Meg said. "That's what she told me. And she asked me to give you that letter. She left on one of the freight wagons heading back to Beaumont early this morning."

Chapter Twenty-Three

Beaumont seemed big and alive as Amanda gazed down from her hotel window at the streets clogged with horses, wagons and buggies, and the board-walks filled with all manner of people. When she'd first gazed out one of the hotel windows several weeks ago upon her arrival from San Francisco, Beaumont had appeared to be a very different place. Had it really changed so much?

Amanda stepped back from the window. No, Beaumont hadn't changed. She had.

Pulling the curtains together against the midday sun, Amanda sank onto the brass bed. All those weeks ago she'd arrived in Beaumont heading up to the Kruger Brothers' Lumber and Milling Company with purpose and drive and big plans for her future. Today she was leaving with a broken heart.

Oh, Jason....

Amanda pressed her lips together, refusing to cry another tear. She loved him, but she was leaving him.

Part of it was Jason's own stubbornness. He was so sure he was right. And so bullheaded that he wouldn't talk to her about his anger. How could anything be solved that way?

But part of her reason for leaving was her own. Amanda pinched the bridge of her nose, pushing away the hurtful memories. She couldn't stay on the mountain for the weddings today. She simply couldn't.

Rising, Amanda paced the room tugging on the sash of her wrapper. When she'd arrived in Beaumont this morning she'd learned that the stagecoach wouldn't be through until supper time. So she'd checked into the hotel, changed into her nightgown, and tried to rest until it was time to go to the depot.

Amanda huffed impatiently. She may as well have stayed in her whalebone corset and stood in the middle of Main Street in the heat of the midday sun for all the rest she'd gotten.

Absently, she stood in front of the mirror on the bureau and tucked stray tendrils of hair into their pins, thinking of the trip back to San Francisco. She'd thought it a rough one, until she'd made the journey up the mountain to the lumber camp. And met Jason.

A little knot of anger formed in Amanda's chest. He'd turned her world upside down. She'd been content to live in San Francisco. She'd been content with the gentlemen there, too. In fact, she'd been happy with every phase of her life in the city.

Until she met Jason Kruger. Now she wasn't happy with anything.

When she'd left the camp this morning, she'd given Meg a letter to pass along to Jason. It simply stated that she was going home, her work on the mountain done.

Now, with the anger in her chest growing, Amanda wished she'd told Jason Kruger exactly what she thought of him. Somebody should do it. And nobody on the mountain had nerve enough. Except for Ethan, perhaps. But right now he was too consumed with his own problems.

"Oh!"

Amanda clenched her fists, pacing at the foot of the bed. She couldn't walk away without telling Jason how she felt. Even though she was certain he didn't want to hear it, she had to tell him—and she would, too.

She glanced around the room at her clothing spread out over the chair, the washstand, the bureau. If she hurried, she could catch one of the freight wagons going up the mountain. Tomorrow she could come back to Beaumont and take the stage home.

Home.

Amanda's footsteps faltered. Home was her little cabin on the mountain, not San Francisco.

Something else Jason had done. Mumbling, Amanda stalked across the room and grabbed a silk stocking from the back of the chair. That man was going to get an earful from her. If he was sorry before that she'd come to his mountain, wait until she got finished with him now.

A knock sounded at the door, indicating the kitchen help had brought up the meal she'd requested. Amanda was hardly in the mood to eat it. She tossed her stocking aside and snatched the door open.

Jason stood in the hallway.

Amanda blinked twice, not sure she trusted her eyes. Finally she blurted out, "What are you doing here?"

"What the hell are *you* doing here?" he demanded.

She saw the deep scowl on his face, the hard lines of his mouth, and that made Amanda angrier.

"I asked you first," she told him.

Jason stalked into the room, forcing Amanda back. He slammed the door.

"I don't give a damn who asked first, I want to know what the hell is going on."

"I'm leaving," she told him. "Is that so hard to understand? I left you a letter."

He yanked it from his shirt pocket and Amanda saw that it was crumpled as if he'd crushed it in his fist.

"You think this is enough?" Jason stepped in front of her, glaring down. "After all you put me through, you think you can leave me a letter, then sashay off to San Francisco as if nothing happened?"

"Nothing did happen!" Amanda frowned up at him, her heart pounding. "Except that I was attracted to a man who thinks I ruined his life."

Jason backed off a step. "I never said that."

"Yes, you did. And you meant it."

"You just got caught up in a family problem. That's all."

"That's *all?*" she echoed, stunned that he minimized it so easily. "This *family problem* has run your life since you were a child. It's why you won't have anything to do with Brandon, why you didn't want women on your mountain, why you don't want me there."

"Look, Amanda, I was mad when I said that."

"But you still meant it."

Jason just looked at her, unable to deny what she'd said.

Amanda continued, "You blame your parents for your unhappy childhood. Your father isn't a strong man. Your mother is a strong woman. You're like her, but you don't want to accept it or admit it, but you're just like him, too."

"That's a lie."

"It's not. Among your brother's belongings are letters from your father to your mother. Love letters."

He glared hard at her.

"Yes, Jason, love letters. I came across them when I helped Brandon unpack. Letters written between your father and mother over the course of their marriage. Your father loves your mother. Loves her so much he follows her wherever she wants to go."

"Like a whipped dog."

"No, like a man in love," Amanda said. "The same as you when you followed me here to Beaumont."

Jason sucked in a quick breath. His face paled. He backed away from her.

"You didn't give it a thought, did you?" she asked. "Just hopped in the wagon and came here."

"I came to get you back on the mountain," Jason told her. "To have you finish what you started."

"I am finished."

"Like hell. There's twenty-three weddings going on—"

"I never attend weddings."

"Why not?"

"It's none of your concern," she said.

"Yes, it is."

"Look, Jason, you've got enough of your own problems. Don't try to tell me how to handle mine."

"And you call me hardheaded?"

The two of them stared at each other, both right, both wrong. Both angry, both hurt.

"You are hardheaded," Amanda said softly.

"I can't argue with that." Jason heaved a heavy sigh. He pulled off his hat and held it in front of him, picking at the brim, then looked up at her and said softly, "But the truth is, Amanda, I don't want you to leave."

"But you don't want me on your mountain, either," she said to him.

He looked at her for a long time before he spoke. "You didn't belong on my mountain. I knew it from the start. You, a fine-looking city woman. Just too refined to live that kind of life."

Jason shook his head, remembering, then grinned. "When you knocked that miner into the water trough, I thought maybe there was more to you than I suspected.''

''I don't know what came over me,'' Amanda admitted.

Jason grew serious. ''But when Brandon got hurt and you took over and started barking out orders, I knew you did belong on my mountain. And I wanted you there. I just didn't know how to tell you. I didn't know how to admit it to myself.''

''You shouldn't keep things locked up inside you,'' Amanda told him. ''You should have told me what was on your mind those times when I tried to talk to you.''

Jason nodded. ''Yeah, I know.''

''And you should stop blaming Brandon for what your parents did.''

He glanced down at his hat. ''You're right about that, too. But, honestly, I don't know what to do with the boy.''

''Talk to him,'' Amanda said. ''He'll tell you.''

Jason shrugged as if he wasn't convinced, but he'd be willing to try. ''So, you'll stay?''

''No.''

''Yes, you will.'' Jason crossed in front of her. ''I love you, Amanda.''

Tears sprang to her eyes as she gazed up at him. ''You do?''

''Yes, Amanda, I do,'' Jason said. ''I tried not to. I fought it. I didn't want to love you. But here I am all crazy in the head over you. Chasing you down the mountain, wanting to take you back home with me.''

"You've been mad at me for days now."

Jason nodded. "I guess I've been mad at a lot of people lately for no good reason."

"I love you, too, Jason."

A big smile broadened his mouth and he walked toward her. Then, realizing he still had his hat in hand, he tossed it on the chair in the corner.

His gaze darkened as he saw her corset, pantalets and chemise draped over the arms and backs of the chair. He noticed her stockings dangling from the washstand.

Jason turned to her again, his eyes taking her in from the top of her head to the tips of her toes, understanding for the first time that she was naked under her robe and gown. His chest swelled.

Amanda's flesh tingled as he looked at her. Warmth crept through her. Jason took her in his arms and kissed her, and Amanda knew there was no place in the world she'd rather be.

He brushed his lips against hers, then deepened their kiss until Amanda responded. She welcomed him inside her, moaning softly at the exquisite warmth of his tongue. Amanda looped her arms around his neck and raised on her toes, pressing closer.

Jason groaned. He kissed a hot trail down her neck, then pulled loose the sash of her robe. His hand closed over the swell of her hip, then lifted to cup her breast. He groaned again.

She pushed against him, feeling the length of him. Amanda opened the buttons of his shirt and pressed her palms against his chest, wiggling her fingers through the curly, dark hair.

Jason claimed her mouth again with his as he unfastened the little buttons of her gown. He lifted his head and gazed down at the white flesh of her breasts swelling outward.

"Oh, Amanda...." Jason wrapped both arms around her shoulders and pulled her against him, kissing the top of her head. He held her that way for a few moments, then took a big breath and set her away from him.

"You know what's about to happen here," he said, his voice heavy.

She nodded. "Yes, I know."

Jason shook his head. "Once we get much further along, it's going to be damn near impossible for me to stop. So if you don't like where this is heading, now's the time to say so."

Amanda smiled up at him. "I like where it's heading."

His eyes closed for a few seconds, then opened again, heavy with need. "You're sure?"

She nodded. "I'm sure."

Taking her in his arms again, Jason kissed her as he pushed her robe off her shoulders. Their mouths still together, he ripped off his vest and shirt. While he hopped on each foot and yanked off his boots and socks, Amanda reached for the pins securing her hair.

"No, wait," he said.

She stopped, unsure of what he wanted.

Jason studied her face, her beautiful hair piled up

atop her head. Then took her hand and led her to the bureau. He stood behind her and adjusted the mirror so they could both see her reflection.

He touched his hands to her shoulders, marveling at her delicate frame, then leaned closer and buried his nose in the back of her hair. So sweet. Jason touched his lips to her neck and felt her shiver.

Slowly, he traced his hand across her shoulder and captured a loose tendril of hair. Soft, silky. He closed his eyes and twirled it around his finger.

When he opened his eyes again his gaze met Amanda's in the mirror. She wasn't frightened, or unsure, or uncomfortable with what he was doing. Anxious, yes. But he was anxious, too. A new sort of contentment settled in the pit of his stomach.

Carefully, he pulled one of the pins from the back of her hair. It tumbled down, covering her shoulder, his hand. He found another and pulled it free. More hair fell loose. Sliding his fingers through her heavy hair, he found each remaining pin and pulled it out until all her hair curled at her waist. Jason smiled, threading his fingers through her mane. He'd wanted to do this for weeks. No, his whole life.

Amanda turned in the circle of his arms and kissed him, hot and full on the mouth. He moaned, lifted her into his arms and carried her to the bed.

She stretched out atop the coverlet, her hair spread over the pillows, her gown open to the waist. He'd never seen anything so beautiful in all his days. Then she smiled, and he was lost.

Jason pulled off the rest of his clothes, tossing them over his shoulder, then got into bed beside her.

He raised on one elbow above her and rested his hand on her hip.

Her hand covered his, stilling him. "I've never—"

He leaned down and kissed her softly on the throat. "The whole idea here is for us to enjoy this," he whispered. "If you don't like something, just say so."

Amanda smiled then, and he lowered his head to kiss her throat again. He captured her mouth then, deepening their kiss until she parted her lips for him. His hand slid upward to her shoulder. He eased her toward him and rubbed her back until she relaxed against him.

The world moved in slow motion for Amanda, while her heart beat wildly. Jason's hands, even calloused from hard work, were soft against her. Gentle. Loving. His lips were hot, his kisses demanding. Her body grew warm, tight, needing to answer the demand of his kisses.

Jason's blood pounded through his veins. He slid his hand down her leg and beneath the hem of her gown, caressing her, pulling the fabric higher until he eased it over her head.

"Oh, Amanda..." he moaned, feasting on the sight of her naked body stretched out beside his.

He dropped his head to the valley between her breasts and kissed her, catching her nipple with his lips, warming her skin with his tongue. She moaned softly and arched against him, wrapping her leg over his and digging her fingers into the hair of his chest.

Jason rose above her, kissing her face, and eased

inside her. She tensed, but he kissed her again and finally she relaxed.

An urgency, a calling, gripped Amanda as she lay locked in Jason's arms, holding tight to his shoulders. The steady movement of his hips became the center of her world. Her body answered, moving with his, climbing, searching until a storm of passion broke through her. She grabbed a handful of his hair and called out his name.

Jason drove himself deeper into Amanda as she gripped him, holding him, his body finding the fulfillment only hers could offer. He collapsed beside her, holding her against his chest.

"So why don't you go to weddings?"

Amanda heard Jason's voice speaking softly at her ear, his head on the pillow beside her, their arms and legs tangled together. They'd made love twice more and were under the covers now, the room dark except for the faint lights of Beaumont filtering through the curtains.

She turned her head to see him. "Because I don't like weddings."

Jason pushed himself up on his elbow and frowned. "You run a matrimonial service, but don't like weddings?"

Amanda turned her head away, gazing at the curtains floating on the cool evening breeze. With his finger, Jason touched her chin and urged her to look at him again.

"Is this what you wanted to talk to me about? That day just before my little brother showed up you asked me if we could talk after supper.'' Jason shook his head. ''I got caught up in my own problems. Too caught up to listen. But if you'd like to tell me now, I'd like to hear about it.''

The comfort of his arms, the closeness of their bodies settled over Amanda like a warm blanket on a cold winter's day. She knew she didn't want to be anywhere else. Only with Jason.

''When I was very young I was engaged to be married,'' Amanda said. ''Everything went as planned. My family spent a large amount of money, the guests were assembled, and the groom never showed up.''

''Damn. He just didn't show up?''

''He sent his brother to explain, as if a public humiliation on that scale could be explained,'' Amanda said. ''He felt we weren't suited for one another. The marriage was a mistake. We wouldn't make each other happy. We shouldn't have been engaged in the first place.''

''It took him until your wedding day to figure that out?''

''Apparently.'' Amanda drew in a deep breath. ''So, as one might imagine, it was difficult for me to trust another man after that, or even think about getting involved with anyone.''

''But you started your matrimonial service?''

She nodded. ''It seemed like the most natural thing to do. This way I could help ensure that no woman was ever left at the altar again. I made it my business to match up compatible men and women so they'd make good husbands and wives.''

Jason shrugged. "Makes sense."

They were quiet for a long time, listening to the thud of hoofbeats on the dirt street outside, the creak of wagon wheels. Faint voices rose to the window occasionally, the words indistinguishable.

"We should go," Amanda said.

"In the morning," Jason answered, snuggling closer.

"Oh, Jason, good gracious," she said, half sitting. "The two of us in Beaumont all night? People will know what we've been doing."

Jarred by her wiggling, Jason raised on his elbow. "You know what's going on up on my mountain tonight, with all those newlyweds?"

Amanda grinned. "Well…yes."

"Then believe me, nobody's going to give you and me a second thought when we come rolling into camp tomorrow." Jason hooked her waist and pulled her close to him again. "Besides, I don't think we're quite done here."

Her heart fluttered. "Really?"

"I've got something I want to show you," Jason said.

Her brows rose. "You have something else I haven't seen yet?"

"Yeah. Look at this." Jason held up his palm.

"I've seen that already," she said.

"Yes, but look at this." Jason pulled the sheet down to her waist and laid his hand on her breast.

A whispered gasp slipped through Amanda's lips.

"See that?" he asked. Jason squeezed her gently. "Fits perfectly."

Amanda gazed down at his dark, sun-browned hand and fingers closed over the swell of her white breast.

''Just the right size for my hand,'' Jason said. ''Not too much, not too little. Perfect. Just like I knew it would be.''

Amanda smiled. ''That's important to you?''

''Oh, yeah,'' he said, and moved his hand away so that his lips could take its place.

Amanda writhed against him, pressing closer. ''A good fit does seem important.''

''Damn right.''

Chapter Twenty-Four

"Miss Amanda? You in there?"

Amanda answered the knock on her cabin door and found Brandon Kruger on her doorstep. Not the Kruger brother she'd hoped for.

The camp had been quiet when she and Jason had ridden up from Beaumont this morning, most everyone otherwise occupied, as Jason had predicted. She'd been surprised not to find Meg or Todd in her cabin, though, and she worried about where they might be.

"How are you feeling today?" Amanda asked Brandon.

He glanced down at his arm still in a sling and shrugged. "Okay, I guess."

Where an adult might have taken weeks to get over so severe an injury, the resilience of youth had Brandon up and around in only a few days. It seemed more a nuisance to him than a worry.

"Jason said for you to come down to the office,"

Brandon said, nodding down the hill. "And he says to bring that catalog of yours with you."

"My catalog of brides?" She was a little surprised by the request, but after all the weddings that had taken place yesterday it was only natural that some of the other loggers would now seek brides.

Amanda fetched her satchel with the catalog inside, closed up her cabin and walked down the path with Brandon.

"I've been at the office working today. Jason said I can work there with him and Ethan," Brandon said. "Guess I'm going to learn about the lumber business."

She smiled. "Really? That's wonderful."

Brandon shrugged as if he didn't understand it, but it suited him all right. As they neared the office, Brandon headed toward town.

Amanda paused before she stepped up onto the porch outside Jason's office, unsure of how to act on this occasion. She'd spent the night in Jason's arms at the hotel in Beaumont. He'd said he loved her, that one time.

Would he take her in his arms when she walked through his office door, declare his love over and over, beg her to be part of his life forever?

Terribly romantic. Amanda smiled at the scene that played out in her mind. It caused her heart to thump a little faster.

Right now, though, it was enough that he loved her. He'd said it. They'd rolled around in bed together for hours. Surely he wouldn't have done that if his intentions weren't honorable.

Amanda's brows drew together. Some men were like that. She'd heard the talk, been warned since she was a young girl. But Jason wasn't like that. Amanda hitched her satchel higher and walked into his office.

He stood at the stove pouring himself a cup of coffee. With a casual glance over his shoulder at her, Jason gestured to the chair in front of his desk.

"Sit down," he said.

Well, so much for professions of love. Amanda placed her satchel on the floor in front of his desk. A feeling of foreboding crept up her spine as Jason stirred sugar into his coffee, tasted it, then ambled to the desk.

"Sit down," he said again, then dropped into his own chair.

"Jason, I—"

"Just a minute." He shuffled through a few papers on his desk, looking them over and finally putting them aside. "We've got some business to attend to."

"Business?"

She wasn't sure she'd heard him right at first, but his cool, casual demeanor assured her that she had.

Amanda slipped into the chair in front of his desk, steeling her feelings.

"I've decided I need a wife," Jason said.

Amanda's stomach clenched and her heart rose into her throat.

"And I want you to find me one," Jason said, leaning back in his chair.

She could only stare at him. He wanted a wife?

And he wanted her to find him one? After all they'd been through, after their night together in Beaumont, he expected her to order him a wife from her catalog?

"Now, first off," Jason said, steepling his fingers over his chest, "I want a smart one."

Amanda just stared at him.

"Aren't you going to write this down?" he asked. "I'm real particular about the kind of wife I want."

Jason found a piece of paper and a pencil on his desk and pushed it in front of her. Numbly, Amanda picked up the pencil.

"Second of all," Jason said, "I want a wife who's not afraid to speak her mind. That's important. I can't abide a timid woman who won't let me know where she stands on every little, tiny thing that comes along."

Amanda opened her mouth to speak, but he wagged his finger at her.

"Write this down," he said. "Next, I want a wife who'll tell me when I'm wrong."

Amanda blinked across the desk at him.

"Of course," Jason went on, "I need a wife who can fend for herself when it's called for. One with a good head for business. One not afraid to take a chance on a business deal, if it's warranted."

Amanda just stared at him.

"She's got to be pretty, too," Jason said. "I like brown hair with streaks of red in it. The kind I can pull the pins out of and watch curl through my fingers. I want a wife who'll let me do that."

Amanda dropped her pencil.

"And see this?" Jason held up his palm. "I want her bosom the perfect size to fit in my hand. Like we were made for each other."

Tears popped into Amanda's eyes.

"Think you can find me a wife like that?" Jason asked.

"Yes," Amanda said, "but she's liable to shoot you first."

Jason grinned and rounded the desk, pulling Amanda into his arms. She laughed and sniffed and brushed away her tears.

He settled her against him. "Will you marry me, Amanda?"

"Yes. Oh, yes, Jason, I will."

Amanda threw her arms around his neck and rose on her toes to meet his lips. He kissed her long and hard and she melted against him.

"All right now, you two, enough of that."

Jason broke off their kiss but didn't let Amanda out of his arms as Ethan walked into the office. Amanda didn't feel embarrassed at being caught. Instead she smiled.

"I've got news," Ethan said. He stopped. "Well, actually *we've* got news."

He reached out the doorway and pulled Meg inside the office. Her cheeks were pink and she was smiling.

Amanda moved out of Jason's arms. "What is it?"

Ethan looked at Meg and gave her fingers a squeeze. She gazed at him and blushed.

"We're getting married," Meg announced.

"Oh, Meg!" Amanda rushed to her friend. They hugged and laughed.

Jason shook his brother's hand, then exchanged a big bear hug.

"Did you run McGee off?" Jason asked in a low voice.

Ethan shook his head. "No. Meg told him last night she'd never forgive him, never love him again. He said he'd give her the divorce she wants, then took off."

"What about her son?"

Ethan frowned. "Todd didn't seem to care much for his pa, after all. Meg talked to the boy and it was all right with him."

Jason raised an eyebrow at Meg, chattering away with Amanda. "So, what have the two of you been doing since last night?"

Ethan elbowed him in the ribs. "Probably the same as you and Amanda."

"Oh, you'll never guess," Amanda said, whirling around, her eyes bright. "Jason asked me to marry him."

Meg squealed. "This is wonderful. Now, we'll really be sisters. Oh, Amanda, I'm so glad I wrote you that letter pretending to be Jason needing a wife."

Amanda gasped. "That was *you?*"

"It was the best way I could think of to get women up here," Meg said.

Ethan slid his arm around her waist. "We're going to have to keep an eye on these two wives of ours. They'll take over the place."

"I think they've already done that," Jason said. He pulled Amanda into his embrace and smiled down at her. "And that's all right with me."

* * * * *

Dixie Browning
and her sister

Mary Williams
writing as

Bronwyn Williams

are pleased to present their new
Harlequin Historical

The Paper Marriage

Former sea captain Matthew Powers knew he needed
help caring for his newly adopted daughter. A
marriage by proxy to a deserving widow seemed
like a good idea—until his Aunt Bess came to town
with her friend in tow, and he found himself falling
in love with the enchanting Rose.

The latest book in

The Passionate
POWERS
series

Available in August 2000

Harlequin Historicals
The way the past *should* have been!

Available at your favorite retail outlet!

Discover the joys of
nineteenth-century America with
four brand-new Westerns from
Harlequin Historicals.

On sale July 2000

THE BLUSHING BRIDE
by **Judith Stacy**
(California)

and

JAKE'S ANGEL
by **Nicole Foster**
(New Mexico)

On sale August 2000

THE PAPER MARRIAGE
by **Bronwyn Williams**
(North Carolina)

and

PRAIRIE BRIDE
by **Julianne McLean**
(Kansas)

Harlequin Historicals
The way the past *should* have been.

HARLEQUIN®
Makes any time special™

Visit us at www.eHarlequin.com
HHWEST8

Where the luckiest babies are born!

Join Harlequin® and Silhouette® for a special 12-book series about the world-renowned Maitland Maternity Clinic, owned and operated by the prominent Maitland family of Austin, Texas, where romances are born, secrets are revealed…and bundles of joy are delivered!

Look for

MAITLAND MATERNITY

titles at your favorite retail outlet, starting in August 2000

HARLEQUIN®
Makes any time special ™

Silhouette®
Where love comes alive ™

Visit us at www.eHarlequin.com   PHMMGEN